SERVANT
THE ACCEPTANCE

L. L. FOSTER

JOVE BOOKS, NEW YORK

THE BERKLEY PUBLISHING GROUP
Published by the Penguin Group
Penguin Group (USA) Inc.
375 Hudson Street, New York, New York 10014, USA
Penguin Group (Canada), 90 Eglinton Avenue East, Suite 700, Toronto, Ontario M4P 2Y3, Canada
(a division of Pearson Penguin Canada Inc.)
Penguin Books Ltd., 80 Strand, London WC2R 0RL, England
Penguin Group Ireland, 25 St. Stephen's Green, Dublin 2, Ireland (a division of Penguin Books Ltd.)
Penguin Group (Australia), 250 Camberwell Road, Camberwell, Victoria 3124, Australia
(a division of Pearson Australia Group Pty. Ltd.)
Penguin Books India Pvt. Ltd., 11 Community Centre, Panchsheel Park, New Delhi—110 017, India
Penguin Group (NZ), 67 Apollo Drive, Rosedale, North Shore 0632, New Zealand
(a division of Pearson New Zealand Ltd.)
Penguin Books (South Africa) (Pty.) Ltd., 24 Sturdee Avenue, Rosebank, Johannesburg 2196,
South Africa

Penguin Books Ltd., Registered Offices: 80 Strand, London WC2R 0RL, England

This is a work of fiction. Names, characters, places, and incidents either are the product of the author's imagination or are used fictitiously, and any resemblance to actual persons, living or dead, business establishments, events, or locales is entirely coincidental. The publisher does not have any control over and does not assume any responsibility for author or third-party websites or their content.

SERVANT: THE ACCEPTANCE

A Jove Book / published by arrangement with the author

PRINTING HISTORY
Jove mass-market edition / September 2008

Copyright © 2008 by Lori Foster.
Excerpt from *Servant: The Kindred* by L. L. Foster copyright © 2008 by Lori Foster.
Cover art by John Blumen.
Cover design by Rita Frangie.
Text design by Laura K. Corless.

All rights reserved.
No part of this book may be reproduced, scanned, or distributed in any printed or electronic form without permission. Please do not participate in or encourage piracy of copyrighted materials in violation of the author's rights. Purchase only authorized editions.
For information, address: The Berkley Publishing Group,
a division of Penguin Group (USA) Inc.,
375 Hudson Street, New York, New York 10014.

ISBN: 978-0-515-14532-8

JOVE®
Jove Books are published by The Berkley Publishing Group,
a division of Penguin Group (USA) Inc.,
375 Hudson Street, New York, New York 10014.
JOVE® is a registered trademark of Penguin Group (USA) Inc.
The "J" design is a trademark belonging to Penguin Group (USA) Inc.

PRINTED IN THE UNITED STATES OF AMERICA

10 9 8 7 6 5 4 3 2 1

If you purchased this book without a cover, you should be aware that this book is stolen property. It was reported as "unsold and destroyed" to the publisher, and neither the author nor the publisher has received any payment for this "stripped book."

SERVANT
THE ACCEPTANCE

Prologue

Boredom was her newest enemy, and since running off from Luther—make that *Detective* Luther Cross—she'd been bored more than not.

Until now, she hadn't realized how much . . . *excitement* he'd brought to her life. You'd think a paladin would have her hands full enough that a nosy cop bent on seduction would have been mostly an annoyance, perhaps even a threat.

Instead, he'd been fucking wonderful. The most wonderful thing to ever happen in her miserable, cursed life.

Shit. Gaby walked along the broken concrete walkway in front of the aged, blackened building until that bored her too, then she leaned back against the rough brick, trying to ease her mind, her body.

Her soul.

Hanging out with hookers was a distraction, but it just didn't fill the space the way he had.

She needed something to happen, anything, to keep her

from . . . *Whoa*. Just then, her instinct kicked and she felt the presence of evil, in her bones, in her guts. Her throat burned, she looked up—and she saw him.

A kid.

Clean-cut and unafraid.

Wrong, wrong, wrong.

The defenses screaming silently throughout her body said that he was the wrong person, in the wrong place—and there could be nothing *right* about his presence here tonight. Pickled with immorality, riddled with holes of depravity, his black aura clung to him like a wet cloak.

He sickened Gaby.

He challenged her.

And it didn't matter to her if he was ten or fifty.

Evil was evil.

Tonight, her boredom would end.

Chapter 1

Standing deep in the shadows of a tall brick building to avoid the glow of a streetlamp, Detective Luther Cross clenched his teeth together. Off duty, but determined, he stared down the sidewalk a good ten yards ahead. His eyes burned and his fury built. Even from that distance, with the moon high in the sky casting eerie shadows over the bleak surroundings, he recognized her.

Gabrielle Cody.

The bane of his existence.

The source of nightmares—and scorching-hot erotic dreams.

Her long thin legs, sleek and toned with muscles, showed beneath a denim miniskirt. Black leather ankle boots replaced her familiar flip-flop sandals, and a loose tank top revealed the outline of the sheath at her back.

Her short dark hair now had vivid purple streaks throughout.

She'd disguised herself in her idea of a whore's garb, but Luther would know that stance, feel that cocky attitude, no matter her outward appearance.

For weeks he'd hunted her, lost sleep over her, worried and ruminated and raged . . . and there she stood, appearing as aloof and untouchable as ever.

Alone.

Deliberately distant.

Taunting him without even trying.

Unsure exactly what he'd say or do, Luther started forward. With her keen perception of her surroundings, Gaby might have picked up on his approach. Very little ever got by her.

But at that moment, a young, lanky boy, maybe twelve or thirteen years of age, came out of an alley. Blond hair showed from beneath a pristine ball cap. Dressed in clean jeans and a button-up shirt, a school-type backpack hooked over his thin shoulders, he bore no resemblance to the homeless or desperate runaways that often choked the crowded streets.

He didn't appear the least shy or reserved about being out of place in the area.

Gaze unflinching, he perused the crumbling building that Gaby protected, sizing it up for some purpose that Luther couldn't fathom.

Gaby focused on the boy.

And when Gaby focused, it was something awesome to witness.

She went rigid, her long bones gathering in defense as she straightened away from the building, then immediately relaxed in the deceptive way appropriate to natural-born combatants.

Not a good sign.

Gaby could attack without warning or mercy, fight with a

frighteningly lethal skill, and her motives remained more elusive than a whispery phantom.

Luther knew this, and accepted it.

But why did the boy interest her?

Forgoing his own disgruntlement for the moment, Luther
picked up his pace to reach her, to protect the kid from
whatever Gaby had planned for him—but not in enough
time.

The boy saw Luther and, for reasons of his own, bolted.

Like an animal of prey, Gaby saw his retreat as just cause
to launch a pursuit.

Shit.

They darted around a dark corner, disappeared into the
blackness of the night, and Luther, not being a complete idiot, slowed and pulled his gun.

He wouldn't shoot Gaby.

But then again, he wouldn't walk into a trap either.

He wanted her, but he didn't trust her. Not anymore.

Maybe he never had.

Using necessary caution, he slunk into the narrow, mucu-
lent alley, closing his mind to the festering odors and willing
his eyes to adjust to the extreme lack of light.

At the far end, he saw movement and slipped farther inside. Finally, with careful scrutiny, he spied Gaby. That long,
lethal blade of hers was held tightly in her hand as she slowly
pushed open a broken door.

Heart pounding, adrenaline rushing, Luther steadied his
hands and his thoughts. "Not another step, Gaby."

Other than a slight stiffening of her tender neck, she
made no acknowledgment of him.

All her fervid scrutiny remained intent on whatever she
saw beyond that door. Even from the back, in the murky

gloom of the odorous alley, Luther noted the changes in her face, the tightening and subtle reshaping of her features that signaled her sense of threat.

He also noted the choker around her slender throat. The choker *he'd* given her.

No. He would not go down this road with her again—not without some explanations, not without *him* being in control.

He tightened his mouth, his heart, and deliberately attempted to breech her concentration. *"Gaby."*

He wasn't surprised that she didn't look toward him; knowing her as he did, he wasn't even certain if she'd heard him. In the past, during a rainstorm and times of danger, he'd witnessed Gaby going into a zone, oblivious to everyone and everything around her until an almost trancelike state enclosed her.

Unwilling to lose her again, even emotionally, he caught his breath, inched closer, and said in a harder, deeper voice, "Gaby, you will listen to me."

By minute degrees, she exposed her awareness of him. It showed in the faint relaxing of her strong, proud shoulders, the ebbing of her immense tension.

Without altering her attention, she warned, "It's not a good time, Luther."

Not a good time. Ha! But just hearing her voice reassured and pleased him. Despite the current situation, his pulse slowed, calmed. "That's too bad." He flexed his fingers around the gun, pleased to feel somewhat in control. "Put the knife down—and your arms up."

As she mulled over his order, her jaw worked. She must have decided to give in to him, because she eased back the tiniest bit—

Something shattered inside the abandoned structure, and

Gaby, realizing her prey had found an alternate way out, slammed the door with absurd force.

"*Son of a bitch.*" In a rage ripened by frustration, she rounded on Luther. "You let him get away!"

Somewhat used to her and her odd manners and coarse language, Luther feigned a negligent attitude and asked, "Him who?"

Now that she faced him, Luther saw that some anomalous emotion had manifested itself in her physical appearance. She looked like Gaby, but then again, she didn't.

He'd seen the odd transformation with her before. Like a quick slithering chameleon, she changed and shifted, her appearance altered subtly, almost imperceptibly. Luther had always been so strangely attuned to her that he picked up on it when, perhaps, others didn't.

Was it a phenomenon left over from her childhood? Some strange illness that plagued her? Or was it just Gaby, as extraordinarily different as she was appealing?

Storming toward him, the knife squeezed in her grip and her pale eyes glittering, Gaby curled her lip. "Now that you blundered in, there's no way for us to know who he is, is there?"

"That's close enough," Luther warned her. With Gaby, he was never entirely certain of her intent, of just how far she'd carry her anger in a physical response.

Disregarding his command, she crowded right up to him, nose to nose, hot breath mingling. "Is it?"

Jesus, he'd missed her ballsy bravado and brash disregard for common civility. He wanted to crush her closer, wanted to tell her . . . *what?*

What was it about her that drew him? Yes, she was different, but it was more than that. He wanted her—in a lot of ways inappropriate to his position as a police detective—to satisfy his suspicions about her involvement in a past case involving the sick slaughter of human beings.

He prayed that Gaby had no part in that. He had no real evidence against her. But he had those gut feelings, almost as staggering as his freakishly strong desire for her.

If he believed in such things, he'd think she'd put a spell on him, one meant to keep him awake at nights, and weary during the day, plagued by the memory of her and the confusion she wrought.

But while he couldn't label Gaby, he knew she wasn't a witch. She was too soft to the touch, too vulnerable despite her harsh attitudes, and much, much too alone.

In their current position, the barrel of his gun pressed into her bony sternum. That bothered him, whether she paid any notice or not. Grinding his molars together, Luther rasped, "Put. The knife. *Away*."

Blue eyes sparking, Gaby scrutinized him. "Ah, what's the matter, cop? You afraid of me now?"

Her sneer deliberately provoked—but she did reach around behind herself and sheath the lethal blade with an alarmingly practiced ease. As she did so, her small breasts pushed against the skimpy tank top.

The hidden dangers of the moment had tightened her nipples.

Despite what he knew to be right, to be sane, the sight of her femaleness, so incongruous with her balls-to-the-wall attitude, drew his attention and sent a fire to sear through his veins.

Anger and lust—it could prove a deadly combination, especially with a woman like Gaby.

A woman like no other.

Scraps of moonlight danced among the purple highlights in her hair. A light sheen of sweat touched her pale, smooth skin.

Her impossibly stubborn chin lifted.

And she smiled. "I won't gut you, Luther."

"Good to know."

Slim brows burrowed down, giving her otherwise plain features a hint of threat. "Not," she murmured low, "without reason."

Since seeing her, Luther rode the edge of fury, and now that the knife didn't pose a threat, he grabbed both her wrists and slammed her up against the brick wall. The gun he still held pressed into her tender flesh, but he couldn't temper himself, couldn't rein in his rage or take the time to holster the weapon, couldn't reason with her or . . . anything.

Chest to chest, thick anger undulating between them, he sought words that would somehow convey all he felt—the resentment and relief, the concern and . . .

Fuck.

So much more.

Ignorant of his mental struggle, Gaby looked at his mouth. "How'd you find me, anyway?" She licked her lips, slow and sweet. "I've been quiet. I've been *good*."

Luther couldn't dredge up a single word.

At his lack of response, her gaze crawled up to his, challenging him and scorching him at the same time. "You know, Luther, I figured on never seeing you again."

That notion didn't seem to distress her at all. Luther wondered if his teeth would turn to dust, given how he ground them together.

Eyes narrowed, Gabrielle tipped her head. "But here you

are." She sucked in a substantial breath, which pressed her body into his. Drawling the words, she said, "Big. Tall. Strong Luther. That golden orange glow around you shows great self-control."

God, she sounded the same, just as confusing and infuriating, as if nothing had happened, as if people hadn't died and monsters hadn't existed.

Her voice softened. "You're holding back, Luther. But what? Anger?" Her attention returned to his mouth. "Or something else?"

Hoarse with an aberrant yearning, determined to maintain control of the situation, Luther pointed out, "You've been knocking around johns." And thank God she had, because her abuse of the flesh-peddling clientele had enabled him to locate her again.

Quiet satisfaction chased away the last remnants of her odd transformation, showing him the Gaby he'd grown to know so well—or at least, as well as anyone could know an enigma like her.

"Only when they deserved it, Luther." She relaxed her shoulder blades against the wall, tilted out her hips to press into his groin. Uncaring of how he held her wrists so tightly, nonchalant to any threat he might pose, she said again, "Only when they deserved it."

God almighty, would he ever figure out her many quirks and idiosyncrasies? Now that he had found her, would she find a way to slip away from him again?

Would she forever unbalance him with a desire so foreign to his nature that he couldn't deal with it, couldn't decipher it or even name it?

"Why, Gaby?" He hadn't meant to growl, to show his loss of discipline, but, damn it, there were so many unknowns with her. A million of them.

Hopefully she caught all that the simple question encompassed.

All that he wanted from her.

❧

Stupid, *stupid* bitch! Heart pounding in a mad relay, he ran far-ther, down an alley, across an empty lot.

Looking back one last time—and seeing no one—Oren Paige squeezed through a broken fence post to enter a closed-off garbage area for a local convenient mart.

A rusty, protruding nail gouged the tender flesh of his arm. Flinching, he examined the wound. "Oh God, no." Tears sprang to his eyes. "Blood!"

Oren stared at the gaping wound. It *hurt*. He squeezed his eyes shut and fought back tears.

A girl would cry.

He would not.

Bottom lip trembling, a soft white hand over the injury, he turned to lean his back against one rotted plank of wood. Bone-deep fear urged him to run; his straining lungs demanded that he catch his breath, get a handle on his astronomical fright.

Slowly, his free hand tightened into a fist and his temper began to boil, chasing away the pain. He had to suppress his fury or he'd be shouting in a temper tantrum that would draw the pathetic hordes looming in the night in this godforsaken area.

This was all *her* fault.

Why had the girl chased him? What did she want? No way had she seen through the disguise.

No one ever did.

He hadn't done anything to her to warrant that absurd pursuit. He'd only wanted to lure a whore, and nobody cared about whores.

They were nasty. Foul. Useless to a better society.

Just as his mother had been.

Nobody missed whores. Nobody wanted them around.

He sure as hell didn't.

He performed a service by ridding the community of their sort, giving them only what they deserved—and allowing his aunt and uncle to partake of the pleasure.

Oren smiled. The bitch he had now . . . well, she wouldn't last much longer. Aunt Dory had yet to learn how to meter her rage, and Uncle Myer couldn't pace himself. All night long, Oren had listened to the stupid bitch scream.

And scream and scream.

Until he'd shut them all down.

Because Oren held the purse strings, his aunt and uncle could be controlled. When threats of disinheritance didn't work, drugs did.

And that boorish slut . . . well, he told her that he'd cut out her tongue if she made another sound. With the other already-mute bitch bleeding to death beside her, she hadn't needed further convincing.

Remembering, Oren's smile turned to a grin.

His uncle's slack mouth.

His aunt's eyes, rolled back in her head.

The whore's white-faced fear.

Shoving off from the rickety wall, refusing to look at the ghastly slash on his soft, pale arm, Oren started back to where his ride waited—in a nicer section of town. To facilitate the rest of his journey, he removed his backpack and dug out what he needed.

Later in the week, he'd return to this hellhole. He'd be sure to avoid the skinny dark-haired girl, and then he'd be more successful. No one would get in his way.

He wouldn't allow it.

What worked on Aunt Dory and Uncle Myer would work on others.

If he didn't keep his aunt and uncle occupied, they'd venture out on their own, and they were so brainless, ruled only by their base desires, that they ran the risk of blowing their whole setup.

But Oren liked things as they were. He liked the house, the freedom, the control he had over others . . .

In his mind, he pictured the dirty tramp, tied to the sparse frame . . . almost broken, almost there.

He laughed out loud.

Yeah, he liked it a lot.

❦

Knowing Luther watched her every tiny move, Gaby turned her head to the side and smirked. Little by little, the grip of the righteous calling subsided, pulling its sharp talons out of her soul, releasing her to deal with more earthbound issues.

Like Luther.

It hurt to keep looking at him, to see how he looked at her.

After the hell of her life, she'd thought herself tough, strong enough to stay alone, to relish her isolation from the pathetic society surrounding her.

But God's truth, walking away from Luther weeks ago had almost destroyed her. She'd needed a purpose, any purpose other than the agony God saw fit to strike her with at His whim.

Luther's breath heated her neck right above the collar that she always wore. Like her association with divine forces, the choker gave her solace.

"Answer me, God damn it!"

The blasphemy bothered her far more than the bone-crushing grip on her wrists. "You know why I left."

"Tell me."

Temper snapping, she jerked her hands loose and shoved him back several feet. That felt good enough that she went ahead and shoved him again, her attack taking him by surprise enough that he stumbled backward and nearly fell on his ass.

As he took a stance against her, his nostrils flared. "Gaby . . ."

"Luther," she mocked. She might be skinny, but when enraged, she had undeniable strength, with or without God's influence.

Leaning in to him, stalking him, she snarled, "I left because I wanted you, all right?"

He planted his big feet and stopped retreating.

His savage expression didn't impress her one iota. "You showed me things you shouldn't have, Luther. But then Mort died and I . . ." The harsh memory of losing her only friend caused the words to strangle in her throat before emerging as a faint whisper. "I felt so guilty, I had to leave."

Straightening on a deep sigh, Luther surveyed her, shook his head, and holstered his gun. "Gaby," he said again, not as a warning this time, but with softened exasperation and what sounded suspiciously like condolence.

"Don't do that." She turned her back on him, resisting the urge to slap her hands over her ears. "Don't talk all gentle and sweet when nothing can ever happen between us." To reinforce that fact, more to herself than to Luther, she said harder, *"Never."*

He had the audacity to laugh. "Bullshit."

Whirling on him, she opened her mouth—

"It's happening, Gaby." To emphasize his point, Luther closed the insignificant space between them. "Believe it. *Accept it.* I can't say when, but I know it will." He looked her over. "*You* know it will, so stop fighting that much, at least."

Meaning he knew she fought everything else? Her commiserable life? Her very existence?

Her purpose on earth?

Okay, so they had that unsettling sexual chemistry thing churning between them. She did accept that. But the rest?

Not possible.

So why did he have to hunt her down and start teasing her with impossible things again? As a paladin, a warrior for God, her life wasn't normal, would never be normal.

She was abnormal—in every way.

Luther couldn't know what she did, and he wouldn't believe why she did it. Normal people weren't summoned by God.

Normal people didn't destroy life in any grisly manner necessary.

Normal people didn't behold the abominable evil that showed itself clearly to her, the evil she was ordered to annihilate.

Like spilled oil in a dirty gutter, it all came back to the surface: her duty, and Luther's inability to ever grasp or accept it. He was a damn cop, and given half a chance he'd arrest her, see her prosecuted, and stand by while unknowing *normal* people saw her locked away.

For life.

And that hurt more than anything could.

Ready to disguise her anguish with anger, Gaby charged forward, and Luther held up a hand to stop her.

"Mort's not dead, sweetheart."

She drew up short. *Sweetheart?* What sappy shit was that? No one called her . . .

Then the rest of what Luther said sank in and Gaby's world tilted. Her knees felt weak. Her heart punched hard against the wall of her chest.

Not dead? But . . .

Weeks ago, Mort had died. She knew it.

She'd *seen* it.

Images burned through her mind with a flash-fire intensity that seared her soul and inflamed her agony.

She saw Mort bravely staying behind in the abandoned building after she'd dispatched the zombielike souls and the monstrous doctor who'd created them. She saw Mort showing his first signs of personal pride, practically glowing with his sense of purpose—God's purpose.

And then . . . Mort falling beneath a madwoman's lust for blood, buried in ashes and dust . . .

"No." Lost on the night breeze, her whispered denial faded into oblivion. She wheezed, trying to draw in needed oxygen, but instead her lungs bloated on the nastiness of depravity and the craven sense of despair.

"Yes, Gaby."

Luther's reassurance didn't touch her. Reaching out, she braced a palm on the roughened surface of broken bricks, her eyes burning and her throat constricted. "I saw . . ."

"What?" New anger sparked in Luther's brown eyes. "What did you see?"

"Nothing." She shook her head. She couldn't let Luther know that she had been there, a part of it all, the biggest part—the part that butchered, hashed, and permanently destroyed atrocities too vile to survive.

He didn't buy it. "You were there, weren't you, Gaby? Mort lied about that much. Admit it."

Luther didn't approach her, didn't touch her. He just waited, watching her, judging her reaction the way he always judged her—with suspicion and cynicism.

He was a good man.

Auras of strength and purpose always surrounded him, a protective halo to remind her of all the ways they contrasted.

That he remained distrustful of her was one good reason to keep her distance. If a do-gooder seraph like Luther
ever found out what she did, he'd never be able to deal
with it.

Reminding herself of that gave her strength, enough to
amass her wits and face him again.

She steadied her palpating heart and locked back her jel-
lied knees. Suspicious, hopeful, she surveyed him. "Mort's
really alive?"

Fed up, Luther reached for her—but this time Gaby was
ready. Exhilarated by the idea that her old landlord and only
true friend might have survived, she ducked out of Luther's
reach and came up behind him.

Her right arm clamped tight around his throat, tight enough
to squeeze his windpipe. "Take it easy, big boy."

The taunt sent him over the edge.

He reacted so quickly, he caught Gaby off guard. In a series of well-timed movements, she found herself slammed
back up against the wall, this time with Luther's big, impos-
ing body plastered to her. Unless she decided to hurt him,
and she didn't want to do that, she couldn't defend herself.

Her bones, her joints, protested and her pride prickled . . .

But oh God, jubilation filled her. Euphoria erupted. She
was better than ecstatic.

Morty was alive.

Luther wouldn't lie about that. He couldn't. Somehow, by
some divine intervention, Morty had survived.

Damn, but she couldn't wait to see the little weasel again.
When she did, she'd give him hell for sure.

Incredulous, Luther snarled. "Don't you dare smile, Gaby."
He bracketed one big, hard hand around her throat, and with
the other pinned both of her wrists high. "Don't you dare act
like nothing is wrong."

Throughout most of her lamentable life, Gaby had had no reason for joy. Now she felt it in spades, and damn it, she couldn't suppress it. Even Luther's pissed-off attitude couldn't dampen her buoyant spirits.

Gaby eyed him, lifted one brow, and when the happiness threatened to implode, she kissed him.

Luther jerked back—but she followed and kissed him again, needing to celebrate the foreign emotion of pure, undiluted happiness bursting inside her.

She'd never felt it before, and she loved it, wanted to cherish it and this moment. It was a first for her, a sign that somewhere in her blackened heart, a real woman lived and breathed and accepted influence from the world that had rejected her so harshly.

Breathing hard and fast, Luther resisted her impetuous onslaught for only a nanosecond before the hand at her throat softened, his fingers slid up into her hair, and he positively devoured her mouth.

Kissing was as new to her as joy, but doubly thrilling. As a creature of instincts, Gaby rubbed herself against him. When that didn't appease, she groaned and bit him.

He jerked back, panting, his face red and his eyes burning like the devil himself.

They stared at each other. Gaby said, "I like kissing you, Luther."

An internal struggle manifested itself on his features. He fought hard, making his beautiful brown eyes blaze and his sensuous mouth tighten.

He swallowed, worked his jaw, then flattened her by asking in a brisk, but affected voice, "Why were you chasing the boy?"

The wind left her lungs. Fucking asshole. Her pride bristled at such a harsh rejection. "Let me go."

"Not until you answer me."

She shook her head; not in denial, but because she didn't have an answer for him. "I don't know why."

"What?"

Because she detested being uncertain in any way, she snapped, "Clear out your ears, cop."

His left eye flinched. "So now we're back to insults, is that it?"

"Hey, I clearly wanted to fuck. You're the one—"

He released her so quickly, Gaby almost fell. Before she could regain her bearings, he'd turned his back on her and paced away. One hand rubbed the back of his neck, the other clenched into a fist.

In a perfect world, Gaby would try to figure him out. She'd want to understand her sudden hurt and why she'd ever, even for a single second, thought a man like Luther, a good, kind, beautiful man, would want any part of her.

But this world was imperfect, in part because of her, in other ways, in spite of her.

Best if she just left, right now, while she still could. She started to do just that.

Luther said, "Please don't go."

"No reason to stay."

Without making a sound, he came to her and his hand closed over her shoulder. In a harsh, hungry whisper, he said, "I want you, Gaby. Don't ever doubt that."

"Yeah, I could tell."

He ignored her sarcasm. "You've been hanging out with prostitutes and now suddenly you want sex. With me. I haven't seen you in a long time. Hell, I wasn't sure if I'd ever see you again. When last I did see you, you made it clear that sex wasn't an option. Hell, you cursed me for making you want sex."

"I have a good memory, and you're saying *sex* an awful lot for a man who just turned it down."

Gently, he turned her to face him. "Just moments ago, you told me it would never happen."

"And it won't."

It was his turn to smile, halfheartedly, crookedly. It made him look so appealing. "I already promised you that it will. But not in a moment of insanity where you might regret it later." Both hands cupped her face. "When I get on top of you, and I will, we won't be in a dirty alley, or in a hurry, and we'll both be clear about what we want."

Those words affected her so deeply that she hid her response. "Whatever. You done with me?"

"No, I'm not. Not by a long shot." With a hand at her back, he started her walking out of the alley toward the street where lamps filtered through a growing fog. "Tell me why you chased that boy. And no bullshit about not knowing why. You always know what you do. You're a very decisive woman."

Okay, so maybe she did know. Something about the kid had . . . reminded her of herself. Oh, he was better dressed than she'd ever been, clean and fresh and healthy. He had normal weight, where she'd always been frail. His eyes were bright instead of sunken with depression and pain.

But something about him, some ethereal aura showed his confusion about his purpose in life.

She was good at reading auras.

It was a talent, not unlike her talent in destroying rancorous evil.

As a child, she'd been adrift in incomprehensible pain and confused direction. The more she fought against it, the worse it got. At times, the pain would ease, but it never completely left her.

That is, not until she accepted her insights, and exterminated the immoral malevolence surrounding her. Then, and only then, could she draw an easy breath.

The blind, the unknowing, summoned doctors for a cure, but they couldn't name the ailment.

Authorities refused to acknowledge it as real.

The foster families who occasionally allowed her into their homes thought her a fraud, a faker, and they punished for the pain.

No one understood, and no one knew how she escaped the agony—no one, except Father Mullond. And that good man encouraged her, coached her, helped her gain direction to her purpose and deception to cover her tracks.

As a man of God, he understood her duty more than she ever could have. He made it crystal clear that if anyone found out, she'd be labeled a murderer, and the rest of her days would be spent in prison, or an asylum—where the pain would gnaw on her all the rest of her days.

And so they'd worked together, Father Mullond and her, an odd pair matched by God. Gaby told Father of her auras, shared with him the first niggling of discomfort, and he, through the confessions of a priest, learned the truths behind her visions.

And ultimately, he gave his blessing to each and every slaughter.

Father had changed her life with his understanding, his guidance.

Then he'd changed it again—with his death.

Chapter 2

The memories sent a shaft of pain slicing through Gaby. She pressed a hand to her gut, and glanced at Luther for a needed distraction. "That boy didn't belong here."

Eyes keen and wary, Luther watched her. "It's a free country, Gaby."

"No, it isn't, not really." A rusted can blocked her path; she crushed it with her heel. "But either way, it doesn't change the fact that he was here for some reason, and he shouldn't have been."

"He looked around twelve or so. A kid. And a scrawny kid at that. Surely you don't consider him a threat to your hookers?"

"*My* hookers?" That made her roll her eyes. "I don't claim ownership to the ladies."

He pressed her. "You consider yourself their protector."

Rolling one shoulder, she said, "It's a purpose. That's all."

"And you need one?"

"Don't you?"

"Maybe."

"Isn't that why you're a cop?" Even as he annoyed her with his persistence, she felt the encroachment of that odd comfort that always ameliorated her edge when she was in Luther's close proximity. She sneered, "You want to accomplish things, make a difference?"

He strolled beside her in silence. "You say that like it isn't possible."

It wasn't. But she wouldn't burst his insulating bubble by telling him so. Not that he'd believe her anyway. Luther was special, but he was also blind to the true depravity of evil.

When she didn't reply, he finally said, "It's dangerous for you to hang out with whores, Gaby. Some of them have pimps—"

"Who get real mean on occasion. I know. I've seen it. And more." God hadn't asked for her intervention with the abusive johns. But she'd given it anyway—and enjoyed herself.

That was something she'd learned since meeting Luther, that righting wrongs—even those simple, quotidian deeds of inhumanity—gave her a great sense of satisfaction, and the feeling that she had some control over her own destiny. She didn't have to base her every act on God's demand.

She, Gabrielle Cody, could sometimes act on her own.

Slanting another glance at Luther, she admired the strong lines of his nose, chin, and jaw, the way an evening breeze disrupted his trimmed blond hair—and she found him so visually pleasing, she wished she never had to look away. "I have an understanding with the men who do claim ownership of the ladies."

Luther muttered a rank curse under his breath, tightened even more, and asked, "Let's hear it."

"Not much to hear." Gaby forced her gaze back to the long stretch of road before them. Haggard vagrants curled in empty doorways; shadowy dealings took place in darkened parked cars; nightlife scurried about, committing conventional crimes and atrocities unworthy of opposition. "They rule the roost, as the ladies allow, but when they cross the line too much . . ." She let her voice fade off, and shrugged. "Shit happens."

"Shit?"

Satiety unfurled lazily inside her. "In the dark," she whispered, "where it's impossible to distinguish a face, things can happen. Things like the slice of a knife where men hope no blade will ever venture." Her palms tingled in memory of that first, light slice—shallow, superficial, and all the more terrifying for it. She could almost smell the fear of her targets, the memory of it pleasantly scorched into her brain. "It's effective."

Luther came to a dead halt. "Jesus, Gaby."

Facing him, she crossed her arms and cocked out one hip. "When I met you, I was pretty damn stupid about all things sexual."

Every muscle in his body tensed. "You were innocent, not stupid."

She shook her head. "No, never."

"Yes." He stepped closer. "There's a difference, Gaby, and I'm well aware of it."

Fool. Luther might not realize it, but she wasn't even innocent at birth. She didn't know what it would be like to have innocence. "I just hadn't much thought about sex, and I had zero action." She looked at his throat, at the open collar of his shirt, and her heartbeat grew heavy. "*After* you, well, I thought about it a lot." Her gaze came back to his. "The ladies taught me things."

He stared, fascinated, horrified. Mute.

"Get your mind out of the gutter, cop!" She reached out and shoved him from his stupor. "I don't mean that I did anything with them."

He rocked back on his heels. "Thank God."

"Yeah, He wouldn't have liked it, that's for sure."

"He?"

She shook her head, unwilling to go into her most personal relationship. "I witnessed a lot of stuff. And I had all these questions—"

Luther pokered right back up again. "You asked *hookers* to educate you on sex?"

"Yeah, but you don't have to announce it to the whole street."

He grabbed her arm and drew her toward the closest building. It didn't offer much privacy, but at least they weren't in the middle of the walkway.

"I thought we agreed you'd come to me."

Snorting, she said, "I'd figured on never seeing you again, remember?"

Through his teeth, he said, "It's not like I could forget."

Ignoring his ire, Gaby added, "Besides, the ladies proved to be real candid about stuff. Way more so than you or Morty ever were."

Tilting his head back, Luther groaned to the starry sky.

"Stop dying on me, will you? I'm just saying, now I have a better understanding on what all the hoopla is about—not that the ladies think sex is all that great. For them, it's a messy chore, but hey, it pays the bills, right?"

Leaning back on the building, his jaw clenched and his eyes zeroed in on her, Luther said, "Selling sex and sharing it with someone special are two different things."

"Even though it sounds pretty complicated and verging

on gross, I think I agree with you. What I felt with you and what I felt when I watched the women—"

"You *watched* the hookers servicing johns?"

Did he have to keep sounding so appalled? "A few times, yeah. Occasionally some perverted creeps will visit, and I need to keep close, for protective reasons, you know. But my point is—"

"I do *not* want you watching that warped shit!"

Damn it, now she forgot her point. "Well, *Daddy*, it's not up to you, is it?"

He loomed over her. "Do not push me, Gaby."

"Or what?" she asked, very deliberately giving him a good hard push.

Silence stretched out while he mentally chewed on his response. "I haven't forgiven you yet for disappearing on me." He brought his nose to hers. "And I'm still suspicious of every damn move you make."

That sobered her and sucked the anger out of her veins. Crestfallen, doused in icy reality, she nodded. "I know."

Her meekness only ripened his fury. "If you force my hand, I swear to God I'll handcuff you and drag your scrawny ass to the station where we can sort things out at my leisure."

She wouldn't—*couldn't*—let him do that. If he ever got her locked away, he might not let her loose again, and that was a risk she couldn't take.

Without the ability to follow God's summons, the pain would destroy her. She knew it, she accepted it.

"I believe you, cop, I really do." Turning away, she said, "And that's why sex can't ever happen between us, never mind my moment of— What did you call it? Insanity? That fits." Strolling off, she added, "You do make me insane."

In a roar loud enough to disrupt the dead, Luther demanded, *"Where are you going?"*

"To see Mort." At least that'd take her a good distance from Luther, and she needed the separation before she got melancholy, or worse, before she broke his jaw. "Is that allowed, cop, or will visiting a friend put me in jeopardy of being arrested?"

In the time that she'd been away from him, Gaby had forgotten the soundless way he moved. Suddenly his hand clamped around her upper arm and he drew her to an uncompromising, but gentle halt.

She didn't turn to face him.

He didn't insist.

Leaning down, his mouth almost touching her ear, he whispered, "Seeing Mort tonight is fine—as long as I know where to find you tomorrow."

"Why would you want to?" she asked, hoping he had a good reason that would miraculously lift the smothering desolation now cloaking her.

Fingertips grazed her skin as he lifted aside her hair and then . . . his mouth touched her throat just above the choker she wore. Damp. Warm. Tingling and exciting. Her heart threatened to escape the bony confines of her chest. Low in her belly, some insidious warmth writhed and wriggled.

Her eyes closed. "Luther . . ."

"When you're like this, Gaby, you're far more likable." He stepped away, met her incredulous, wide-eyed gaze, and smiled. "Meet me here, tomorrow, at seven. It's important."

"Bastard," she hissed.

He looked down at her tightened nipples, lifted a taunting eyebrow, and insisted, "I need your promise, Gaby."

Slow and exact, she crowded toward him. "I can promise to make you a fucking choirboy if you ever again pull a stunt like—"

In a cheerful mood directly opposite of hers, he laughed,

yanked her in for a fast smooch on her mouth, and released her again. "Heard it, and heard it again. But wouldn't it be easier to just promise me?"

God, he was dangerous to her state of mind. Grudgingly, she said, "I'll be here."

"Be careful tonight."

"Fuck you."

A shake of his head showed his disapproval. "Same old Gaby—except with new clothes and hair."

Self-consciousness crept in. "That's the ladies' doing."

"The hookers?"

"They said if I was going to hang around, I needed to fit in." Truthfully, she'd enjoyed their efforts. They'd painted her hair, and she'd grilled them on the how and why of sexual variations. Not a terrible trade-off.

"I like it. But then, I liked you before, too." He touched her chin, looked at the choker he'd bought her, still around her throat, and then left.

Gaby stood there until he'd rounded the corner. Since he headed toward the building where she now lived, she would have been worried—except if he knew where she lived, he wouldn't have exacted a promise from her to meet him on the street.

Right?

She started to follow him, just to make sure, but changed her mind. Seeing Mort was more important.

Tomorrow she'd deal with Luther.

❦

Luther waited around the corner until Gaby had time to leave. When he checked, he saw her walking away, her stride cocky, her presence commanding. His gaze stayed glued to her narrow hips until she faded into the darkness.

Until recently—until knowing Gabrielle Cody—the protector in him would never have allowed a woman to wander the drug- and crime-ravaged area alone. During the day, the neighborhood was a cesspool of corruption where fights broke out every hour, flesh was traded, and drugs were purchased.

At night, the lowest kind of miscreants crawled out, willing to snuff life for a smoke, or sometimes, just for the pleasure of it.

Gaby could care for herself though. She'd proven that time and again.

Still, Luther took out his cell and called Morty Vance, Gaby's old landlord.

He answered on the second ring.

"'Lo?"

"It's Luther."

"Hi, Luther. What's up?"

Cutting to the chase, Luther said, "I found Gaby."

Silence. And then: "You *found* her? How is she? *Is she okay?*"

"She's the same, Mort." Well, not really, but he didn't have time to go into it. "She's on her way to see you. She should be there soon. If she doesn't make it, let me know."

"She's coming here alone?"

Guilt nudged in, but Luther snuffed it beneath other priorities. "I couldn't go with her. I have things to do." Important things. Urgent things. "She'll be fine."

"Shit. Which way is she coming? I'll meet her halfway."

Bemused, because a near-death experience had neatly matured Morty into a man almost overnight, Luther told him her direction. "You be careful, too, Mort. Stay in the light."

He laughed. "I'd never find Gaby if I did. She's a woman who clings to shadows. But yeah, I'll be careful. Thanks, Luther." The call disconnected.

A woman who clings to shadows.

Didn't he know it? When she chose to be, Gaby was an adumbration of humanity, every bit as obscure and hazy as the shifting shadow of a half-moon. Gaby could be there one minute, and if he dared to blink, she disappeared. Part of Luther believed she'd wanted him to find her; if not, he probably never would have. Gaby had many talents, among them the ability to blend into nothingness, to be no one, to . . . not exist.

Putting the phone back in his pocket, Luther headed toward the motel where he'd bet Gaby lived. It was an eyesore, a den of iniquity, but unless summoned, the police turned a blind eye to the crimes committed there.

He'd deceived Gaby on purpose, pretending he had no clue where she resided. For that he wouldn't feel a single iota of guilt. He didn't trust her.

He couldn't.

If he got a chance to talk to the call girls, maybe the manager of the motel, without Gaby aware of it, he might get some new insight on her.

At least, that was the plan.

The building sat close to the street with only a broken, littered walkway separating it from the curb. Most of the windows were painted black or shielded with dark coverings. The red paint on the front door peeled away like blistering skin from a harsh sunburn.

In raunchy poses that exposed overused body parts, three women lounged around. As Luther approached, they sized him up with guarded cynicism—and intuitively recognized him as a cop.

That didn't convince them to close their legs or their mouths. Lewd comments, void of any real offering, would have brought a blush to a man unaccustomed to such human dreariness.

Luther stopped in front of a redhead wearing layered makeup and smoking a cigarette with ravenous appetite. "I have some questions."

After blowing smoke in his face, she grinned wide enough to show two missing side teeth. "This ain't the information desk, sugar."

"Is the manager inside?"

She laughed. "Now, sugar, you know he ain't gonna talk to you neither."

Looking up three stories, Luther guessed that Gaby would be up top somewhere. "I'm looking for Gabrielle Cody's room."

"Yeah?" She took another hungry drag on her cigarette. "Who's that?"

Luther could be patient when need be. "Tall, thin girl. Quiet. Deadly."

The whore shrugged. "Don't ring no bells."

"What's your name?"

She eyed him. "Betty."

"Well, Betty." Luther pulled out his badge, and finished by saying, "Either you start talking, or I bust all three of you."

Flicking away the cigarette and straightening with apprehension, she demanded, "For what?"

Using the edge of his badge, Luther tapped the inside of Betty's fleshy thigh. "Indecent exposure, for starters. You'll probably be held up for hours—and that'll make it tough to reach your quota for the day, now won't it?"

In rapid succession, sounding like a pack of pissed off banshees, the women told him to fuck himself in ways unimaginable, and surely impossible.

"Fine." Luther pulled out his radio. "Have it your way."

From behind him, a man said, "Hold up, cop."

Luther turned, found a tall, lean, and muscled man behind him. Given certain traits, he likely had a mixed racial background. Given his clothes and attitude, Luther knew he was a pimp.

"And you are?"

Through narrowed eyes partially concealed by blue-tinted sunglasses, the fellow watched him. "An innocent bystander." He grinned to show off a gold tooth. "What do you want with the girl?"

Sensing an ally, Luther moved closer. "Actually, Ms. Cody is a friend more than anything. I want to know what she's up to, that's all."

Luther stiffened when the man withdrew a knife from his back pocket, but he only flicked it open to clean his nails. "Tell you what, cop. If you'll get her out of my hair, I'll help however I can."

Viewing his assistance as traitorous, the women started grumbling and grousing to themselves. The man shouted, "Shut the fuck up! Get off your lazy asses and head up the street a ways."

"I was taking my break," Betty protested.

Jaw locked, the man took a threatening step toward her. "You want a break, bitch?"

"No, Jimbo." She ducked, covering her head until she realized he had stopped short of reaching her. Then she hurried away.

"Stupid bitches," Jimbo spat as he moved back to rest his spine on a lamppost. "Lazy sluts, every fucking one of them."

Rage simmered inside Luther. He detested men like Jimbo, men who abused those smaller or weaker than himself. "Just so you know," Luther told him, "I wouldn't have let you touch her."

They stared at each other until Jimbo grinned.

"Don't need to knock Betty around much. She knows her place." He examined the knife blade. "The bitch you're talking about don't, though. She's fucking psychotic."

The rage threatened to boil over, but Luther kept his tone calm. "Why do you say that?"

"She bought a shitload of stuff to barricade her room. Got reinforced locks on everything—and that was before I said shit to her."

"Before?" If Jimbo had given Gaby one second of grief, Luther would take him apart. Oozing menace, disregarding the knife, he crowded into Jimbo's space. "What exactly did you say to her?"

Jimbo sized him up, and saw more than Luther meant to share. "I only asked her what she was thinking, moving into a whorehouse. But she don't say much. And when she does, she wants to talk with her fists."

"She *fought* you?" God almighty, Luther would kill her himself.

Jimbo laughed. "Nah, man, I don't fight with the bitches. Besides, she doesn't work for me."

"If I thought she did," Luther said quietly, "I'd kill you."

Jimbo paused, rethought his position, and went back to his nails. "She moved in, took over, and turned that piss-hole she calls a room into a fortress." He folded the knife and slid it back into his pocket. "Makes me wonder what kind of trouble she's expecting—and how it might affect my working girls if it shows up."

"Did you ask her about it?"

Scoffing, Jimbo said, "Prickly bitch don't talk to me. She just looks at me like she'd like to skin me alive. But I know why she did it. She figures Carver will be after her, on account of the way she cut him up and all."

Worse and worse. Just how much trouble had Gaby gotten into since Luther last saw her? With growing exasperation, he asked, "Carver?"

"Yeah. Raggedy-ass hillbilly punk used to work this corner." He eyed Luther, looked around. "I don't want trouble with Carver."

"You should worry more about me, and less about him."

"My man." Jimbo grinned with amusement. "I'm not worried 'bout either of yas, but I'd sooner make money than have a hassle. And with you, I think we can work out a deal."

"I don't deal with the likes of you."

"If you want to keep the bitch alive, you're going to have to. Because it's a fact, Carver will come looking for her. If we can work in harmony, then hey, I'll drop you a line when I hear word of the plan. After that . . ." He shrugged. "It'll be up to you if you wanna play her white knight."

There was a plan. Jesus. "I'm listening."

"I want Carver and the woman out of my hair. When he comes after her, you can catch him in the act and put him away for good."

"Not a problem." Anyone planning to hurt Gaby made his shit list real quick. "Anything else?"

"Yeah. You'll get the woman off my corner for good."

Luther asked, "What does it matter to you if she's here or not?"

"She interferes with business and gives the whores uppity ideas. Right now, she's only an annoyance, nothing more. I want her gone before she really starts to piss me off. Deal?"

Taking the time to breathe deep and long, Luther looked up at the sky, breathed in the humid night air and released it slowly. When he knew he could speak without ripping off Jimbo's head, he faced him.

At six three and two hundred pounds, Luther was bigger than many men. His weight was all muscle; he stayed in shape and kept up with his defense training.

Against him, a jerk-off like Jimbo didn't stand a chance.

The urge to destroy the psychopathic little cretin trickled ice through Luther's veins, but he was a man of law, not a vigilante—and not a one-man defense for Gaby Cody's twisted lifestyle.

The lecture of reason helped Luther to rein in the urge for destruction—but it didn't stop him from planting a single vicious punch to Jimbo's solar plexus.

As the smaller man doubled over, wheezing and heaving, Luther caught the front of his shirt and turned to slam him into the wall of the building. "Do I have your attention, Jimbo?"

When Jimbo only coughed and choked, Luther rattled him. "You miserable little bully, suck it up and listen to me."

"Yeah, man," Jimbo gasped. "Yeah. I hear ya."

"I'll gladly take care of Carver. In return, there better not be a single hair on Gaby's head disturbed. If anyone touches her, if you let *anyone* get close enough to hurt her without telling me, I'll make you the sorriest little shit this city has ever seen. Do I make myself clear?"

Arms folded around himself, Jimbo turned his head to the side and puked. Luther released him with alacrity. "Fuck." Stepping back out of range, Luther fulminated against the injustice of abuse. "For a man who likes to threaten women, you sure can't take a punch yourself."

Jimbo dropped to his knees. He gagged again, but kept down the putrid remains of his gut. After a couple of seconds, he wiped a sleeve over his mouth, spat, and swallowed. "You didn't need to do that."

"No, probably not. But I wanted to." Catching him by the shoulder, Luther pulled him back to his feet. "Now tell me about Carver and why he'd want to hurt Gaby."

Jimbo nodded a little too quickly.

"Lie to me, and that last blow will seem like a lover's tap." Even as Luther hated himself for indulging a bully's mentality, he gave a grim promise: "I'll be sure to break no less than three ribs. Believe it, Jimbo."

Shrugging off Luther's hold, Jimbo said, "Yeah, got it, dude. Just give me a second."

Checking his watch, Luther saw that Gaby should have reached Mort already. How long she'd remain there, he couldn't guess. Her less favorable qualities included unpredictability.

Why he felt so drawn to her, Luther couldn't say. But he'd laid eyes on her, and it had all been downhill since. There was some ethereal, elusive quality to Gaby that had him in a stranglehold. "I'm about out of time. Spit it out."

Jimbo wiped his mouth again, looked around to ensure they hadn't drawn notice, and stared up at Luther. "One of Carver's whores gave him some lip, and he smacked her around some."

"Gaby saw this?"

"Yeah." Grinding pain strangled Jimbo's laugh. "That psycho cunt didn't like it one bit, I can tell you that. But she kept her trap shut, so Carver ignored her."

Lingering on the periphery of an insane rage, Luther whispered, "You are dumber than you look, Jimbo, do you know that?"

"What? It's the truth, I swear."

Shaking his head, as much at himself and his absurd code of chivalry as Jimbo's obtuse sense of propriety, Luther said, "Call her one more name, make one more slur, and I'll—"

"God damn it, man, I can't think with you threatening me!"

Luther fought for control. "Carver hurt the girl?"

"Broke her jaw, I think. It wasn't real bad. I've seen worse beatings."

"I take it you didn't offer to help her?"

"Hell no, man. You don't get between that shit. And I figured my girls could learn some from it, ya know? But sometime later that night, Carver was attacked."

"By whom?"

Jimbo shook his head. "Carver ain't sayin', and the whore he was with didn't see nothin' before he kicked her out of his bed. Word on the street is that Carver was lying there, taking a snooze after a good plow, and *boom*!"

"Boom?"

Jimbo shrugged. "His girls found him tied to the bed, sliced up all over. Not deep cuts, but a pool of his own blood had soaked into the mattress. His face, his body, hell, even his dick was worked over." As Jimbo spoke, an oily, nervous sweat showed on his brow. "That was some fucked-up shit, man."

Luther had a hard time containing himself. He knew it was Gaby, had heard her practically admit as much. "He's lucky that whoever it was didn't kill him."

Digging out a smoke, Jimbo said, "Lucky hell. It was a damn threat to everyone. I ain't seen him, but I hear that Carver is still shook up. He's lying low until he gets healed, and then he'll want revenge."

Against Gaby.

Grit scratched at Luther's tired eyes and acid burned his stomach. Hoping for a convincing bluff, Luther asked, "What's this have to do with Gabrielle Cody?"

Jimbo moved a few cautious steps away from Luther. "I don't know what it is, but that girl has everyone spooked. She goes around like a fucking ghost, unafraid, silent in that damned eerie way of hers, and everyone assumes she had something to do with Carver's attack. Some think she put a hex, or some shit, on him, and others think she hired someone to cut him up. All I know is, if you care about her, you ought to get her away from here before Carver does a number on her."

If Luther tried to take Gaby away, what would she do? For certain she'd fight him. Independence was the stronghold of her nature. "I told you what would happen to you, Jimbo, if anyone hurts her."

"Hell, man, I'm leaving psycho chick alone." With trembling hands, he lit the cigarette and sucked hard, making the tip glow hot. He relaxed on the tangible effects of smoke filling his lungs, nicotine polluting his system. "Look, cop, the woman . . . Gaby—"

"No," Luther warned. "Don't say her name. I like hearing it from your mouth even less than the insults."

"What the fuck, man!" Jimbo exploded. "Do you want to hear this or not?"

"Finish."

"She—*that woman*—keeps the johns from hurting my girls so they can keep working. Far as I'm concerned, if she hadn't pissed off the wrong people, she could've hung around. But she's made enemies and that means I have to look after things."

A group of thugs came around the corner. They were still

too far away to see much when Jimbo threw down the cigarette. "That's my posse. I gotta split."

Luther pulled out a business card and held it out to him. "Don't forget what I said, Jimbo. If you hear anything at all about Carver, I want to know."

"Yeah, right." He snatched the card and slid it into his pocket. "If you want to check her room, it's all the way at the top, in the attic."

That prickly animosity resurfaced. "How is it you know that?"

"Fuck no, man, don't make wrong assumptions. The bitches knock on her door sometimes, but I keep my distance." Jimbo started away. "That attic wasn't livable before she moved in. It sure as hell ain't a place to visit now that she's in there."

Dismissing Jimbo from his thoughts, Luther turned and went into the building. Dim lighting left long shadows in the foyer. Two metal-legged chairs with cracked plastic seats sat at the bottom of a tall staircase. Under the front window sat a loveseat, and on that was a woman curled into the corner, sleeping soundly, her clothes as much off as on.

A wooden desk, rotted with age, carved with graffiti and sticky with unknown substances served as a check-in point. Behind it, keys on plastic rings hung from a pegboard on the wall. All but three keys were missing from their hooks.

No one sat at the front desk, and Luther didn't bother ringing the bell. Taking the dark stairs two at a time, he went up. He heard coarse laughter, a few squeals, some crying. Bedsprings squeaked. The sound of a slap rang out.

His stomach cramped.

He didn't want Gaby here.

But where else did she belong? He didn't know her well enough to say.

At the top of three stories, only a narrow staircase remained. It led to the attic.

Gaby had chosen to be here. There had to be a reason.

This time, before she escaped him again, Luther would get some answers—one way or another.

Chapter 3

As she traversed through dreary shadows, avoiding streetlamps and caustic denizens, Gaby festered on her damning misconceptions. So much wasted time, so many spent emotions that she didn't have to spare.

After seeing Morty die—or thinking he had died—she'd given up writing her popular graphic novels. Because Mort had served as her contact to the publishing world, writing and illustrating the novels seemed pointless. Sending the completed novels to an unknown source could initiate unwanted exposure.

It was too risky.

But without an outlet for her pain and despair, a yawning, caliginous wasteland had split open inside her. At times it had felt alive, devouring her one painful bite at a time.

Knowing that Morty lived opened up endless possibilities.

Stories ripe with both fabrication and fact winged through her beleaguered consciousness. An extant drive to put pen to paper conflicted with the urgent need to *see* Mort, to have his survival as a visual fact, not just a repeated truth.

A loud voice shattered her ruminations.

Up ahead, uncaring of who might see, an obese woman snatched up a stocky kid and shook him hard, berating him for following her.

The boy looked about ten.

He wanted his mamma; she wanted a john, possibly to pay for food, more likely because she was no more than a base whore lacking emotion for the well-being of her child.

Gaby's heart wrenched, and she fought the urge to intercede. Only the truth that she couldn't change the woman kept her away.

Sinking back against a wall, Gaby watched as the boy turned and, with a broken expression, ran away.

Just as she, at that age, had so many times run—even when there'd been nowhere to run to. Not until she'd been almost grown. Not until . . . Father.

For one awful, desperate moment, their initial meeting crept into her memories. If only she'd known him when she was that young and needy. If only he'd been there to help her deal with the duties heaped on an adolescent paladin.

But it wasn't until she'd turned seventeen and was on the streets alone that Father found her. Whenever she thought of those desperate times, she again tasted the fear that filmed her throat and left its burning scum on her teeth and tongue. She felt the rippling agony of demand for action, and the incomprehension of what to do about it.

Father had stumbled upon her in her weakened state, and to his credit, he'd tried to help.

No one else had approached her, asked or listened. No

one else had encroached at a time when her defenses were
lost to her.

"What's in your mind, child?"

*The voice came from far away, biting into her agony.
"Death. Death."*

"For yourself?"

*The torment twisted her, bowed her body like a soul pos-
sessed. "No," she whimpered. "For another."*

*A cool hand touched her brow. She shied from the aber-
rant act of comfort.*

"And that would be . . . ?"

*"I don't know his name." Speaking of her sins, her dark-
est cravings, should have cast her straight to hell. Instead, it
freed her. "He's there. At the end of the alley." She curled
tighter, squeezing her arms around herself, begging herself
to be silent, but the words erupted. "I don't know why, but I
need to destroy him."*

After a thoughtful pause, he said, "Wait here."

*The priest left her, as was right and proper. But within
minutes, he returned. Without a word, he sat beside her in the
abominable alley, uncaring of his robes or the refuse that
surrounded her, that was her.*

*Finally, after a long time, he said, "You would truly kill
him?"*

"Yes. Oh God, yes."

*"I don't see how." He lifted her hair back, put his hand
around her upper arm. "You're so young, a small child . . ."*

*"I would rip him to shreds with my bare hands!" The de-
monic voice sounded like someone else, but just saying it
sent a fire raging through her, making the pain wan beneath
a surge of pernicious strength. She panted hard, looked at*

the priest and saw his shock, his fear, and his curiosity, perhaps even understanding.

Sickened, expecting the worst, she tried to turn away.

He held her face. "Look at me."

And when she did, he said, "Do it."

Permission energized her. The strength amassed, so powerful that she felt inhuman. Superhuman.

"If you can destroy him," Father said with a calm that soothed her, "then you should, because my dear, no one else will." He smiled, patted her cheek, and said without judgment, "I'll wait here."

"Gaby?"

She jerked. Still held by the bellicose nostalgia, she reacted on instinct. Grabbing her confronter, she put him in a deadly hold—and heard a choking laugh.

"God, Gaby, I've missed you," the strangled voice said.

Mort. "You idiot!" She loosed him with a shove of temper. "Don't you know better than to sneak up on me?"

"Sneak?" Even in the darkness, she could see his grin. "I almost walked into you, you're standing there so still." He threw his arms around her, and she was stunned by his strength.

Morty Vance, landlord and wannabe friend, had always been just shy of a complete wimp and a spineless worm.

Now he had muscle tone; Gaby could feel the new strength in his limbs. And he exuded . . . confidence.

What the hell? "Mort? Is that really you?"

Using the back of his hand, he swiped away a tear. Of happiness? Shit.

"Of course it's me," he said around a robust laugh, and he didn't look the least bit self-conscious about weeping like an infant. "Luther called to say you were finally coming over, so I hurried out to meet you."

"Luther called you?"

Ignoring her question, he let his gaze roam all over her. "I almost didn't recognize you, Gaby, you look so different!" He held her at arm's length. "Look at you!"

Feeling like a freak with the way he gawked, she shook him off. "Stop it." Two gangly youths walking by tried to mean mug them, but one vengeful glance from her and they kept on going.

Mort beamed. "Same old Gaby where it counts, I see."

Now what the hell did he mean by that? "I altered the façade a little, that's all." Changing clothes and hair had been necessary camouflage to help her blend in. "It's nothing."

"You have nice legs."

Without even meaning to, Gaby surged up nose to nose with him, oozing menace and prickly beyond all measure. "Do you want me to demolish you?"

To her shock, he kissed her nose. "No." Then he bear-hugged her again, and all Gaby could do was stand there, arms and legs stiff, head back as far as her neck would allow, as she suffered his excess of affection.

"Come on," he said as he finally turned her loose. He clasped her hand. "Let's go to my place so we can catch up."

She didn't budge. "I'm going to kill you, Mort."

He laughed, held his hands out in surrender. "I'm sorry, Gaby. I really am. I know you're not into public displays. It's just that I really have missed you. Where did you go? Why did you leave me?"

Leave him? He smiled as he spoke, but a shitload of hurt shone in his pale blue eyes. He'd been her first friend.

Her only friend. Because he'd insisted. Little by little he'd forced his way in, and now he thought she'd abandoned him.

Gaby's stomach burned with guilt, and she hated it. With all she'd done—the people she'd dismembered—hurting one landlord's insignificant feelings shouldn't factor in.

But it did.

Father was a confidante, a teacher, pseudo-family. But he hadn't been as compassionate and caring, as . . . affectionate, as Mort.

Damn him for doing this to her.

Taking a cocky stance, she rolled her eyes. She meant to sound flippant, but instead, at the last second, the words emerged rife with aching loss. "I thought you were dead."

He blinked hard and fast. "Dead?"

Out of her element, Gaby lashed out, thwacking him on the shoulder and turning to walk a wide circle. "You were caught in that damned abandoned hospital. It exploded. I saw you go down, Mort."

"You'd already left."

She shot around to face him. "I came back for you!"

"You did?"

It was too much. She hadn't expected to feel this . . . this . . . whatever. She didn't like it. And it was Mort's fault.

"Fuck it." She strode away, her long legs eating up the pavement—until Mort rushed around in front of her.

"I'm sorry." His feet braced apart, expression forbidding, he blocked her. "I didn't know."

She couldn't believe it. Had the world gone topsy-turvy on her? Composure slipping, she snarled, "Get out of my way."

"No."

"No?"

Mort's scrawny chest expanded on a deep inhalation. "But Gaby, even if I had known what you thought, I couldn't have done anything about it, could I? You walked away and I had no idea where to find you. I thought you had taken off for good."

Still incredulous, she repeated, "No?"

He shook his head. "Please. Let's go to my place and talk. Your room is still there. You can move back in—"

The groan erupted with volcanic force. Worse and worse. She didn't want to hurt Mort again, but moving back was out of the question. Disgusted, she grabbed his hand and dragged him to the curb to sit. "Park it, Mort."

He parked.

Pacing behind him didn't do one damn thing for her temper, so she finally dropped down beside him. The short skirt, always an annoyance, rode up. But what the hell? It was too dark for anyone to see, and she didn't give a flip anyway.

Putting her elbows on her knees, she let out a breath. "I can't come back, Mort."

"Why?"

Being questioned by anyone was as new as friendship. But she supposed it came hand in hand, so she cut Mort some slack. "I can visit, but I can't live there. And no, don't grill me. I can't, and that's that."

"Where are you living now?"

"Over at the corner of Fifth and Elm."

He drew back. "But that's—"

Eyes narrowing, Gaby said, "Yes?"

With new insight, Mort took in her hair, the length of her exposed thigh, and he blanched. "No way."

She punched his shoulder hard enough to nearly topple him off the curb. "Of course not."

"It's a disguise?"

"It's me, a freak of nature, fitting in the best I can." The only real disguise was her pretending to be a normal human.

"Oh, Gaby." He started to hug her again, and she warned

him off with a single look. He settled back and smiled. "You're special, but you're not a freak."

"Says the dork." She gave him a fond look. "I'm not sure you're in a position to know a freak if you see one."

"Maybe," he agreed, accepting that he wasn't a popular figure himself. "What I don't get is, if you've been so close, how come Luther didn't find you sooner? He's sure been looking."

"I know."

It wouldn't hurt to tell Mort a little about what she did, how she'd secured new quarters and a modicum of anonymity. Before they'd parted ways, Mort had witnessed some of what she did. He didn't understand it all. He couldn't. But he knew that she killed only when ordered to.

In whatever way necessary.

"You remember when I asked you about sex?"

Mort stiffened, looked around, scooted a few inches away. "Yeah, uh . . ."

"Oh, for crying out loud. Stop squirming. I already know what I need to know now, no thanks to you."

His gulp could be heard above the normal night sounds.

Rolling her eyes, Gaby cut to the chase. "I was looking for a place to hole up when I heard a hooker fighting some guy. He'd tried to take the goods without paying, and she wasn't happy about it."

"Oh God."

"I made him pay, that's all." Given her mood at the time, she'd reveled in the punishment more than she should have. The show had impressed the woman and later her friends, left them awed and feeling empowered. They saw her as their own superhero—and Gaby, in need of cover, hadn't dissuaded them of that absurd notion.

To simplify all that, she said, "The woman appreciated my help."

Mort's incredulity hit her in waves. "I'll just bet she did."

"I don't think anyone had defended her, in anything, for a very long time."

"Which is probably why she's making a living off the streets." He gave her shoulder a brief squeeze. "Good for you, Gaby."

Gaby well remembered the hooker's esteem that prompted the offer of a place to rest up, and later an introduction to the rest of the girls who frequented that particular flophouse for prurient transactions.

Other offerings followed the initial gratefulness; fleshy proposals were proffered, some meant to show appreciation, some, oddly, from sincere interest. Most were in the way of a bartering tool for future services rendered.

Pity for the women, distracting concerns of her own, and a healthy interest in Luther, kept Gaby disinterested in anything physical with the women. They ribbed her, but respected her decision. Instead of sexual exchange, they'd worked out a deal that suited them all: Gaby got her meager rent paid on the upstairs room, and she protected the girls whenever need be.

"Anyway," she said, getting back on track, "I stick around and when they need me to, I protect them, or collect for them."

"And in the process, learn a few things?"

"You could say that." Giving unnecessary attention to her nails, Gaby asked, "So how's your business been?" Mort's apartment building abutted a comic store that sold underground graphic novels, some, like her work, in high demand. Mort had no idea that his business kept her in business, and supplied her meager livelihood.

He accepted the change of topic with a great show of relief. "Slower than usual. I'm waiting for a new *Servant* novel to bring in the customers. It'll be here soon, I hope."

New to the whole friendship, sharing, chatting business,

Gaby searched for more conversation, but came up empty. "Anything else going on?"

His shoulder touched hers with fond camaraderie. "I have a girlfriend now. I'd love for you to meet her."

Gaby's jaw went slack. No words came to her. *Mort* and *girlfriend* were two concepts she'd never envisioned aligned together.

Her lack of response didn't slow down Mort. "You might have met her," he enthused. "She's a detective who works with Luther, and she's beautiful."

Still blank brained, Gaby waited.

He filled the silence. "Her name is Ann Kennedy. I really care about her."

"Ann Kennedy." Oh yeah, she knew that name. She'd seen the woman with Luther, and she'd felt . . . jealousy. It sucked big-time, mostly because an emotion like that had no place in her brain, or in her life. She wasn't a woman fashioned for consocation of any kind, but a romantic alliance was out of the question.

Being a paladin meant being alone.

Having Mort as a friend was risky enough.

Being more than a friend to Luther could risk it all.

She squeezed her eyes shut. Denying it didn't remove the yearning.

"Yeah," Mort said, "Luther knows her."

"You said that." Luther had claimed they were only friends. If the woman had an interest in Mort, then obviously an earthbound seraph like Luther wasn't her speed.

Some things in this fucked-up world never made sense.

"She's blonde," Mort continued, "slim, big dark eyes . . ."

Fashioning a gun with her fingers, Gaby shot herself in the head.

Mort laughed. "Come on, Gaby. Is it really so odd for me to have a significant other?"

"Damn straight, it is. But, hey, I'm happy for you anyway." Unfortunately, she'd have even more reason to avoid Mort if he had a damn female cop hanging around him. But looking at Mort, at the soft yellow aura drifting around him, assured her of his optimism for this new relationship. He was content, if still a little shy, and Gaby couldn't bring herself to quell his happiness in any way.

When she kept her visits few and far between, he'd figure out the situation on his own.

Obtuse to the inner workings of her mind, Mort put his hands to his knees and turned to her with buoyant exuberance. "Maybe we can double date sometime."

Gaby's wide eyes zeroed in on him and she nearly choked. He *had* to be joking.

"You know," Mort prompted, taking her expression for confusion. "You and Luther, and me and Ann . . ."

"Ain't happening, Mort. Not ever." Shoving to her feet, anxious to get away, Gaby said, "Look, I gotta go." She needed to be by herself so she could digest all the frivolous changes pervading her structured and severe existence.

"Already?" He hovered close, as if by his mere proximity he could keep her there.

She stepped away from him—away from temptation. "Yeah. I just wanted to drop by to—"

His solemn gaze caught hers. "To tell me you thought I was dead?"

"Well . . . yeah." Her brows beetled. "Usually word on the street is reliable, but I haven't heard shit about you, so I had no reason to believe that you'd survived."

He kicked at a small rock by his feet. "I've been busy

with Ann, but we mostly stay in. I figured it was best to lie low for a while."

"Lie low?"

He shrugged. "I wasn't sure if anyone was looking for you or not. Other than Luther, I mean. He's been going nuts looking for you."

"Yeah?" Not that it mattered, but still . . .

"He's grilled me a dozen times. That was bad enough—I didn't need anyone else questioning me. I didn't want to take a chance on screwing up our story or anything."

A shifting shadow caught Gaby's attention, and she looked across the street at an abandoned, tireless car in the unlit lot of a failed business. It looked as if it had been there some time. "Well, it's old news now, and Luther already found me. If anyone else bothers you, send him my way."

A faint shift in what should have been a stationary shadow made her eyes narrow. Someone lurked there. She sensed it.

Given she had no divine warnings raping her body, Gaby decided it wasn't the worst of corruption, not the truest of evil.

Not the evil she hunted.

But all the same, she sensed a malicious cretin. Through the onerous years, Gaby had learned to trust her prescience, and knowing she was about to engage intoxicated her.

To protect Mort from any fallout, Gaby moved in front of him. "Stay back."

With panic filling his voice, Mort asked, "What is it? What's wrong?"

"Don't know yet." Going still inside, collecting her sui generis abilities around her, Gaby stared across the way into the aphotic lot. She willed the vague shapes of re-fuse into recognizable forms. The car was a good distance from them, but after a time of concentration, Gaby picked out a hunkered, human form.

Before the thought had finished forming, she had her knife in her hand. "Something is about to happen, Mort." Her heartbeat thickened with excitement. "Maybe you should go."

He stunned her by saying, "Not on your life."

Lacking time to argue, Gaby said, "Then stay the fuck out of my way. I'll try not to hurt him, but he doesn't share the same intent toward me, and this could get vicious."

Moving the threat away from Mort the best she could, Gaby stepped out to the street just in time to meet the nigrescent apparition charging toward her. A macabre mask of sunken eyes and distorted, gaping mouth concealed the attacker's face. Dark clothing obscured the body type.

A stray beam of moonlight reflected off a long, heavy pipe swinging from one substantial arm.

Oh yeah. This fellow meant business.

He meant to maim her—or more.

Perfect.

Satisfaction aggrandized, sending a flow of torrid anticipation through Gaby. She braced her booted feet apart, flexed her rock-steady knees, and whispered, "God, I needed this. Thank you."

In the next instant, the pipe came crashing down toward her with thunderous force. Reflexes on automatic, Gaby ducked the pipe before bringing her elbow back hard and fast. She smashed it into the masked face, heard the crunching of nose cartilage, and waited to see if that would end the fight.

A rank curse brought a brief pause, but didn't quell the attack. The pipe swung again, and again missed her. She was too fast, too agile for the likes of this cretin.

This time Gaby kicked out a knee, and watched the attacker's leg buckle. He almost fell, stumbled instead, and took another vicious swing at her head.

An enthusiastic opponent, for sure.

Determined and stupid.

Leaving her few choices in the matter.

The weapon hit the paved street with a deafening clash. She thought she might have heard Mort scream, but she tuned out all distractions to get in the zone, to deal with this threat.

To . . . destroy it.

Taking advantage of the assailant's bludgeoned state, Gaby brought her blade straight up—and felt it burst through vessels, fat, and muscle.

She joined her hands together, pushed hard and deep, and experienced the satisfying sensation of deflecting off a bone.

An agonized scream rang out, this one from the man pierced by her blade.

Thanks to his persistence in trying to do her harm, it was even easier to ignore than Mort's distress.

Tugging out the knife against the natural resistance, the suck and drag of wet, fibrous flesh, Gaby stepped to the side and, for only a heartbeat, waited.

As she assumed, her strike ended the fight.

The clunky pipe dropped to the ground with a clattering echo. Her adversary's knees buckled. The body slumped.

Disappointed that she'd had to use such extreme measures, Gaby muttered, "That was hardly worth the effort."

Gigging this son of a bitch had done little to alleviate her burgeoning belligerence.

The recondite disguise served no purpose now, but what did she care who her attacker might be? Craven souls, both insignificant and exalted, crawled over the surface of the earth with annoying sedulousness.

The more Gaby accepted her life's duty, the more she relished taking on them all, with or without God's specific mandate.

No, she didn't care who this inconsequential gnat might be.

But Mort did. Creeping closer, he asked, "Good God, Gaby. Who is that?"

Knife still in her hand, now crimson with gore, Gaby shrugged her tense shoulders. She kicked the fallen figure with the toe of her boot. "Hey, my friend wants a name."

She said it, and then it struck her all over again.

Her friend.

Would she ever get entirely used to the concept?

Mort wanted details on this attack because he *cared* for her. She sensed his misguided tendency to protect her—never mind that, moments before, he'd screeched like a little girl.

As a dark puddle of blood blossomed around him, the assailant slumped to his side in a protective curl more appropriate to the womb than a dirty street.

Voice shaking, faint, he said, "Carver hired me . . . to kill . . . you."

"Yeah?" Gaby knelt down, curiosity now piqued. "You failed big-time, huh?"

In a barely audible whisper, the man said, "He'll kill me now."

"Nah, I doubt it. You'll be dead before he can get to you."

Mort said, "Gaby," with a lot of worry. "Why would anyone want you dead?"

"I don't know." She nudged the man. "How come he sent you after me?"

There was a strange gurgle, then the body went flat, sprawled on the pavement, limp and still.

She looked back at Mort. "Think you ought to call someone before he really does expire?"

Mort chewed his bottom lip, his brows pinched. "I suppose." But he didn't rush to do it, further surprising Gaby. "He wanted to kill you, Gaby. He tried to cleave your head open with that pipe."

"Shake it off, Mort. The clown wasn't even close." She stood again and held out her hand. "Give me the phone."

With grave reluctance, he said, "No, I'll do it. You need to clean that knife."

"True." Bending at the waist, she jerked off the man's ridiculous mask, saw a face gone slack in near death, and said, "I don't recognize him. You?"

Shaking his head hard, Mort said, "No." He looked at Gaby. "Who's Carver?"

"No one important." She used the mask to clean off as much of the blood and gore as she could. To the naked eye, the knife looked spotless. The naked eye wasn't good enough. Soon as possible, she'd do a thorough job.

She slid the weapon back into her sheath.

"You should probably go," Mort told her.

Not a bad idea, really. As he punched in 911, she asked, "What will you say?"

"That I couldn't see much, but after the fight broke up and a body was on the ground, I figured I'd better call." He held up a finger, and spoke into the phone. "Hey, yeah, I have an emergency. Yeah, a guy's been stabbed. He's hurt real bad, might even be dead."

Gaby marveled at the lack of emotion in his tone. Sure, he'd screamed out during the attack. But after that, he'd quickly gathered himself.

The Mort she used to know would have been a nervous wreck after witnessing an altercation that resulted in a limp, bleeding body.

This Mort took charge, accepting that some things were inevitable—and necessary.

After giving the police their general location, Mort disconnected the call.

He'd impressed her, and it took a lot to do that these days. "Thanks, Mort."

"Thank you. For coming back. For being my friend." He turned solemn, distraught, far too grave. "Thank you for doing what others won't. What they can't."

"If you get maudlin, I'm smacking you."

The corner of his mouth kicked up, and for the very first time since meeting him, Gaby thought he might not be such a slimy-looking little guy.

Confidence, control, changed his appearance as much as a summons changed hers.

"No, I won't," he said. "But I've thought about you a lot, Gaby, about the burden you bear."

She reared back, threatening him, and Mort laughed before holding up his hands in surrender. "Fine. I know you don't need my thanks. Now go before they get here. And make sure you scrub that knife clean."

Bossing her? He really *had* changed. "I know what to do."

Silent, he walked beside her toward an oppressive alley no doubt filled with more human vermin. "We need to know why Carver wants you dead."

What the hell? Gaby glared at him. "Wrong, Mort. *We* don't need to know anything. Go back to your place and visit with your girlfriend. Forget about this."

His sigh was loud enough to send a rat scurrying away. "Gaby—"

"I can take care of myself, and you know it. As for Carver, you can leave that numb-nut to me."

Drawing back, Mort stared at her with disapproval. "You know why he's after you, don't you?"

Good God. Bossing, questions—was there no end to his

intrusion? "You want me to go, or stick around to chat with the cops?"

Frustration put back his scrawny shoulders. "Go. But, Gaby? Promise you'll come to see me again."

"Yeah, sure. Eventually." It wasn't a lie. She'd be back.

After she wrote the rest of the newest *Servant* novel.

And had a little one-on-one chat with Carver.

And met again with Luther . . .

"Damn," she said, only half under her breath, "having friends can be a pain in the ass."

Mort smiled, lifted a hand to wave, and when she was almost out of range to hear, he said, "I love you, too, Gaby."

She nearly tripped over her own feet.

A masked man with a pipe hadn't fazed her.

Mort's affection, on the other hand, scared her half to death.

Chapter 4

Oren travelled up the clean, wide street to the stately mansion. Unlike the area he'd just left, in this community the crime rate was almost nonexistent. Money had its uses, and in these aloof environs it ensured privacy and well-being, forming the perfect purlieus to the atrocities committed in the basement of the mansion.

Oren unlocked the front gate with a passkey and, forgetting himself for only a moment, practically skipped up the long, paved walkway to the curved stairs leading up and into his lavish world.

Beneath the high, covered porch, no light penetrated, and he let the giggles escape. Before long, he'd have a new one—but for now, he'd make do with the slut they already had.

Except for prominently displayed paintings and sculptures, the cavernous foyer was empty when he let himself in. To his left was the massive formal dining room. Aunt Dory sat at the end of the long mahogany table, nursing a whisky and talking to herself.

Oren detected blood on her hands, and worry wormed through his deranged giddiness.

What had the stupid cow done now?

To his right was the study, and through the open door, Oren saw Uncle Myer sprawled in a leather chair, his close-cropped graying hair standing on end, his shoulders slumped. He wore only dirty boxers, gaping open to expose his with-ered member.

Lip curling, Oren let the rage boil. God, he despised their ignorance and slovenly ways. They sickened him—but they were his cross to bear.

And they afforded him the life he craved. The power. The salacious immorality.

Neither of them made note of his entrance, so he ignored them both and went through the family room to the kitchen. Taking the elevator down to the unused servant's quarters, his anticipation bloated. He neared the deep bowels of the magnificent stone house, but heard no sounds.

No whimpers.

No muffled pleas for mercy.

Only a silent peace filled the air, and buzzed like annoy-ing gnat in his brain.

By the time Oren reached the basement, his heart punched a fevered crescendo against his ribs, so hard that it pained him. Nearing panic, he vaulted out of the elevator, rushed through the game room, and burst into the extra stor-age area.

He drew to an inflamed halt.

Eyes wide and unseeing, mouth agape in a now silent scream, the lifeless body of the woman hung in an obscene sprawl from tightened restraints.

Bruises mottled the body.

A trail of semen splattered her white thighs and belly.

Oren swallowed back bile and disgust. Almost by rote, his expression affixed in loathing, he walked past the body to the wall where multiple devices of torture hung in disarray.

Stupid bastards couldn't even put their tools away properly.

Without quelling the odium he felt for his family, he stared at a clamp, a knife, various prods and whips . . . and settled on a short, vicious crop. He turned with steely resolve.

When he reached the upstairs again, he saw that Aunt Dory hadn't moved.

He paused in the doorway, letting his rage ripen. As he calmly entered the dining room, prepared to dispense with his own form of justice, she finally looked up.

At first, her muddy brown eyes went to his clothes, before leaping back to his face. Would she dare mention his garb?

Of course not.

"Now, Oren . . ." Voice trembling, she looked at the crop.

Fat people lacked speed and agility and she couldn't quite get out of her chair fast enough. "It wasn't my fault! I didn't mean to—"

The crop landed across her shoulders, and that felt so good to Oren, so satisfying, that he drew back and landed another, and another.

Her screams exceeded the punishment, bringing Uncle Myer rushing in.

"Oren!"

Seeing the depraved man he called "Uncle" by need, only incensed Oren further. He turned his back on Dory. Myer's flaccid and overused cock hung out from open unwashed boxers.

A perfect target.

Uncle Myer backed up, but not fast enough. The crop lashed across his lap, cutting into exposed flesh and causing a dehiscent burst of blood and screams.

Uncle Myer fell to his knees. He curled both hands over his privates, but that only allowed Oren to lash his vein-riddled hands, his rawboned arms.

Between his aunt and uncle, the cries were deafening. Breathing hard, detesting the shrill assault on his ears, Oren threw the crop across the room.

"Now," he snarled in accusation, his voice nowhere as deep as he would have preferred, "we have to dispose of the body." He looked at Dory. "Tonight."

Her tears mingling with the snot shining on her upper lip, Dory said, "But, but shouldn't we wait until—"

Fury spun Oren toward her, and he kicked out at her bulging ankles, her padded shins.

"*Wait?*" he screamed. "You want to wait?" He kicked her again, and she fell from the chair in gargantuan array. "You *know* how dead bodies start to stink. If she stiffens up, it'll be twice as hard."

"Stiffen up? But . . . she just died."

Killing her would only cause Oren more grief, so he reined in the desire and tugged on the long, unleashed length of his hair. He didn't like his hair loose, but at times like this—as in other times—it served its purpose. "It only takes a couple of hours for it to start, and by tomorrow morning she'll be in a complete state of rigor mortis. Then we'll have to wait for the proteins in her muscles to decompose. It could take several days."

Dory blinked at him in horror.

"Do you want a dead, rotting corpse around here for days, Dory?"

She looked so stricken that a sick thrill ran through Oren.

His mouth curled. "Maybe I should put you in the basement with her. In the wine cellar. You could watch the process and maybe then you'd remember it."

Going white, Dory whimpered, "Oh, Oren, no . . ."

"Of course you're right," Uncle Myer said, showing a semblance of gallantry as he tried to come to his wife's aid. "We'll do it tonight." As he spoke, he examined his now swollen and cut member. Seeing the abuse inflicted on the old shriveled appendage, his mouth trembled.

Oren felt small satisfaction at their suffering. But not enough. "Both of you, get downstairs and bundle her up in an old blanket. I'll decide where to dump her."

Dory audibly gulped down her relief. "Did you want to . . . change?"

"No. We shouldn't be spotted, but just in case, better that I be seen like this." He pushed his hair from his face. "Uncle Myer, you'll drive. Put her in the trunk of the car in the garage."

"Of course." Myer headed for the elevator.

Built under the house and abutting the storage area, the garage gave them the perfect exodus. No one would notice anything other than a family heading out for a drive.

As his imbecilic relatives left him, Oren paced, formulating his plans.

He'd need another body right away.

Already, he shook with the need to dominate, to prove his mastery.

And there was no one here, no one to accept his superior will. His throat burned at the loss, at the anger festering inside him. But he couldn't kill his relatives. He needed them.

He'd once been a child on his own, passed from one house to another. It had been unbearable. Suffocating.

When they learned of his inheritance from his father, his aunt and uncle had come quickly enough.

And just as quickly, Oren had discovered that they were just as sick and twisted as his mother had been. They were weak, perverted, and they made the perfect façade. He could do as he wished with impunity, and no one would ever know.

No one.

The river. Yes, perfect.

That's where he'd take her. Let the hungry carp and wide-mouthed catfish feast on her destroyed flesh. In the less savory neighborhoods, he could access the river away from houses, away from humanity.

He'd have to watch out for vagrants and criminals, but he'd take a gun for protection.

Aunt Dory, when threatened, proved an adequate shot.

Thinking of Aunt Dory again spurred his discontent with their excesses. He hoped they both bled. He hoped they hurt ten times more than he was hurting.

It'd be a good lesson for them.

It was no more than they deserved.

Rubbing the back of his neck, trying to ease the tension, Oren went to the basement to supervise. He instructed Uncle Myer to wash and dress properly, just in case they were spotted. He told Aunt Dory to fix her hair and dry her tears. There was no time for self-pity, not for the likes of them.

Within an hour, they were on the road. The headlights of the black Mercedes cut through a dense fog clinging to the roadway. A timorous sliver of moon quailed behind thick gray clouds. Dory and Myer shared pointless chitchat from the front seat, with Myer driving.

In the backseat, closest to the corpse compressed into the

cramped trunk space, Oren rode in silence. He pressed his back firmly into the seat, imagining how the body had gotten unnaturally twisted in order to fit, getting closer to it, relishing the nearness.

It gave him some small solace, a taste of dominance, but not enough.

He needed another tramp.

Tomorrow.

Nothing could get in his way. Not even the skinny bitch with the spooky, perspicacious eyes.

✱

After a writing marathon that ended with several completed chapters and filled her small room with the actuating scents of ink, paper, and idealism, Gaby stowed her tools in the special storage box she'd procured for just that purpose. The lockbox, fashioned to withstand fire and attempts at theft, held her treasures in the safest manner possible to one like her.

Though she'd been locked away in her room all day, writing without consideration for breakfast or lunch, no one could guess why. No one could know that she translated heinous reality into a fictionalized account of her pathetic life.

She *was* Servant, the female lead in her graphic novels. Romanticized surely, softened and more heroic, more human—just as normal people insisted their idols be. The series had proven mega-popular with the underground crowd.

And then it had proven popular with everyone.

No one realized that Gaby wrote and illustrated the stories. That she *was* the stories.

Far as she knew, no one even suspected her of being more than a homely, lonely, antagonistic bitch.

Except Luther.

Glancing out the window, Gaby saw that the day had melted away. He would be visiting her soon.

Intrusive bastard.

Real-life hero.

Gaby closed her eyes, despondent. Had Luther insisted on seeing her today because, as he'd said, he missed her? Or because he distrusted her?

Perhaps both?

Edgy with conflicting emotion, Gaby tucked the lockbox into a camouflaged niche carved into her box spring, and straightened her covers. As she exited the room that was as circumscribed as her existence, she double locked the reinforced door. With her privacy secured, she headed out into the public hallway.

The motel served as a safe place for assignations all day long, but at this time of early evening, things were just starting to heat up. Gaby heard faked moans, unenthusiastic laughter, and the more distinct sounds of flesh slapping on flesh.

She paused, watching the lewd displays happening in the stairway, down in the foyer, in an open room. When she'd first moved to the motel, curiosity had kept her watching.

Now, there was nothing new for her to see.

Sex, bought and paid for, lost its luster early on.

The more she observed, the more sadness infiltrated her soul.

Tuning out the acquainted sounds of business, she decided to station herself on the middle floor where she could keep an eye on the girls until Luther's arrival. No need to sit out in the heat. When a cop showed up near a whorehouse, it caused a buzz; she'd know.

Putting in her tiny earphones and turning on the digital audioplayer, Gaby settled back against the peeling wallpaper.

She enjoyed the music Luther had given her as a gift. She never tired of listening to it. So she could hear any cries of distress, need, or intrusion, she kept the volume low.

Usually the music lent her a strange sort of equanimity, lulling her, quieting her turbulent disquiet.

Tonight, her thoughts raged.

Residue from yesterday's conflict?

Gaby dismissed that thought almost as soon as she had it. Mort would tell her later if the man survived, and even if he didn't, she couldn't care. The more she accepted her duties, the less they staggered her.

The man had wanted her dead. He'd likely killed before.

The strength of his muddy, convulsing aura exposed his laziness. The rotted black holes added an indication of severe imbalance, both in morals and mental ability. The man was a bottom-feeder, and if he passed, the world would be a better place.

No, she didn't care. More likely Carver's audacity caused her tension.

How dare that bastard hire another to have her snuffed? He was such a chicken-shit moron.

For underestimating her in such a big way, Carver would pay.

Maybe. If the mood struck her. If not . . .

Distracted from her ruminations, Gaby watched a suited, middle-class man climb the stairs with Bliss, one of the younger hookers.

Bliss didn't belong here, but then, who did?

No one.

Yet here they were: Gaby; the hookers who'd accepted her; the pimps who tolerated her; the men who, thanks to sickness, debauchery, loneliness, or misguided emotion, sought them out.

And Luther.

God knew he belonged here least of all.

He came through a need to right wrongs, to prevent injustice.

To visit her.

Her jaw tightened. Looking like a painted angel and chatting like a magpie, Bliss climbed the stairs with the man's hand held in hers. He wore an anticipatory smile on his smug face.

When they neared Gaby, she ensured the john felt her gaze; he stiffened in alarm.

Gaby didn't give a shit.

She wanted the slimeball to feel her warning.

Hurt Bliss, and you'll pay.

Gaby was . . . partial to Bliss. Maybe because of her young age. Maybe because Gaby knew her better than she knew the others.

Possibly it was because in some small, indefinable way, Gaby recognized something of herself in Bliss. That didn't make sense, but then, nothing of her life could be rationalized.

Given the heat of Gaby's stare, Bliss had to take a moment to soothe the man before leading him to a meager room. After she got him in the door, Bliss leaned out, gave Gaby a goofy, teasing look of reprimand, and blew her a kiss.

It was something a younger sister might have done, and it pained Gaby as much as an arrow through her heart.

Not that she'd ever let Bliss know.

When the door closed, Gaby went back to her contemplation of Carver. Hard music filled her ears, pulsing through her veins, finding a cadence with her angered heartbeat.

She decided that if she got bored and needed the exercise, she'd find Carver and . . .

A swift bolt of tension impaled her, burning her soul and then spiraling into her veins with awesome speed until every part of her body burned with acute agony. The sensation was familiar, and grindingly painful.

It gained momentum, gnashing Gaby's muscles, boring into her heart.

Ah. So this was why she'd felt the tension.

Only one thing ever delivered on her this prodigious pain: Tonight, she had deific duties to attend.

Loosing the ear pieces from her ears, Gaby sucked in deep breaths until she could isolate the pain, compartmentalize it for later use. She forced her constricted muscles to flex and pushed up to stand on her feet.

It looked like her meeting with Luther would have to be postponed.

Luther would be pissed.

And truthfully, she'd miss him. She hadn't wanted to admit it, but she'd looked forward to seeing him again.

Focusing on Luther better enabled her to bridle the pain, keeping the worst of it at bay.

In the furthest reaches of her mind, she heard one of the hookers saying, "Gaby?" And then with very real caring: "Oh God. What's wrong with her? What should we do?"

Fuck. Did her face look different?

One of the more distressing things to come from her relationships with Luther and Mort was the realization that it wasn't only evil incarnates who showed their authentic natures through bodily appearance.

Gaby also suffered the affliction. By shared accounts, when called to duty, she looked different. Luther swore she wasn't hideous, just altered in some way he could never elucidate.

Mort, when seeing her thus, was frightened.

Knowing she had to remove herself from the women before they witnessed too much, became too suspicious, Gaby swallowed hard and managed to whisper, "Butt out. I'm fine."

"Don't be silly, Gaby," Betty said with her thick accent. "You're sick. I can see it. So what can I do?"

Sick? Well, that was preferable to beastly. "I'm fine, I tell you."

"You ain't," Tiff insisted. "Come to my room. I'll—"

Bliss's softer voice interrupted the others. "Gaby? What's happenin'? How can I help?"

Gaby dredged up a believable snicker, and a thick dose of vitriol. "Like I need help from any of *you*? Not likely." In a daze, guided only by her inner sight, Gaby started on her way.

"Stubborn to the bitter end," Betty lamented.

"And proud," Bliss added.

"Hey," a guy called out. "I ain't paying for this!"

Gaby ignored them all.

Now that she'd given in to the summons, each footfall grew stronger, more determined than the one before it. Her muscles became more fluid, her movements faster, more agile.

She left the lugubrious presence of the motel and stepped into hazy sunlight congested with street noise, human virulence, and malodorous dormancy.

No incarnation of evil lurked about.

Instinctively, Gaby knew that she needed her car. The distance this time would be too far to traverse on foot. For protective purposes, Gaby kept her Ford Falcon parked well away from the motel. Still, with God-enhanced speed on her side, she reached it in only minutes. Keys hidden in the hubcap kept her from having to carry them on her person.

No one messed with her car.

Why would they? Despite the automobile's reliable running condition, it looked as deserted, as broken as any rust-ravaged heap in the junkyard.

Because a speeding car was more obvious than a woman racing on foot, Gaby worried whenever she had to drive to a destination.

She had no driver's license.

No IDs at all.

The less anyone knew of her, the simpler her complicated existence became. She had to trust that God would guide her safely, as He always had, to wherever she needed to be.

It was unclear to Gaby just how far she could travel within a paladin's duty. Atrocities happened around the world; she felt only those in her small corner of society. If she couldn't reach the malefactor, she couldn't stop the evil committed.

It was a huge conflict in the cycle of what she did, how she justified her actions. If her ability wasn't far-reaching, how much did her existence really matter?

As if to wring the doubts from her consciousness, more pain squeezed through her. Gaby gave in to the agony so that it could help her focus.

Navigating by divine intervention, she made the journey by rote, unseeing and unhearing. Her muscles knotted and wrung in agony, in the urgency of the moment.

The sun began its descent just as she reached the bank of a slow-moving, murky river. Dusk left everything dirty, cheerless and gray. Coasting her car up alongside a tree, Gaby put it in park and turned off the engine.

Through the distortion of her ability, her *gift*, she saw nothing amiss. Clouds rolled in. The rippling surface of the river turned silver.

Her pain receded—and under the circumstances, that wasn't good at all.

Fresh alarm replaced the hurt; only two things ever caused

Gaby's suffering to abate: Luther's close proximity, or a missed opportunity.

Breath catching and knife in hand, Gaby jerked around in her seat, looking out the rear window, searching the landscape, the prickling of scrub brush and dead trees. She saw wide-open spaces. There was no way for Luther to be nearby without her seeing him.

Relief turned her spine to jelly and she slumped almost boneless in her seat. She didn't want Luther to see her like this—ugly, murderous.

More capable than any human being should be or could be.

The abnormal effect Luther had on her would always leave her agitated. He got physically close, and despite the veil of God's emphatic instructions, she saw more clearly.

Rather than the evil within, she saw the human side of her target.

She saw the destruction she wreaked.

She saw her own vulnerability.

Luther affected her as no one ever had. He softened her, robbing her of a crucial edge.

During weaker moments, Gaby wanted to thank him for that. But when reality crashed around her, she knew it was far too dangerous to let him disturb her vantage over iniquity.

Shaking her head to clear Luther from her thoughts, Gaby opened her car door and stepped out. Her knees still felt weak, but a humid breeze struck her, thick with the foul odors of the river, and that motivated her.

As if it had never been, her pain evaporated altogether, leaving her sick at heart and muddled in spirit.

Raw with regret.

She was too late—but how could that be? It had never happened before.

She was *always* on time. Tonight, she hadn't even struggled with the summons. The whores hadn't let her. They were there, observing her, leaving her no choice but to give in and comply before they saw more than they could ever comprehend.

So . . . what did it mean?

Had God given her a unique directive? Perhaps, this time, He wanted something aberrant, something other than a total destruction of evil about to corrupt.

As silent as a wraith, Gaby walked away from the car toward the riverbank, awaiting guidance with each step. The heels of her boots sank into the loamy soil. Weeds prickled her ankles. Mosquitoes thought her a feast and dined on her flesh with gusto.

Gaby searched the riverbank, the rocks, the washed-up tree limbs, swirling moss and reeds . . .

Oh God. She went stock-still. She'd seen plenty of dead, massacred bodies.

She'd done the massacring herself.

But this . . . this was different.

The body—a bloated, waterlogged sponge on the shoreline—wasn't dead by her hand. Someone had killed, and dumped the body, and God sent her to . . . what?

Find a murderer?

Maybe before more murders took place?

Okay, fine. But then, why the awful, wracking pain? Why the urgency?

From a distance, Gaby could tell that the body had been in the river for the better part of a day. There was nothing urgent in a rotting corpse.

Unless it was someone she'd recognize.

Vision narrowing, Gaby stared at the white body while a

litany raced around her mind. *Please, don't let it be Luther. Please, don't let it be Mort.*

She calmed herself and studied what she could see—a rounded hip, a mutilated breast.

Not a man, but a woman.

The stench of decayed fish and humid refuse burned Gaby's nostrils as she inhaled, exhaled, breathed in again.

Feet leaden with dread, Gaby crept closer. Long slimy fingers of green sea moss teased over the carious body, impelled on each lapping wave, tickling, receding, rolling in and over it again, and again.

Trepidation took a toll. Gaby forced the approach, and the human form became more distinguishable. Arms. Legs.

Open, unseeing eyes.

The torso and thighs were badly cut. All over. Long, thin slices made with a very sharp blade.

A blade not unlike her own.

Carver? Was the bastard sending her a message? Had he killed an innocent woman because he couldn't kill Gaby?

Mottled bruises almost disguised the features of the deceased, but Gaby recognized her.

Not just any woman, but a woman she knew.

One of the hookers.

An . . . acquaintance, but not really a friend.

Blinking hard and fast, Gaby forced herself to stay there, to take it all in.

Could Carver have done this?

And if so, why?

If not Carver, then . . . the problem multiplied exponentially.

Long bleached hair swam on the constantly moving surface of the river, catching on reeds, hiding tiny fish that pecked at the rotting flesh.

Gaby sniffed, remembering how the other hookers had told the woman that her hair was over-bleached, that it felt like straw. Now, floating around the victim, the hair looked so soft.

A cloudy film covered the open eyes, but Gaby could see that they were dark brown. It was an odd combination, one she wouldn't forget.

She sniffed again, tasting the atrocity of the scene before her. Lucy. Poor, poor Lucy. Her death had been gruesome. Given the shape of the corpse, she'd suffered, a lot.

Gaby went from gasping in upset, to straightening tall and strong with restorative outrage. Somehow, some way, she'd find out who did this, and regardless if it was Carver or not, she would avenge Lucy.

That's why God had sent her here, she was sure. To let her know. To make her aware.

To put her on guard and to prepare her to act.

Gaby said a final farewell to the woman she hadn't known well, but had pitied all the same. She didn't touch the body. She didn't dare.

Her insides clenched and her guts gnarled. She looked around, but this particular section of river was far from picturesque. There were no riverboats, no fancy hotels or restaurants.

Along the shore, remnants of fishing excursions remained: rotted carp heads, a broken reel, foam cups, and a broken lawn chair. Farther out, empty railroad tracks led to nowhere that she could see. In the distance, tall stacks from a factory billowed thick white smoke in the darkening sky.

There was no place for someone to hide, but then, at this deserted location, secrecy wouldn't be necessary.

Had the body been dumped here, or had it floated here?

For one of the very few times in her life, Gaby wished for the impossible—she wished for company.

She wanted Luther. He'd know what to do.

That made her snort. Luther would take her into custody first, and ask questions later.

Mind made up, Gaby backed away from the grisly scene. Hating herself and her necessary choices that, at this particular moment, felt cowardly, she went to her car. Sitting inside the open door, she removed her boots and checked the soles for any evidence of dirt or debris.

Once they were clean, she started the engine and drove in the opposite direction from the motel where she resided. It'd be safer for her to take care of business in a different part of town.

She found a self-serve carwash and took infinite care in cleaning her shambles of a vehicle, making sure all river mud or indigenous weeds had been removed. There was no one around to see her, no one to later identify her.

The moon crowned the black sky, again reminding her that she was supposed to meet Luther. Now, there was no reason to rush. He'd be too busy to concern himself with her.

On a dark, dangerous stretch of road, Gaby stopped at a pay phone. She called the police station and reported the body, giving the sparest of details, and disguising her voice.

When the officer started to ask questions, she hung up and quickly drove away. Taking her time, she coasted through the slums, making note of children still at play, drug exchanges, a few fights.

By the time she parked the Falcon in the lot, the night dwellers had crawled out like cockroaches, crowding every corner, watching every movement for an advantage over another.

During Gaby's walk toward the motel, a tall black man hailed her, offering her pills, needles, or whatever else she might need.

Burning with hatred, sick over Lucy's fate, Gaby fixed her

gaze on his, letting him feel what she felt. He backed up several steps, spewed a few vicious insults her way, and loped off. Someone laughed. Another person screamed.

Gaby kept walking. There were people who deserved to suffer, and she sensed this was one of those people.

Dreading it, steeped in guilt, Gaby approached the front of the motel. She had lost one of them when she'd made it her duty to keep them safe. She'd failed.

And Lucy had suffered because of it.

As one set of whores exited the motel, several others went in. They stayed busy hustling for johns, harassing those who turned them down, all in all faking an enjoyment that Gaby knew they couldn't feel.

With little conversation, she started to go up to her room. Bliss stopped her. "Gaby?"

She turned, saw Bliss's upset, and jumped on the opportunity to indulge in destruction. "What's the matter?" Gaby stomped toward her. "Did someone do something to you?"

Bliss blinked at her ferocity before twittering a laugh. "No, silly, it's nothing like that. I've had a good night."

Meaning she'd made an adequate amount of cash. Gaby's guts burned. "Then what is it?"

Reaching out to touch Gaby's shoulder, Bliss said, "I just wanted to ask about you. If you're okay."

Gaby reared back. What the hell? "Of course I'm okay. Why wouldn't I be?"

"I dunno. You looked pretty sick before and now you look kinda sad. It's not like you."

Looking beyond Bliss, Gaby saw Jimbo standing alone, taking in the exchange with suspicion. Overall, Jimbo treated the women no differently than they expected. Gaby had yet to see him cross the proverbial line, to do anything to engage her wrath.

Wrapping her fingers around Bliss's upper arm, Gaby pulled her farther away from the bright streetlamp and into the dark shadows of a door overhang. An outraged cat screeched and vaulted away.

Jerking in startled surprise, Bliss screeched, too. "Ohmigod. That poor l'il kitty scared me half to death." She knelt down and made kissing noises. "Here, kitty, kitty. I won't hurt you."

Impatient, Gaby said, "The cat's gone, Bliss."

"Did it look hungry to you?" she asked as she straightened.

Compassion got a stranglehold on Gaby, all because Bliss was worried about the animal. Not for herself. Not for a lifestyle that put her in peril against nutcases and disease alike. But for a stray cat.

Another small piece of her heart warmed, melted, and turned to mush. Taking Bliss's arm to regain her attention, Gaby said, "I need to know something, Bliss." She cleared her throat, and her mind, and got right to the point. "When's the last time you saw Lucy?"

Chapter 5

Nervously twining a long lock of her brown hair around her fingertips, Bliss said, "I dunno." She stared up at Gaby. "Why? Are you mad at her for something?"

Frowning over that bit of absurdity, Gaby asked, "Why the hell would I be mad at Lucy?"

Bliss's rounded shoulders lifted. "I dunno. But you look pretty pissed right now." She licked her lips. "And you're kinda hurtin' my arm."

Gaby dropped her hand so fast that Bliss stumbled back. Until then, she hadn't even noted how the girl strained against her hold.

"I'm not mad," Gaby repeated evenly, trying to prove it through a moderate tone and temperate disposition. "It's just that I need to talk to her, but I can't find her. That's all."

Bliss frowned in thought. "It's been a couple of days, I think." She reached out and removed a cobweb from Gaby's hair.

Grooming her? Great. Just fucking great.

Teeth sawing together, but expression as affable as she could manage, Gaby said, "Try to remember, Bliss. It's important."

Lowering her head, Bliss concentrated, and finally said, "You know, I haven't seen her since the first of the week. Do you think—?"

Rather than let Bliss's mind start wandering down the wrong path, Gaby interrupted. "What was she doing when you last saw her?"

"Workin', as usual." Her blue eyes studied Gaby's hair. "Well, sort of." Distracted and far too familiar, Bliss urged Gaby to sit on a step, then she went behind her and, after retrieving a tie from her pocket, began finger-combing Gaby's hair back into a ponytail.

It was the oddest thing to have another woman touching her, but the hookers were a familiar lot, free with physical contact. They did each other's hair and makeup, modeled clothes for one another, gave advice, and all in all, grossly intruded into Gaby's personal space.

Gaby would never get used to it, but she had learned to tolerate it.

Sort of working? "What does that mean?" She tried to twist around to see Bliss, but enrapt in her chore, Bliss didn't release her hair, and Gaby gave up. "Who was she with? Can you describe the guy?"

"Actually . . ." Bliss put the tie in, securing the short ponytail. "It wasn't a guy. Lucy was talking to a girl."

Whoa. Okay, Gaby knew some of the ladies did whatever, and *whoever*, for cash. But she hadn't known Lucy to favor other females.

It seemed more likely that she'd made an incorrect

assumption. She turned toward Bliss. "For business? Or was she maybe chatting with another hooker?"

"Neither." Bliss laughed, reached out, and tugged a few strands of hair loose over Gaby's ears. "There," she said. "That's real pretty."

Pretty would never be a word ascribed to Gaby. The compliment left her prickly with embarrassment. "Then who was she?"

"I dunno. I'd never seen her before. I'm pretty sure she wasn't from around here." Bliss licked her thumb and wiped a spot on Gaby's forehead.

Swatting her hand away, Gaby asked, "Why do you say that?"

"She was young. Not really pretty, but . . . sort of refined-like."

"Dressed fancy, you mean?"

"No. She was dressed real plain." Bliss smoothed a wrinkle out of Gaby's shirt. "The reason I noticed is because—" Suddenly Bliss's eyes widened and she looked beyond Gaby.

Gaby stiffened, waited.

"Gaby."

And there it was, that voice she'd never forget, the one she sometimes heard in her dreams, and in her daydreams.

The voice that made her stomach punchy and her breath short.

How the hell had Luther gotten so close without her knowing it?

Bliss met Gaby's gaze, giggled at her expression, and rolled her eyes. She stood and smiled widely. "Hey there, Luther."

"Hello, Bliss. How are you?"

"Fine, thank you." She smiled over the formality, which was surely foreign to her.

"I'm sorry to interrupt you two girls during such a fascinating exchange—of words and deeds."

Bliss giggled again. "I was jus' fixin' her hair." Around
Luther, Bliss's lack of good grammar became more apparent
than ever.

"You did a beautiful job."

Beaming, Bliss asked, "You're on the wrong side of town,
ain't ya?"

"For a reason." Luther's big hands settled on Gaby's
shoulders with warm weight and outlandish possession. "I'm
sorry, Bliss, but would you mind if I had a moment alone
with Gaby?"

Gaby, who still hadn't turned to face him, couldn't seem
to get her vocal cords to work. How much had he heard?
How much had he *seen*?

A tidal wave of heat washed through her. Insane! Since
when did she give a shit what others thought of her?

Since Luther, that's when.

Before Gaby could object, the decision was taken away
from her.

"Be my guest." To Gaby, Bliss said, "We can talk later."
She gave a fingertip wave and headed off.

Gaby watched as Bliss made an almost immediate assig-
nation with a young man who appeared to be waiting specifically for her. Then she felt Luther's fingers gliding over her
ponytail and she shot to her feet.

Jerking around to face him, she scowled. "What the hell
do you want now?"

His hand fell from her hair to her cheek and lingered
there. Looking at her mouth, now set in hard lines, he said
simply, "You."

For a nanosecond, Gaby's tongue stuck to the roof of her
mouth. Bliss's presumptuous way of primping her hair was

disconcerting enough. For Luther to continually state a sexual desire for her rocked her very foundation.

Ill humor combusting, Gaby shoved Luther away from her. "Hands off, cop. I'm pissed at you."

"You always are." He smiled and sighed. "So what's the problem this time?"

Grumbling, because she couldn't dare admit to missing him, maybe even needing him, Gaby said, "I doubt you want to hear it, and it's for certain I don't want to hear your solution for it, so forget it."

"Not this time." He caught her hand and pressed money, wrapped around a note, into her palm.

"What's this?" Gaby started to separate the cash from the slip of paper, but Luther's hand curved over hers.

Leaning close, he breathed into her ear, "You're in disguise as a hooker, if you'll remember. Well, I'm just keeping up appearances." His hand tightened. "You should do the same."

Heady with the richness of his scent in her nostrils, Gaby took a moment to gather her defenses against his effect. When Luther separated from her again, she looked at his face, and saw too much.

No one could call her a dummy. Aware of Luther's urgency, Gaby smiled. "Sure thing." She stuck the cash and the note in her pocket. "Let's walk."

His body didn't budge. "I thought maybe we'd go to your room."

"You thought wrong." Her eyes narrowed. "And the next time you go poking around up there, I'll have something to say about it."

Luther went still, decided against subterfuge, and shrugged. "How did you know?"

Gaby couldn't say for sure, but when she'd first returned

to her rooms, she'd sensed that someone had been there, snooping around. The door hadn't been disturbed, so no one had entered, but only because she'd made it so difficult to do so.

"I'm astute—and you're far from stealthy." She looked behind her at a noisy duo of men haggling price with Jimbo. "Now do you want to get away from here, or what?"

With a strange sort of affection, Luther said, "You are so damn difficult."

Still watching the prospective johns, Gaby shrugged. "Not to people who leave me alone."

"And that," Luther said, taking her hand, "is something I can't do."

Gaby shot him a look, but he'd turned away and was determined to take her with him.

Did he infer an affection, or duty to his job as a cop?

She gave token resistance as Luther, maintaining his hold, towed her down the dark stretch of roadway, but they both knew if she wanted loose, she'd be loose, and he'd be hurting.

At least, she knew it.

Luther persisted in the farcical theory that he could hold his own against her.

And usually he could—because usually she hesitated to hurt him.

"You can let go now," Gaby told him.

"I don't want to."

His big hand swallowed hers, warm and secure in an extrinsic way. Gaby rolled in her lips, fought with herself, and said, "Okay."

The night breeze carried the cries of a baby. Somewhere nearby, glass broke. A car alarm went off, adding shrill stridency to the chronic bedlam.

Fingers entwined, they walked on.

The mood was nice—and deceptive.

With her left hand, Gaby retrieved the note and read it. Her innards churned. *A prostitute has been murdered. I have to talk to you.*

So, after seeing the body on the riverbank, Luther had rushed to her? Why? Did he suspect her of mutilating that poor girl, or did he hope to grill her for information on it? She'd covered her tracks, so surely he couldn't know she'd already been there, that she was the one who'd called it in, that she—

"I was worried, Gaby."

They were two blocks away and around a corner. Thoughts stalled with his admission; Gaby scowled at him. "Worried about *what*?"

"You." Before she could react to that, he held her face in hot palms, his long fingers tunneling into her hair, and he kissed her hard and fast. "Sick with worry."

Damn, but every time he put his mouth on hers, he tasted better. Hotter.

She was fast becoming addicted.

Confused, and a little turned on, Gaby had to remind herself to be cautious. Luther couldn't know she had prior knowledge of Lucy's death. "Is kissing your answer for everything? Anger, worry, lust—"

"Around you, yes."

"Huh." Mouth twisting, she said, "That's kinda sad, Luther."

He laughed, but there wasn't much humor in the low, rumbling chuckle. "Somehow, in some indefinable way, you're irresistible, whether you want to admit it or not."

Cocking a brow, Gaby looked down at her long, lanky, curveless body. "You're so tired, you can't see straight. Is that it?" He did sound exhausted. And strained.

"I'm fine." He nodded at the note in her hand, then gestured her toward a bench where they could talk. "Let's sit down."

"I could use a rest." Gaby sauntered past him and slouched onto the bench. Legs straight out, arms folded over her middle, she examined the toes of her boots. "So you were worried, huh? Wanna tell me why, or were you just planning to smooch?"

Luther sat beside her, but he didn't relax. Elbows on his thighs, his hands hanging between his knees, he looked defeated with concern. "I know you have enemies, Gaby."

"Yeah, who doesn't?" She couldn't be sure, but she assumed everyone, even normal folks, had others who detested them. Human nature wasn't forgiving or accepting. The most pious in society were generally also the most harshly judgmental.

Turning his head to look at her, Luther said, "You read the note."

"Yeah." Gaby chewed her upper lip. "So a hooker was murdered, and you're talking about it to me . . . why?"

"She was cut up real bad. Beaten. Probably tortured."

Gaby knew all that, and still, hearing it from Luther's mouth, seeing the turbulence in his aura, pained her.

"Who was she?"

He studied her in silence for several long moments. "You know her, Gaby."

Trying to hide her reaction, Gaby drew in a breath. "One of the girls in my motel?"

His smile quirked. "So now it's your motel?"

Annoyance pinched her face. "No. But I stay there. That's what I meant and you know it so stop being an asshole."

He sighed. And he took her hand, cradling it on his thigh,

offering an unfamiliar comfort. "I'm pretty sure she stays there. She was out front the other day when I came around asking about you."

Eyes widening, Gaby asked, "You did what?" She tried to pull her hand back, albeit without much determination, and Luther held on.

"Her body was dumped in the river, but she was dead before that." He lifted her hand to his mouth and kissed her palm. "I'm sorry, Gaby, but when I got on the scene and realized where I'd seen her, all I could think about was that maybe it was a warning."

Caution kept her temper in check. "To who?"

Luther slumped, holding her knuckles to his forehead. "Carver wants revenge on you."

Alarms shrieked throughout Gaby's system. "What the hell do you know of that?" More frantic now, she tried to free herself. They ended up in a real struggle that brought them both off the bench.

Luther locked his arms around her, squeezing the breath from her lungs. Gaby knew she could head-butt him, knee him in the crotch, any number of moves that'd get her free real quick.

But oddly, his need for the embrace quelled her more violent tendencies. "Luther?"

"I hate this, Gaby."

"This?"

In a sudden turnaround, he thrust her back from him, and began to vociferate in a mean snarl, "Fearing for you, because you're too goddamned stubborn to fear for yourself. Trying to protect you when you fight me every step of the way. Wondering how to get through to you, if I ever will, or if eventually I'll show up only to find you—"

His pain and frustration became her own.

Which meant his lust became hers, too. After all, he'd taught her what she knew of the volatile, volcanic emotion. For her, Luther and lust were synonymous.

Gaby threw herself against him and plastered her mouth to his. His hands clamped on to her shoulders as if to push her away; instead, he crushed her closer.

His tongue pushed past her lips. One of his hands went to her tush and, in a display of his awesome strength, he lifted her off her feet, meshing their lower bodies, letting her feel the steel of his erection.

"Luther?" Her head swam, her blood burned. And at the root of all sensation was a powerful need that she didn't know how to appease.

"God, woman, you make me insane."

He kissed her more gently this time, again using his tongue to taste her deeply, slowly. So hot.

But by small degrees, he left her, a wet kiss, a small lick, a kiss to the corner of her mouth—and he was gone.

Eyelids heavy and heart thumping, Gaby tried to focus beyond the haze of desire. "Luther?" she said again.

He let out a long, aggrieved breath. "I hate myself for saying this, but the timing is off for what I want to do. And history being what it is, that makes me wonder if you distracted me on purpose."

A splash of ice water couldn't have done more to cool her ardor, or bring her out of the sensual fog. Arms crossing under her breasts, Gaby struck an obstinate pose. "Come again?"

Cynical and bitter, Luther ran both hands through his hair. "Enough, Gaby. If after I've gotten some answers, you want to pick up where we left off, you know I'm more than willing."

"Ha!"

His teeth locked and his eyes burned. "But *first*, I have questions, and God help you, you will answer them."

She turned on her heel and started away.

"I'll arrest you."

That brought her back around. "For what?"

He closed the small space she'd just gained. "I have a firsthand account of you attacking Carver with a knife."

That had to be a lie. No one had seen her go near Carver. She'd made sure of it. Confidence wavering, she went on tiptoe to say into his face, "Bullshit."

He didn't withdraw, and this close, Gaby saw the golden flecks in his brown eyes sparking with ire and determination.

His aura, usually the golden hue of great control, now wavered with quick-tempered red, swirling around Gaby, engulfing her.

Luther meant business, no doubt about it.

"You have the knife. I have a dead prostitute sliced up and thrown in the river. Put those three things together, and you're the closest lead I have."

Damn. It did sound plausible. If she didn't know herself, she'd be looking at her as a suspect, too.

Taking advantage of her moment of uncertainty, Luther cupped her chin. "Trust me, Gaby. I'll either get my answers, or I'll haul your skinny ass to the station tonight. Late as it is, you won't be out of there until morning, at the earliest. Longer, if someone other than me decides you sound guilty as hell."

An invisible fist squeezed her windpipe. She couldn't swallow, could barely breathe. Giving herself over to Luther's dark gaze, she asked simply, "Do you believe I killed her?"

"No."

Relief washed over her. "Then—"

"But I think you can tell me things. And Gaby?" He kissed her again. "You will. Right now."

Oren watched the skinny girl and the tall man exchange money, whisper, and finally make off for their trick.

So she was a whore, like the others. Somehow, he hadn't figured her for that type. She was too . . . off-putting to be in the flesh trade. And too skinny. Too plain.

In his experience, even the homeliest whores had curves. Big chests and bigger posteriors, welcoming smiles and tired eyes. They wore revealing clothes and painted themselves to advertise their trade.

Not that woman.

No, her eyes weren't tired at all. They were laser sharp and she just watched everyone and everything with a hatred that cut clean.

Maybe it was a specialty of hers, that antagonistic attitude. Did men pay her extra for it?

Did she, like he, favor dominance?

Interesting. Oren smiled at the thought.

Perhaps later, when the need arose again, he'd take her and see just how well she fared as a supplicant. Breaking someone as strong-willed as her would last longer, and provide extra enjoyment.

But for now . . . yes, the youngest of the whores finally finished her duty with her most recent john and returned outside.

With the pimp otherwise occupied and the skinny watchdog off with her own trick, Oren finally had his chance. He waited near the corner, out of sight, until she strolled toward him.

"Excuse me?"

She looked up, tipped her head at the sight of him, and frowned. "Hello."

Putting just the right quaver in his voice, Oren said, "Could you . . . you help me? Please?"

She looked behind her, fretted, and then came toward him. "Help you how? What are you doin' out this time of night? You don't look like you belong around here."

"I don't. I'm lost, and I'm scared." He let his bottom lip tremble. "I want to go home."

"Shhh, now. It's okay."

She started to touch the hat on his head, and Oren stepped out of reach.

Luckily, she read that as fear. "I'm Bliss. What's your name?"

Oren thought quickly, and said, "Matt."

"How old are ya, Matt?"

"Twelve." He shuffled his feet, peeked at her from under the brim of his cap. "I was with my older brother at a party, but I got mad at him and decided to walk home. Now I'm lost and my mom will kill me if she finds out."

The stupid cow melted with sympathy. "Well, we won't let that happen, will we? If you want to come with me, we can call your brother and—"

"No!" Covering up, Oren said, "I don't know his number. But he's probably still at the party. If you walk me back there, I can pay you. I promise."

"You don't need to do that."

"But I want to. We're rich. My brother throws away money. He'll give you some, I swear. He doesn't want my parents to find out that he let me leave, or he'll be in trouble, too."

Undecided, Bliss again looked around the building and

down the street. She turned back to him. "I guess it'd be okay. Is it very far away?"

Oren pointed. "It's down that way. I just don't want to go back by myself."

She held out her hand. "Okay then, Matt. We'll go together."

Grinning to himself, Oren slipped his hand in hers. "Thank you." The anticipation sparked and ignited, making him giddy. He reached into his pocket with his free hand and fingered the syringe that made compliance so easy.

Not yet. Not yet.

He had to get her closer to the plain sedan he drove for just these occasions.

"You okay, little buddy?"

"Yes." Excitement made his voice croak, and he bit his lip, trying to contain himself. His breathing deepened. His palms got sweaty.

God, he loved this part the most. He couldn't hold back. He saw the car, was within a few feet of it. "This way."

As they walked past the vehicle, Oren observed the surrounding area.

He saw no one. They were alone.

Empty buildings towered around them, ready to muffle the screams sure to come. Inflamed, aroused, he withdrew the syringe and flicked off the cap. It hit the pavement with a near silent ping.

Yes, yes, yes.

Shaking with excitement, Oren tugged on Bliss's soft hand. "Oh, Bliss?" he teased in a singsong voice.

She turned to look at him. "Hmmm?"

Vicious, hard and fast, Oren jabbed the needle into the base of her throat, just above her collarbone.

With a high-pitched scream, she flailed back, staring at him in blank astonishment. She tried to look down at the needle protruding from her neck, then just as quickly began to stagger. "Wha . . . ?"

Oh, God, the look of utter shock on her stupid face.

The dawning horror in her big blue eyes.

Relishing it all, Oren withdrew the keys and with the touch of a button the doors unlocked. "Don't fight it, Bliss. There's no point. No, don't be afraid, my dear. Fear won't help. Yes, here you go. Inside. That's it."

Eyes going vague, as amiable and placid as a newborn kitten, Bliss allowed him to lead her into the backseat of the sedan where she slumped in a foul heap of open legs and lifted skirts.

Oren took in her disarray with distaste. Yes, she deserved this. Every single second of it.

Repulsed at the touch of her smooth flesh, Oren shoved her legs inside and closed the door. She'd be out cold any second now, and she'd stay out until he had her well caught in her restraints.

Uncle Myer and Aunt Dory would be euphoric. For them, the joy was in the play, not the pursuit. Plebian fools. They had no imagination.

No motivation.

Without him, they'd still be sitting in the squalor of their small apartment, feasting on cheap porn and each other. When he'd first met them, he wasn't sure if they could be trusted. But bloodthirst lurked inside the most unassuming people. It smoldered in the bosom, bound by principle and morality, until someone daring broke the fetters.

He was daring.

And once circumstances occurred to call their fetishes

into action, circumstances that *he'd* manufactured as a test, their true natures broke free, shattering forever their mundane existences. Now they served him.

And he indulged their desires. A perfect union.

Ripping off his hat and removing his backpack, Oren climbed behind the wheel. He got the satchel-type purse from the backpack, and the sandals, then removed his jacket to reveal a young woman's T-shirt. He stuffed the jacket, hat, and sneakers into the backpack, and put it all in the oversized purse.

Within one minute, he'd transformed himself from a boy to a young, but legal-aged woman.

Driving out of the area, he passed low-class establishments, but he knew if anyone noticed him, they'd see only a woman.

Never Oren.

Never that.

The only one to ever see him, really see him, was the skinny whore with the too-intense eyes.

Maybe it was thoughts of her that distracted him, but Bliss was sitting up, slumped against the rear side door when Oren finally brought his attention back to her.

She didn't look well. Eyes closed, body weaving, she clutched the car door.

Stupid sow. "The door is locked. There's no escape," he enjoyed telling her. "You should rest. Believe me, with what I have planned for you, you'll need your strength."

She moaned, delighting him.

"You'll be constrained in handcuffs, gagged so I don't have to hear your ridiculous begging, and every inch of your body will be explored to find your breaking point of pain. You'd be amazed, you slut, how much the human body can take before giving in to death. I predict that you'll last for days, if not a week. That is, as long as I temper Dory and Myer's appetites. They can be gluttons when it comes to deriving pleasure from another's pain."

Oren smiled at her through the rearview mirror—and she gagged.

Outrage coursed through him. "Don't you dare!" Frantically searching for the window release while still watching her, Oren lowered the window. "Hang your head out, you stupid pig. *Hang it out!*"

Oh God, she didn't.

Through the mirror, Oren watched in disbelief as she swayed away from the door and gagged again, this time more convulsively.

"You listen to me, you detestable tramp. If you *dare* vomit in my car, I swear to you, I'll—"

She hurled, not just in the car, but all over the back of Oren's head.

Shock stripped him of thought and reaction. He felt the hot, loamy ooze dripping down his hair, seeping into his neck, his ear cavities, slipping over his shoulders and on to his chest.

It almost made him vomit as well.

Slamming on the brakes, he knew he'd kill her now, right now—and in the next second, she toppled out the open window and hit the street hard.

Oren's mouth fell open. No. She didn't.

How dare she?

Bliss screamed even as she pushed herself up to her feet.

Two thugs on the corner looked up.

Screeching, her voice raw and weak, Bliss made a haphazard race down the street. She didn't even care that puke stained the front of her clothes, or that she babbled like a drugged idiot.

Men in front of a bar started toward her.

Fury made Oren see red. Damn her, he had no choice but to drive away now, before anyone approached him with questions. The stupid bitch had robbed him. Because of her and her weak stomach, he'd have to go home empty-handed.

With puke on his neck.

Seething, he made a vow to return, soon, and when he did, he'd make sure she paid. *They'd all pay*.

In the most painful ways he could devise.

Chapter 6

"Tell me what happened with Carver."

Walking away from him, Gaby went to the building and slumped down to sit with her back against it, her knees up.

Even in the dim light, Luther could see the crotch of her plain white panties, her long calves, her pale thighs. Salacious heat set his blood to boiling. His dick twitched, but then, around Gaby, twitchy was a way of life.

But more than that, more than anything carnal, he felt Gaby's isolation, and he hated it.

Unfortunately, he couldn't give in to it. Not yet. Not now, with a murder to be solved.

Standing over her helped Luther keep the emotional distance he needed to think with clarity. "Tell me what happened, Gaby."

"Fine." She scratched at a bug bite on her shoulder. "Carver hurt one of the women." She shrugged. "So I hurt him."

Luther had known the facts, but still, the dispassionate,

almost flippant way Gaby retold the story bothered him. He
wanted to see her care. About something. About him. "Which
woman? Give me a name."

"Winnie."

Luther searched his mind, but couldn't dredge up a resemblance to go with the name. "You know her well?"

"No, but what does that matter?" Elbows on her knees,
Gaby dropped her forehead down and crossed her wrists at
the back of her skull. Voice muffled, she intoned, "No man
has a right to hurt a woman."

"I agree." Abuse of any kind enraged him. "Unfortunately—"

"Yeah, they're prostitutes. I know. And I accept their life
choices, I really do. They let men knock them around as a rou-
tine part of their day. It's as commonplace for them as eating
is for other women." Her hands curled into fists. "But there are
always limits, and Carver took it too far. He hurt her."

Aching to touch her, Luther whispered, "It wasn't the first
time."

"No." Her shoulders tightened. "But then Bliss was under
his control."

Ah. He'd realized early on that she and Bliss had an affinity, a bond of sorts.

And that meant . . . what? That Gaby had to get Carver in
line? "You take responsibility for Bliss?"

"She'd lived on the streets for a long time."

Another child society had ignored, and forgotten. Luther
softened more. "Until you moved her in near you."

"Something like that. I thought it'd be better, but with
Carver still around . . . I won't let anyone hurt her, Luther."
She made a small, choking sound, and Luther could tell it
hurt her to admit, "She's so young, and so sad, that I can't
help but care for her."

Her distress proved more than Luther could take. Giving up, he sat down on the mucky, debris-covered concrete beside her. Being closer to Gaby, shoulders touching, helped.

A little.

"Let's try this from another angle." Staring at the moon-glow on her smooth skin, Luther asked, "Does Carver know for sure it was you who attacked him?"

Her shoulders twitched with a grunt. "How should I know? He's dumber than a rock." She lifted her face, showing Luther red eyes and total dejection. "But even if he does, so what?"

So what? Exasperated, Luther stared at her. "He's an unconscionable degenerate out for vengeance."

Gaby's lip curled with disdain. "Carver can't hurt me." Not seriously. She was too strong, and healed too quickly.

But others . . .

Her insistence of indomitability kept Luther awake on too many nights. "If Carver was involved with the murder of that woman—"

"I'll find out," Gaby said as a matter of course. "I doubt if he was, but he won't be able to lie to me."

"No." Luther couldn't get more than that single word out of his mouth. Every muscle in his body clenched in denial. He'd raced here to protect Gaby, not to encourage her into harm's way, not to send her after a sick bastard with a penchant for torture.

Gaby didn't look at him. She picked through the gravel on the sidewalk beside her until she found a pebble that appealed to her. She rolled it between her fingers, pitched it away.

He could practically see her thoughts churning.

Finally, she looked at him, her gaze so exigent that he couldn't look away. "I know this will be tough for you, but you're going to have to trust me."

He shook his head.

"Yes."

Given her past behavior, how she'd disappeared on him without a word, she asked too much. Luther meant to remonstrate with her and instead, his voice raw, he asked, "Why the hell would I trust you when you don't trust me?"

For long moments, their gazes clashed. "There is that."

Damn it.

"So you need some reasons. Well, let me see." Gaby stared at her hands as she dusted them off, then propped her elbows on her knees. "How about, because you care for me and you don't want me hurt, and letting me do this my way is the best possible insurance you can get that I won't be hurt."

Seeking control, knowing it to be well out of reach, Luther closed his eyes. "Just tell me where I can find Carver." He opened his eyes, willing her to try things his way for a change.

"Sorry, no." Her eyes darkened with regret. "There's no point. He won't tell you anything. You and I both know that."

Obstinate to the bitter end. "But you think you can make him talk?"

"If he knows anything worth telling, yeah, I can." Her affect revealed no modesty in her ability. "For sure when I finish with him, he won't want revenge on me. He'll just want to stay the hell out of my way."

Putting his head back against the rough bricks, Luther laughed. "Jesus, Gaby. You leave me no choices."

Lacking concern for his dilemma, she said, "Yeah? Meaning what?"

Did he, and his circumstance, truly not matter to her? Could she be that indifferent to him? "If you'll recall, I'm an officer of the law."

"No shit. Trust me, you being a cop isn't something I'm likely to forget."

"Right." She'd infused as much insult in that statement as she could. Luther glowered. "So you have to know that I can't condone willful acts of violence."

"Didn't ask you to condone it."

Throttle her or kiss her—it was a toss-up which one Luther wanted to do the most. "Now that you've told me, I can't sit here twiddling my thumbs while you . . . you . . ." He trailed off, unsure how to phrase what she might have planned, when she was so capricious he couldn't guess what she'd do.

He only knew it wouldn't be good.

"What?" Gaby prodded, half-turning toward him, her skirt still hiked too high, her antagonism a live thing. "What did you think I was talking about doing?"

Her posture finally proved more than Luther could take. Curving his hand around her slender upper thigh, he said, "That's just it, honey. With you, I never know."

Gaby looked at his hand on the inside of her thigh, covered his fingers with her own, and—a shock of pain punctured her burgeoning concupiscence.

Luther felt the withdrawal, a commutation of combativeness over sexual awareness. Gaby stiffened on a gasp of breath and her light blue eyes went first unseeing, then sharp with an insight that was strangely empyreal.

"Gaby?"

Clumsy with pain, she hurried to her feet and stared at nothingness as her chest heaved in an effort to draw in breath.

Luther tried to clasp her arms, but she brushed him off as easily as she'd shoo a fly. She took a step forward, then another.

"Damn it, Gabrielle Cody, don't you dare—"

In the next instant, a bloodcurdling cry erupted from

deep inside her, a shout of purest agony and harshest denial.

The fine hairs on Luther's nape stood on end. He whispered, "Gaby?"

And she was off, running full out, her muscles fluid with grace and speed. Luther gave chase, shouting her name, giving it his all but oddly unable to catch her.

Arms pumping and legs churning, she rounded a corner, then another.

Where the hell was she going? The hard, full-out run left Luther's lungs laboring, and sweat glued his shirt to his back. Lagging several feet behind Gaby, they charged past a drug deal turned battle, past a drunken trio who shouted obscenities at them, and past a homeless woman who almost tripped him up with her cart of discarded wares.

Finally, they hit a long, dark street and Gaby paused, posed in combat mode.

But not for long.

Her first step was tentative, her second long and sure. *"Bliss."*

Luther saw beyond Gaby to where she was headed.

There in the middle of the road, clothes torn, neck bleeding, staggering with her eyes closed and her arms out, was poor, young, too helpless Bliss.

Oh no, Luther thought. Not again.

Gaby reached Bliss just as she went limply into her arms; Gaby didn't stagger as she held Bliss mostly upright.

Even as he hurried forward to help, Luther surveyed the area. He saw a group of thugs hanging out, and knew he'd have to question them before they scattered. Across the street, an old white woman, hunched over from age and depression, scurried off.

Luther narrowed his eyes, but couldn't make out the license plate on the dark sedan screeching away.

"Son of a bitch." It needed only this. He loped up to the two women and relieved Gaby of Bliss's deadweight. "Is she okay?"

Grim, furious, Gaby smoothed back Bliss's hair. "No. She's not."

Supporting Bliss with one arm, Luther retrieved his radio and made an authoritative call for assistance and an ambulance. "I've got her," he said to Gaby, and gently lifted Bliss into his arms. Her head lolled against his chest. Her hair hung over his arm. She was soft, warm, but so still it scared him half to death.

He headed to the curb.

Without moving, Gaby shouted, "Where are you taking her?"

Knowing she needed his control right now, Luther tried for a calm and even tone. "I'm just moving her out of the street, that's all. An ambulance is on the way. We'll get her to a hospital and have her checked over." He looked up, caught Gaby's stark, taciturn countenance. "It's okay, Gaby. The paramedics will know what to do."

Bliss roused herself to mumble, "No. Please. No hospitals." Vomit clung to her hair and the corners of her mouth. Her pupils were wildly dilated, unseeing. "No, please."

"Shh, Bliss. It's all right. I promise." Luther looked back at Gaby. Still, she hadn't moved. She stood there in the middle of the street, heaving in impotence and paralyzing rage. Somehow, he had to reach her. "Come over here, Gaby. I need your help."

She took a step forward, then halted again. Her hands fisted. Her face contorted.

Oh no. She couldn't transform in that special way of hers. She couldn't run off to do God knew what. He did need her. Here, and now.

More sternly, Luther repeated, "Come *here*, Gaby." Bliss hung boneless in his arms until he lowered her to a bus-stop bench. Her arms flopped over the sides. Her loose blouse, now torn, nearly exposed a breast.

A raised, circular welt shone bright red on her throat. Hypodermic? Given the force of the needle's puncture, not self-inflicted.

Bliss moaned, and Gaby was suddenly there, beside the bench, her knees on the rough concrete.

Luther waited for her to comfort Bliss.

Gaby caught Bliss's face in her hands. "Who did this to you?" Her harsh, raised voice startled Luther. *"Give me a name, Bliss."*

There was no answer.

Luther touched her shoulder. "Gaby, this isn't the time."

She didn't relent. "Tell me, Bliss. Describe him."

"Not . . . not a him," Bliss said.

"A woman?"

Bliss's fair brows pulled down and her face scrunched in pain. "I don't know. A boy . . ."

"A boy?"

Bliss moaned. "No. I don't know."

Gaby gently shook her. "You're not making any sense. Give me a target, Bliss. Man, woman, kid—you tell me, and I'll do the rest."

After another moan, Bliss's head lolled to the side, as if she'd again lost consciousness.

"Let her rest." Luther squeezed Gaby's shoulder. "She's been drugged."

"I can see that," Gaby snapped. "Someone tried to take her.

Someone tried to—" Excess emotion strangled the words. She swallowed convulsively.

Bliss moaned again, tried to lurch away, and both Luther and Gaby went on alert.

"It's okay, Bliss," Luther told her. "Everything will be okay now."

"I only wanted to help," she murmured. "He . . . he said he needed help. Then he . . . she . . . oh God."

Nudging Gaby to the side, Luther pulled out a hanky and wiped the vomit from Bliss's face, tried to dab it from her hair. "You're safe now, Bliss. You're with me, and with Gaby. You're safe."

"I'm sick." Pitifully weak, she curled her arms about her stomach and gagged again, but nothing more came up. "He stabbed me with something."

"So it was a guy?"

"I don't know . . ." She touched a hand to her head. "He seemed so nice, but then she was going to do awful things to me. She said it, but I already knew it. I *felt* it." Bliss's faint voice broke on a sob. "Oh God, oh God, *oh God*."

"Two of them," Gaby decided aloud. "There were two of them. A woman and a man."

Bliss continued to sob. "No. Somehow he . . . he was a she. Or . . . I don't know. I'm sorry, Gaby, so sorry, but my head hurts."

Gaby stared up at the sky.

Luther locked both hands behind his neck. He wanted to kill someone. He wanted to know who would do this to Bliss. Damn it, he wanted to know *why*.

After a moment of internal struggle, Gaby put her palm to Bliss's cheek, and the girl quieted. Luther could tell that Gaby was unsure how to console her friend, how to comfort her. Embracing was foreign to her.

Any signs of affection were anomalous to Gaby's austere life.

Pulling himself together, Luther held out his hand to her. "Come here, Gaby." He had no problem with affection, and right now, he wanted, needed, to hold her.

But, of course, she stepped away, stiff, angry, unreachable in her grief.

Sirens cleaved the mundane sounds of night in the slums. Flashing lights rebounded off brick façades, concrete and odorous filth.

Giving Gaby some time to herself, Luther spoke to the paramedics as they approached. He directed the officers in the cruiser to question the people standing around, taking in the scene with the same indifference they'd give to a television commercial.

As soon as Bliss was loaded into the ambulance, he turned to talk to Gaby—and found her gone.

Rank curses burned his throat, but he swallowed them down. He didn't want the others to know she'd evaded him. Again.

Think, Luther. He paced . . . and it came to him.

Carver. She'd go after him, Luther knew it.

Now all he had to do was find him first.

Skin still itchy and too tight, lungs heavy with lead weights, Gaby strolled the dark streets looking for her prey. She asked numerous questions, gave innumerable threats, and finally got the answers she sought.

Carver would be warned; he'd be waiting for her.

She rejoiced in that certitude.

The arcade and pool hall next door to Carver's abode

overflowed with obstreperous activity. Gaby didn't flinch when a bottle broke a few feet behind her. She didn't slow when a drunken sot propositioned her.

When two leering punks accosted her, she laid them out with ease. One hit his head on the pavement and stayed still. The other held a broken jaw and slunk off in haste.

Rounding the front of the building, where Carver would least expect her, Gaby looked up at the structure. The second story had fire escapes, which would make it easy for her to gain entrance if she could reach them.

The gutters running down the side of the building barely adhered to the brick. They'd be of no help to her. But pipes of some sort ran along the exterior walls, and those should support her exiguous weight.

It wouldn't be easy, but she didn't want easy.

She wanted proof.

Upending a garbage can without care to the clatter she made, or the mess she left, Gaby moved it close to the building to give herself a leg up. Adjusting her fingers until she had an adequate grip on the thick pipe, she strained her muscles and chinned up. The toe of her boot caught in the brick, and she pushed up higher, stretching out with her left arm until she felt the cool iron of the fire escape.

After gaining that purchase, the rest of the climb was easy.

Ascending higher and higher, Gaby made it to the correct floor, crawled in through an open window, and passed through a home of devastation and apathy. She closed her ears to the crying babies, the blaring television, the drunken revelry in the kitchen. Without anyone paying notice, she walked on through and went out the front door into the hallway.

Two doors down, her knife in her hand, she knocked on Carver's hideaway.

The door opened to a bulldog of a guy prepped to grapple.

Gaby watched him display his discolored teeth in an earnest smile of anticipation—and she slugged him in the temple with the hilt of her knife. He collapsed forward, she moved, and he fell into the hallway. Behind him, Carver stood in frozen disbelief.

Gaby narrowed her eyes at him. "If you run, I will catch you, and then I'll make you a choirboy. Do we understand each other?"

He backed up, hit a wall, and looked around for assistance. Finding none, he nodded.

Hilarious.

If only Luther had even an ounce of this man's reverence for her ability. But he didn't. He accounted her no proficiency at all.

Gaby shoved the bodyguard's heavy legs out of her way, shut the apartment door, and locked it. Still holding her knife, she glanced at Carver and pointed toward the tattered sofa. "Sit."

Seething, Carver swallowed hard and moved to park himself on faded, flowery damask. "Haven't you done enough? What the fuck do you want now?"

Silvery scars showed on his ruddy skin.

Scars she'd given him.

It was nothing compared to the hurt he'd inflicted on women throughout his miserable life. "I want answers. I want the truth. If you lie, I'll know it. Do you believe me?"

"Yeah." His nostrils flared. His mouth pinched. "I believe you."

"Did you murder Lucy?"

His face went pasty white. He croaked, "Lucy's dead?"

Tapping her knife blade against her thigh, Gaby stalked

closer while measuring his honest response. "Dead, tor-tured, diced, and thrown in the river."

Eyes bulging with fear, Carver shook his head. "I never touched her." Just as quickly, he blanched and recanted that statement. "No, wait! That wasn't a lie."

"Sure sounded like one to me."

He rushed into garbled speech. "I didn't *kill* her. I swear it. I've slapped her around—you already know that. But I didn't want her dead. I wouldn't. I swear."

Gaby tipped her head, studying him, but . . . she believed him. More than that, she *knew* he was telling the truth. "What about Bliss?"

Like a fish out of water, his mouth flapped open and closed until he managed to whisper, "She's dead, too?"

Almost, Gaby thought. So close. In the marrow of her bones, she knew the person who'd tried to take Bliss, the person Bliss had somehow managed to escape, was the same who'd murdered Lucy.

Gaby inhaled deeply.

So why was she bothering Carver?

Because she'd desperately wanted it to be him? Because, in the end, she had wanted it to be that simple?

Rubbing her eyes, Gaby said, "She's not dead. Someone stuck a needle in her neck and tried to kidnap her. She es-caped."

"How?"

"I don't know." Sheathing her knife, Gaby said, "You had nothing to do with any of it, did you?"

"No."

Of course not. She'd known it, but damn it . . . well, at least now she had it verified. "You still plotting against me, Carver?"

"No!" He shook his head hard. "I just want to be left alone. I don't—"

A prickle slithered down Gaby's spine, belying his words. She gave Carver a gentle study, and tsked. "Now you're lying."

Panicked, Carver lurched to his feet and held out both meaty hands. "Okay, okay, so I had wanted to get to you. You cut me all up! But . . . I don't anymore. I consider us even. I swear."

"Stop swearing."

Losing control, he lunged for her. Gaby went to the ground with him, rolled, and buried her knee in his gut. He let out a "woof" but didn't slow. With the palm of her hand, she smashed his nose, and at almost the same time, drew her knife.

That gave Carver pause. Quick and easy, Gaby put three additional slices on him—one on his right forearm, one on his chest, and one over his abdomen.

"You wanna play now, Carver? You feeling froggy enough to take me on? Well, come on then." She egged him forward. "Let's play. I'm more than ready."

He wiped the blood from his nose, stared at the blood seeping into his clothes, and crumpled down on his ass to sit on the threadbare carpet. "No. No, I don't want to . . ." He squeezed his eyes shut. "Damn you, woman, can't you just leave me alone?"

Yeah, she should. She was wasting her time here. "Maybe. If you leave me alone."

Before Carver could reply, someone pounded a heavy fist against his door. "Carver? Open up right now or I'm knocking down the door."

Luther.

Damn, he was good. Impressed, Gaby bent close to Carver, snaring him in her gaze. "Tell the cop nothing about me, and then we're even. You got that?"

"*Cop?*" He stared with horror at the rattling door. "But I don't want to talk to no cop!"

"Tough tittie. He's here, and you can take my word for it, he won't be leaving until you've answered all his questions. Unfortunately for you, he won't be nearly as easy to convince as I am." Gaby grabbed his chin. "Do we have a deal?"

"Yeah, sure. You weren't here." Carver looked back at the door, turned again, and said, "But what if . . . Hey, where'd you go?"

Out on the ledge, Gaby listened, almost smiling. The door crashed in, Luther's booming voice shouted her name, and Carver, true to his word, said, "There's no one else here. What do you want? What do you mean, breaking in my door?"

As Gaby scampered back down the bricks, she didn't hear anything else. But she pictured Luther's red face, his hot temper.

Then she pictured him holding Bliss in his arms. A whore with puke in her hair. A woman bleeding.

And Luther had held her like a delicate child.

Gaby's feet touched the pavement and she sighed. There weren't many men like Detective Luther Cross, and it sure made him hard to resist.

But until she figured out what evil incarnate had tried to hurt Bliss, until she destroyed that evil, she'd do well to stay clear of the good detective.

Sometimes, *most* times, her life really sucked.

Chapter 7

Still seething, but also . . . scared, Gaby strode into the hospital.
She wasn't afraid for herself.

She feared for Bliss.

From the day she'd met the young girl, she'd felt compelled toward protectiveness. Gaby had first saved Bliss from a despicable john who had grossly abused her, and wasn't done.

One look at Bliss, and anyone could see the lifelong sadness in her blue eyes, the despondency emanating from her smiles. Her life had been hell—much like Gaby's.

Gaby had felt an immediate affinity to her.

But whereas Gaby had strength of purpose, Bliss still wandered, clinging, needing . . . as yet unloved.

Until Gaby, no one had ever protected Bliss. No one had ever really cared for her at all.

How Gaby knew that, she couldn't say, except that when she looked at Bliss, she saw herself.

And it hurt.

Now Bliss needed her more than ever, but she'd found out nothing. The animus remained at large, out there somewhere, pursuing, conspiring.

Unless Luther had better luck with witnesses, which she doubted, they'd have zilch to go on.

A dark car.

An attack.

Nothing more.

Gaby's head pounded, her guts churned, and her eyes burned. She would not let anyone or anything hurt Bliss. She wouldn't.

Somehow, some way, she'd—

"'Bout time you showed up."

At that carefully even voice, Gaby spun around, and there stood Luther, tall, powerful.

Furious, despite the lack of venom in his words.

Unconcerned with his mood swings, Gaby turned and headed toward him. "How's Bliss?"

His nostrils flared. His gaze all but seared her. Turning sideways and indicating a hallway, Luther said, "This way."

Well . . . regardless of how he'd modulated his voice, his aura burned scorching hot, so Gaby didn't know if she wanted to follow him. More cautious now, she asked, "Are you taking me to see Bliss?"

He didn't look at her. His hands landed on his hips and his chest expanded. Fury worked his jaw. "Come. With. Me."

Uh-oh. Sounded like he meant business. Truthfully, she was too damned enervated to spar with him right now. Never, not once, had she ever feared Luther. She sure wouldn't start now.

"Fine. Whatever." Gaby sauntered past him. "Don't get your boxers in a bunch."

Her sarcasm must've tipped the scales, because Luther imploded. Snatching up her arm, he lifted her to the tips of her toes and propelled her forward before she could even think to object. When they reached a private room, he practically slammed her inside.

"Hey!"

He shut the door and with theatric temper, lifted his hands up and off her as if he thought touching her would inspire mayhem.

Something had gotten to him, and that worried her. An invisible fist clenched her heart and compressed her lungs. "Is Bliss okay?"

Scorn distorted his features. "Do you even care?"

The rancor slapped her with blinding force, almost bringing tears to Gaby's eyes. It almost hurt too much to speak, forcing her to a whisper. "You miserable prick."

God, how she wished she *didn't* care.

Wanting to escape, to be alone with her detestable self, she reached for the door.

Luther wrenched her back around. "Don't."

Keeping her head down, Gaby didn't dare look at him. Usually she'd be in fighting form. Under different circumstances, Luther's audacity would find him flat on the floor.

But this time . . . she didn't have it in her.

Everything she knew herself to be—her only purpose in life—did her no good right now. Bliss was vulnerable, and she couldn't figure out how to help her.

"If you care, why the hell did you run off and leave her? Why did you abandon her?"

Explanations weren't her strong suit, but for some reason, Gaby needed Luther to understand. "I wanted to find whoever tried to take her."

"That's *my* job."

A pressing weight stooped her shoulders. "Then . . . that leaves me with no purpose at all."

He edged closer, vibrating with rage, ready to lose his control. Leaning down, each word sharp with contempt, he said, "You could have consoled her. You could have been her friend."

Damn, those tears were determined to spill over. Gaby shook her head—and felt like a fool. "The thing is . . . I don't know how to do that."

Silence stretched out. Muffled voices drifted over the intercom. People passed by in the hallway. In the distance, a faint siren intruded.

Luther's hand tangled in her hair, smarting a little, but so what? He sounded hoarse and despondent as he cursed her. "Damn you, Gaby."

Yeah right. "I was damned long before I met you, cop."

Bending down, he touched his forehead to hers. His breath rushed against her cheek. His voice softened. "Don't say that."

Fine. She'd say nothing at all.

"Damn it." He pushed her head to his chest and held it there, then locked his free arm around her.

She'd gone from accepting his scorn to caught in his secure embrace. He held her tight, crushed her close. His heartbeat pumped against her cheek. Heat, scented by his big body, wafted around her.

Why did he want to comfort her now? He'd been so angry, on the verge of truest rage. What event could possibly inspire both emotions . . .

Oh God.

Thoughts and images raced through Gaby's consciousness. Had Bliss . . . *died?*

Bliss had shown a bad reaction to the drug used on her.

People died from adverse drug reactions all the time. Who knew what had been injected into her, how much, or how toxic it might be?

Just as Gaby started to collapse, Luther set her back from him. "She's fine, Gaby."

She heard him, but after such numbing fear, she had a hard time grasping the truth. "You're sure?"

"As sure as I can be at the moment. I stayed with her until she was in the ambulance."

Gaby's eyelids sank shut. Luther said she was fine. Hurt, certainly, but not expired as he'd made her think.

Fury replaced the remorse, and Gaby slugged him in the ribs with enough force to repay him for that awful panic. "Thanks for scaring me half to death!"

He barely grunted. "I can't make any guarantees on how she fared after she reached the hospital, because I had to chase after *you*."

So now it was her fault that he was so nosy? "No," Gaby said, "you didn't."

"Yes," Luther said, grabbing her shoulders and rattling her witless, "I *did*."

Being manhandled didn't sit well with Gaby's temper at the best of times. This sure as hell wasn't the best of times. "Get your mitts off me right now." She tried to shrug him away, but he didn't budge.

"Oh no you don't, not this time." Luther's grip held her secure.

"I'm warning you . . ."

"You want a battle, Gaby?" He released her and stepped back. "Well, come on, lady. Bring it. I'm more than fucking ready."

Wow. Gaby eyed Luther up and down. Seeing that his temper was more frayed than her own, she no longer had any desire to pulverize him. "Did you drag me in here for a reason, or just to expend some anger?"

Luther's pointing finger nearly poked her in the nose. "We're coming to an agreement, you and I, one you'll abide by."

"Is that so?"

"Damn straight it is, or so help me, I'll—"

"Arrest me, I know." Gaby flapped a dismissive hand at him. His threats had never carried much weight, and right now, they meant less than nothing to her. "That's your answer to every damn thing that happens, isn't it?"

"I'll arrest you," Luther confirmed, "and you won't get a chance to visit with Bliss." He stared her in the eyes, unrelenting, firm in his resolve. "How do you think that'll make Bliss feel? Or do you even care how she feels?"

Low blow. "Bastard," she hissed.

"Sticks and stones, Gaby."

Her biceps twitched with the urge to brain him. Just one solid sock, right in his handsome face. He might not be so appealing with a crooked nose.

But no, she couldn't, wouldn't, do that. Even now with his fury boiling over and red-hot anger tingeing the outer perimeter of his aura, shades of pure altruism encompassed him.

Luther epitomized all that was good and pure.

She, on the other hand, epitomized the cold slam of justice. "So tell me the damn terms of this agreement, and make it fast, before I lose my good humor and flatten you."

Luther took a calming breath. "I want you to work with me on this, not on your own. That means that whatever you know, I want to know."

Huh. He wanted to play partners? Ridiculous. "And vice versa?"

He surprised her by saying, "Yes."

Dropping back against the wall, her eyebrows raised, Gaby blinked at him. "No shit?"

Running a hand through his hair, Luther paced away from her. For the first time, Gaby noticed his disheveled state. Wrinkles marred his untucked and sweat-stained shirt. Dirt splotched his slacks. He looked haggard and tired and fed up.

Guilt gnawed on her. But what could she have done to make any of this easier on him? She had her own hardships to deal with.

"It sickened me," Luther said, "to find Bliss in that shape, drugged and hurt and scared half to death."

"Me, too."

"I keep seeing that tortured corpse on the riverbank, knowing how badly the woman suffered."

"Me, too."

He caught Gaby in his gaze. "I know it's going to happen again."

Gaby wasn't a mind reader, but this time, she didn't need to be. "Hold up a minute. You're thinking it could happen to *me*?"

"If you keep charging in without caution—"

"I don't do that, but even if I did, you don't need to worry about me. It's Bliss, and women like her—"

"Like her?"

"Helpless." Ordinary. Normal. Real. Gaby choked down the damning words. "Women who, because of their lifestyles, are vulnerable to sick pervs like our guy who's still running loose." Because she'd failed.

"If it's a guy," Luther pointed out. "Bliss was pretty confused about it all."

"She'll be able to tell us more when she's recovered." Gaby was counting on it.

"Maybe." Luther waved that away. "But unless I stop it, we're going to be finding more corpses."

"Yeah." More likely, Gaby thought, she'd be the one to put an end to things, but she didn't want to devalue Luther's contribution, or his sincerity. "I take it you have something in mind?"

"If we work together, me in my official capacity, you with your street information, we have a better chance to catch the guy responsible before anyone else gets hurt, or killed."

Hell no. Gaby's eventual success depended largely on Luther staying unaware of the scope of her metaphysical, even supernatural, ability. But she couldn't tell him that. "Sounds like a plan."

He straightened, moved closer to her again. "You said I didn't trust you. Well, I'm going to trust your word that you'll tell me everything you find out."

Shit. "Luther . . ."

"I'll trust you to be careful. I'll trust you—but you have to trust me, too."

Damn it, did he have to drag her nonexistent integrity into this?

A voice over the PA called for Detective Cross. Luther didn't move. He waited, and Gaby, seeing so few choices, accepted his offer. "Fine."

He nodded and reached for the door.

When he had it open, Gaby said, "But Luther?"

He looked back.

She felt on the precipice of something insane, unimagined—something once so far out of reach that now loomed within her grasp.

If she went through the threshold, it could liberate her.

Or kill her.

Luther turned to fully face her. "What is it?"

Taking a huge leap of faith, Gaby whispered, "Believing what I tell you isn't always going to be easy."

For a long moment, he said nothing. Then he reached out his hand for her.

An olive branch. Acceptance. Maybe more?

Hating her own weakness, Gaby took his hand.

His fingers curled warmly around hers. One corner of his mouth lifted with humor, with relief, and with promise. "I've found that where you're concerned, Gabrielle Cody, nothing ever is."

A plump, gray-haired doctor met Luther and Gaby in the hallway outside of the room where Bliss rested. "You're her family?"

"Not quite." Luther showed his badge, then introduced himself.

The doctor held out a hand. "I'm Dr. Bolton. I apologize for your long wait. The patient—" He referred to a clipboard. "—Bliss, was drugged with a high dose of Midazolam."

High dose. Gaby seethed. When she found the one responsible, she'd get her retribution.

Well, except that Luther hoped to tag along, and he might be averse to her chopping up the jerk and feeding him to the carp in the river.

Unaware of Gaby's frothing anger, Luther asked, "Midazolam? That's one of the date rape drugs, right?"

The doctor nodded. "It's a powerful anesthetic used in minor surgery because it leaves patients unable to remember what has happened to them."

Luther glanced at Gaby, then back to the doctor with frustration. "In other words, it's perfect for kidnapping someone."

"I'm afraid so." Dr. Bolton took off his glasses and rubbed tired eyes. "In this patient's case, she had an adverse reaction to the drug, which affected her breathing and caused the vomiting. We flushed out her system. Her stomach is calmer, and she's resting easier now, but I'd like to keep her overnight for observation. I don't expect any problems, so she should be able to go home in the morning."

Both men excluded Gaby from their discussion, which suited her just fine. It gave her time to let her thoughts connect into some sort of coherent order.

Luther rubbed the back of his neck in a show of exhaustion. "Is Bliss able to answer some questions about the attack?"

"Physically, she's stable. Other than some bruises and scratches, which I gather she sustained while escaping the car, she doesn't have any serious injuries."

"So I can talk with her?"

The doctor tapped his eyeglasses against his thigh. "It won't hurt anything, but I don't know how much help she can be at this point. Emotionally, she's still very confused and upset. Midazolam often has a residual 'hangover' effect. Your young lady was given such a large dosage that she's still suffering the effects of sleepiness, impaired psychomotor and cognitive functions. Overall, she seems very confused about what happened to her."

Every word caused Gaby more pain. She could only imagine Bliss's discomfort and fear.

"How long till her head clears enough to tell us what happened?"

"Hard to say." A nurse came to the doctor with a message. He read it, then returned his attention to Luther. "It may persist into tomorrow. In fact, she could feel drowsy, tired, or weak for two days or more."

"Jesus," Luther swore.

The doctor commiserated with a pat on Luther's shoulder. "Don't push her. The quality that makes Midazolam medically valuable, namely clinical amnesia, is precisely what enables others to use it as an effective date rape drug. Victims are unable to give an accurate account of what happened to them, and testing for the drug is difficult. It breaks down rapidly and disappears from the system within forty-eight hours, making its detection in criminal cases problematic. In this case, because of her reaction to the drug, we were able to do a blood test right away."

Remembering the violent way that Bliss heaved, Gaby asked, "It's uncommon for most people to get as ill as she got?"

The doctor studied Gaby only a moment before replying. "Fortunately for surgery patients, yes. But because of how she reacted, I'd like someone to stay with her for a few days, just to keep an eye on her."

"She won't be alone," Gaby told them, vowing it as much to herself as to anyone else. "Can we go in to see her now?"

"By all means. But be patient if she falls asleep on you."

Luther thanked the doctor as Gaby moved to the door.

She abhorred hospitals. Too much of her time had been spent trapped within the sterile walls, her ears assaulted by the clinical concern of staff. Father's disease had left him lost in his own misery, a stranger in a disease-defiled body. But Gaby, hale and hearty throughout it all, had obtained a visceral detestation of all things related to hospital care.

Father had died a slow, agonizing death, and Gaby, with her special ability, had felt it with him.

She felt it still—whenever she entered a hospital. Her pulse raced, her skin became clammy. Her throat ached and her stomach burned.

But this was a different situation. This was Bliss, and she *would* be okay.

Pushing the door open, Gaby strode in with the feigned comportment of a person in charge. At the first sight of her friend, she stalled.

Bliss lay limp in a sterile white bed, her brown hair clean but matted, her makeup smudged everywhere it shouldn't be. The faded, striped hospital gown swallowed her feminine frame, making her look like a small, defenseless child.

"Hey," Gaby whispered, unsure if Bliss slept or not. Equally unsure if she wanted to wake her.

Bliss's eyes opened with drowsy delay, focused on Gaby, then filled with glistening tears. *"Gaby."*

It was the oddest thing, to be wanted like this.

To be needed. Trusted.

Propping her hip on the side of the narrow cot, Gaby scowled down at Bliss, but kept her voice soft. "Now, Bliss, don't you dare start bawling. There's no reason. It's okay. You're safe now."

"No." Her bottom lip quivered as she clutched at Gaby's arm. "Please." Casting frightened, leery glances at Luther, she implored in a low, hushed voice, *"Get me out of here."*

Standing at the foot of the bed, Luther studied her. "How old are you, Bliss?"

As if in great pain and immeasurable panic, Bliss groaned aloud and dragged the bedsheet up to her chin.

Gaby rolled her eyes. "Relax, Bliss. Luther's no dummy. He's already figured out that you're underage and likely a runaway."

Luther said nothing.

Gaby patted Bliss's hand. "He's the heroic sort, which means he's not going to let anyone send you back to a situation worse than the one you're in now."

With mocking irony, Luther agreed. "Worse than this? That's hard to imagine."

Bliss groaned again.

"Luther," Gaby warned, "you know what I mean."

He touched Bliss's small foot tenting the sheets at the end of the bed. "You can trust me, Bliss. Gaby's right. I just want to know that you're safe, and I want to catch the person who did this to you. Those are my only concerns right now."

Hope filled Bliss's expression. "But . . . they keep asking me questions about my real name and stuff."

"You're confused," Gaby told her. "The doctor said so. You don't have to tell anyone anything, not if you don't want to."

New tears filled her eyes. "I am confused. I know you want me to tell you what happened, but . . . I can't really remember nothing important."

Appreciating Luther's silence, Gaby took Bliss's hand. "Just tell me what you can remember."

"I sort of remember talking to a boy." Pain flashed in her blue eyes, but her aura coruscated around her, dancing in shades of yellow—the color of mental activity.

Gaby glanced toward Luther. She hadn't forgotten the boy that Luther let escape her. And seeing the guilt on his face, she knew that he hadn't forgotten either.

"A boy? What did you talk about with him?"

Bliss shook her head. "I don't know. And . . . I'm not even sure it was a boy." She pressed fingertips to her temples. "I can almost see him. But I remember a woman's voice."

A boy and a woman? "Can you tell me what she looked like?"

Bliss shook her head.

Luther stepped closer. "What did she say?"

Her fingers curled into fists. "She was really sick, telling me awful things. Cruel things. But . . . some of the things she didn't say. I just . . . knew them." Bliss looked up at Gaby, shuddering anew. "I sound like an idiot."

"No, you don't. You sound like someone who was attacked and hasn't gotten it all together yet. That's all."

Bliss hesitated, breathing hard, then she reached for Gaby's hand. "I remember thinkin' that I had to get away from her any way I could. Because, Gaby, I knew if I didn't, I'd . . . die."

The bitch had really scared Bliss. Gaby wasn't sure how to calm her, except to say, "I'll find her, Bliss. I swear I will."

Bliss squeezed her eyes shut. "I want to leave here, but I'm . . . scared of going, too. Dumb, huh?"

"Not dumb at all." Gaby leaned down. "But I'm not going to let anyone hurt you, Bliss. I want you to believe that."

"*We're* not going to let anyone hurt you." After frowning at Gaby, Luther circled the bed to stand opposite her. "Bliss, do you remember how old the boy was? What he wore? Anything about the car?"

Bliss's brow puckered as she struggled with her thoughts. She shook her head. "I'm sorry, Luther."

"You said the woman said sick things to you. Do you recall any of it?"

"She . . . she told me I'd need my strength." Saying it aloud leeched more color from Bliss's face. "That's it. I can't remember nothing else."

"Did she have an accent of any type?"

"She sounded really happy. She was almost giggling. That scared me more than anything."

Luther touched her shoulder. "One witness said he saw a woman driving away from you, but he didn't see anyone else. He didn't see a boy."

Bliss shook her head. "Maybe it was just a woman, then. But I ain't sure. I've been trying and trying, Luther, I swear.

But I can't picture him or her or nothing. I can't picture no one."

Again, Bliss cast an unsure glance at Luther, then leaned in closer to Gaby. "I remember knowin' what would happen to me. But I don't know how I knew it. I just . . . did." She chewed her trembling lips, looked at Luther, then away. "There's a room . . ."

An eerie sliver of dread snaked down Gaby's back. "A room?"

"I sort of . . . saw it. But I didn't."

Gaby leaned closer, cautious and curious. "It's okay, Bliss. Just tell me what you saw."

"It was awful, Gaby. A room full of stuff to hurt people. Places to tie them down. Things to use on them. Like a dungeon maybe."

"In a house?"

"I think so, but I ain't sure about that. I just . . . well, I know the room is there."

Gaby sat up a little straighter. Did Bliss have the curse, or was it just her reverence of Gaby that made her believe such things?

Aware of Luther standing beside the bed, frozen in disbelief, Gaby tried not to give herself away. "Can you tell me what it looked like, specifically? Concrete walls, or paneling, or plaster? Painted walls? Lights?"

"It's a big room." Bliss closed her eyes. "Dark wooden walls with fancy trim on everything. Really bright lights. Blood and flesh and . . ." Her eyes opened, stark with horror. "A lot of people have died there."

Looking like a thundercloud, Luther stared at Gaby, then at Bliss. "How would you know this, Bliss? Did the woman maybe say something?"

"No." Bliss continued to fret. "But I remember seeing it real clear, and knowin' that's where she wanted to take me."

"It's okay," Gaby told her. "A lot of people have special sight in a situation like yours."

"Special sight?" Luther repeated.

Gaby ignored him.

So did Bliss. "I also knew you'd come to help me, Gaby."

"I've been your protector—"

"No," Bliss said. "Somehow, I *knew* that if I got outta that car, you'd come to help me."

Luther went rigid.

Gaby squeezed Bliss's hand. The poor girl shook all over. It was a dilemma to be solved later, she decided. For right now, with Bliss so muddled and afraid, she wouldn't draw any conclusions.

Except that . . . "Luther, I wonder if it's the same boy."

He looked relieved for some sound logic instead of psychogenic phenomenon. "The same kid you were chasing when I found you again?"

"Could be."

"I guess that depends on why you were chasing him, doesn't it?"

Allowing Bliss to retain her death hold on her hand, Gaby settled more comfortably on the side of the bed. "I sensed he was up to something. That's all."

"Murder? Torture?" Luther scoffed. "You sensed he was up to that?"

"If I had, he wouldn't have gotten away from me." In no mood for Luther's lack of faith, Gaby smoothed back Bliss's hair. "I'm going to take you to Morty's for a while. You'll be safe there, and it's not too far away, so I can visit you whenever you want me to. What do you think of that?"

Bliss said nothing.

She'd fallen back to sleep, her hand still clutching Gaby's.

"It's a strange coincidence," Luther said, thinking aloud as he paced the small room. "For you to be after a boy, and for a boy to be after Bliss."

"Tell me about it." Gaby only wished she had a sound connection to share. But she didn't.

Was it the same kid? She wasn't sure. But she didn't believe in coincidence.

Luther rounded the bed to stand in front of her. "Where did you know him from?"

"I didn't. Until that day, I'd never laid eyes on him before."

Hands on his hips, Luther said, "So you just saw a kid, disliked him on sight? What the hell would you have done if you'd caught him?"

"He was where he shouldn't be, and I didn't like it." She thought about that, about her intentions that day, and her dead certainty that something was wrong. "Until he ran, I'd only planned to talk to him." Gaby loosened Bliss's hold, then pulled the sheet up over her. "But he did run, which seems real suspicious if you ask me."

"Me, too." He nodded toward Bliss. "At least now it does."

"I'll know him if I ever see him again."

"That's a start."

And a dead end. Knowing Luther wouldn't let it go, Gaby stood without touching him, brushed Bliss's cheek one last time, and walked out of the room. Though her hands were steady, vengeance and rage commingled inside her.

Freed from the confines of Bliss's room, Gaby breathed in the cool hospital air and drooped against the wall, eyes closed as she waited for Luther.

When she heard the quiet click of the door and felt him beside her, she said, "I want to kill someone."

"I know." He smoothed her hair. "Me, too."

He *knew*. Gaby looked at him. He hadn't remonstrated with her for her bloodthirsty desire. He'd . . . commiserated.

"You want a truth, Luther?"

"That'd be nice." His fingers continued to play with her hair. It was something Gaby had noticed early on, this strange fascination Luther had with her unkempt, mostly forgotten hair.

"This is hard for me."

"I know. Me, too."

She shook her head. He didn't get her meaning. "No. I'm not like you, Luther. I'm hardwired to react." Fisting a hand, Gaby pressed it against her abdomen. "Here, inside me. Everything that *is* me is screaming for me to do something."

"But you don't yet know what to do?"

She put her head back again and squeezed her eyes shut. "I don't have a fucking clue."

"Me neither." Luther's hand left her hair and instead curved around her neck.

His palm was hot, a little rough. Exciting.

Lost in a vortex of extraordinary need, Gaby opened her eyes to look at him. "Sucks, huh?"

"It's frustrating." He crowded into her space, big and powerful, sharing his heat, his scent. "If we're patient, if we work together, we'll get it figured out."

"Being patient means someone else could die."

"That's an impasse cops face often. It takes persistence to solve a problem, but all the while, you know someone's life could be on the line."

Gaby trusted that eventually she'd get the one responsible—but how many women would be hurt first? The only thing she knew with any certainty was that the bastard who'd tried to take Bliss would act again.

And again.

Somewhere along the way, he'd screw up and then she'd have him. God willing, that'd happen before another woman was tortured and murdered.

"Gaby?" Luther now had both hands on her neck, his thumbs stroking along her jawline.

How could thumbs on her chin turn her on? Maybe she was a degenerate of some sort. A sexual deviant.

With every breath she took, her chest brushed Luther's, heightening her strange tension.

Her innate reactions sickened Gaby; she shouldn't be thinking such carnal thoughts while Bliss lay drugged and frightened in a hospital bed.

Unwilling to look him in the eyes, Gaby said, "Yeah?"

"There's been a lot said today that I'd like to understand."

She snorted. "I can imagine." Her endogenous perception to all things evil would confuse a saint. Of course a solid citizen like Luther would be confused by it. "Shoot."

"What do you mean that you're hardwired to react?"

That got her gaze on his. He tried to look passive, when Gaby knew Luther was anything but. "Can you handle the truth?"

In some infinitesimal way, he hardened all over. "Yes."

Gaby twisted her mouth. Maybe Luther believed that calumnious statement, but she knew better. If she gave him the whole truth, he'd be calling for the guys with the straightjacket.

A quarter-truth would serve for now. Later, if he didn't freak out too much, she could share more.

Oh God, what was she thinking?

"Don't think," he said, as if he'd read her mind. "Just open up to me."

"You asked for it." Slipping her fingers through his belt

loops, Gaby urged him closer. Feeling Luther, being with him, filled her with copious emotion and turned his aura effulgent. She liked that.

Watching him, Gaby nudged her pelvis into his hips—and saw the slight tightening of his facial muscles, felt the quickening of his pulse.

No time like the present. "When evil is near, I know it."

Jerked from her deliberate enticement, Luther studied her face, nodded. "Explain evil."

"Why? You know evil, Luther. You've dealt with it plenty of times."

"I want to hear your definition."

"Fine. There are bad people, and then there are true corruptions passing themselves off as humans. They don't deserve to breathe the same air as others. They don't merit rehabilitation, or a life in prison, or even an easy death."

Some of the erotic energy flowing through his aura began to fade. His hold now felt more restraining than tender, his fingertips pressing into her nape.

Gaby defied him with a look. "What's the matter, cop? Too much for you?"

Challenged, Luther held silent for a heartbeat, then he relented. "Yes, I've known evil like that. It's a sad hazard of my profession."

Poor Luther. He wanted so badly to accept her, that he tried to find correlations in their lives and attitudes. "Did you know that evil as soon as you saw it?"

Distant memories passed over his features. "On occasion. Most often, no." His eyes narrowed. "People can be deceiving."

Not to paladins. Not to freaks like her. "They don't deceive me, Luther." Just to keep him off balance, Gaby lifted to her tiptoes and kissed his mouth hard and fast. "Ever."

Wary now, Luther set her away from him. "And when you recognize evil, what do you do about it?"

"Me?" Leaving him no illusion as to her facetiousness, Gaby said, "But Luther, I'm just a woman. Whatever could I do?"

Rather than take the bait, Luther dragged her back to him and this time the kiss was slow and deep, scorching hot, mesmerizing.

Claiming.

Gaby thought about struggling . . . but what the hell?

She needed this.

She needed *more*. Of him.

Little by little, she understood that sexual need caused at least part of her frustration, sleeplessness, and fractious demeanor.

For Luther.

When he ended the kiss, Luther also ended all contact. He released Gaby, stepped back two paces, and watched her.

Collapsing against the wall, Gaby touched her now swollen and tingling lips.

And sighed.

Maybe sharing with Luther wasn't so unthinkable. Maybe, just maybe, she could ease him into the abomination of her life.

"Wow. I'm starting to like that more and more."

He didn't smile. "When Bliss said that she knew you'd be there, what exactly did she mean?"

With sexual awareness coursing like hot lava through her veins, Gaby watched Luther with new eyes. "You'd have to ask her."

He tried a different tack. "What do you think she meant?"

Oh no. Not so soon. It was time to get out from under Luther's spell.

Willing strength into her bones, Gaby pushed away from the wall. "Bliss was drugged, disoriented." Gaby turned and started down the long corridor. "Who knows what she might've meant? Maybe she said that just because . . . I'm a friend."

"And her description of the room?"

"She fantasized it because of her fear. For her, that'd be the worst to happen, so in her mind, she knew it would happen."

"You believe that?"

No. She believed Bliss. "Maybe." In only a few steps, Gaby decided, What the hell? He wanted to know more, so she'd tell him more. "I do believe in mind reading, though I'm not a mind reader myself."

Rather than doubt her, Luther nodded. "How does it work?"

"I've never really studied it, so I'm not sure. But I do know that people have auras, and a lot is revealed through an aura."

"You've mentioned auras before."

Gaby peered up at him. "Right now, your aura is a muddy shade of violet. Want to know what that means?"

"Sure, why not?"

"Violet usually represents the ability to handle affairs with practicality. But that darker shade is pure erotic imagination." Gaby tilted her head at him. "You're asking about Bliss, but your thoughts are divided."

"Guilty." Not the least bit ashamed or hesitant, Luther said, "I always want you. I've told you that. But now's not the time, so back to Bliss . . ."

Wow. He did know how to keep her off-kilter. "My theory is that fear naturally heightens sensory perception, so even someone unfamiliar with reading auras could pick up on them when scared witless. Bliss said the woman who took

her giggled. That sounds pretty fucking sick to me, so I figure she was giving off some glaring vibes on her intent."

"And the room?"

"If there is a room, and the demented bitch was thinking
about taking Bliss there, she might have picked up on that."

He chewed his upper lip before saying, "Okay, I can buy
that, I suppose."

"Yeah, right. People like you are the reason that the ab-
stract prospects of the human mind and the intangible realm
behind matter are treated as hocus-pocus."

Luther whistled. "All that, huh?"

Her temper sparked. "Don't poke fun at me, Luther."

"Actually, I was thinking there are many depths to you.
Some of them are a little loony, but somehow you make it all
sound reasonable, and believable."

She stayed silent, but Gaby felt the nearly tactile sensation of his narrow-eyed attention on her face.

"So, let's try this another way."

Oh shit. Why couldn't he just give it up?

"How did you know Bliss was in trouble?"

Gaby's heart tripped. She walked faster, harder. Questions
on Bliss she could handle. Questions on her own preternatural
acuity were hitting too close to home. "I don't know what you
mean."

"When she was being attacked, somehow you knew it."
Stewing over his own memories, Luther thought it out without Gaby's help. "You couldn't see her, and you couldn't
hear her. But somehow you knew what was happening all the
same. And that isn't the first time it's happened with you."

"Don't be—"

"We were talking," Luther reminded her, "then you suddenly went on alert. I saw it in your face that something was
wrong. I didn't know what—but you did."

Gaby kept walking.

Luther kept pace with her. "At first, your movements were a little jerky, as if you hurt all over. But then you were facile, and so fast, I could barely keep up."

"You're a slowpoke wimp, what can I say?"

"No, Gaby. I'm in good shape, and you know it. My legs are longer and stronger than yours. I have more power. But you outran me."

Gaby snorted. "If this is about wounded ego, Luther, I don't have time."

"It's about you, Gaby."

"A boring subject."

But Luther wouldn't let it go. "You somehow knew Bliss was being threatened, didn't you?"

No, no, no. "No."

Luther snagged her arm and they both stopped.

"Tell me another truth, Gaby. Did you know that evil had her?"

Chapter 8

Tonight, one way or another, Luther knew he had to get some answers. Women's lives were on the line, and somehow Gaby was involved.

He didn't know how, but he knew he had to keep her safe—whether she wanted his help or not.

Gaby kept her back to him, but she paused.

Luther didn't push her. He just waited, and after a moment of visibly churning thoughts, she said, "I've heard that most cops have intuition. Do you?"

It wasn't what he'd expected, but the answer was easy enough. "Sometimes."

Rubbing the back of her neck and flexing her shoulders, Gaby considered his response. "Sometimes, huh?"

"It's not the same as what you're saying, Gaby. I get a bad feeling, but I don't see things clearly. They aren't spelled out for me."

"No, of course not." Glancing over her shoulder at him,

Gaby said, "But do you get that kick in your gut, that churning sensation in your blood when you just know something is wrong?"

Damn it, he did. But not the way it seemed she had.

Her light blue eyes pinned him. "Do you trust your instincts?"

No need to hesitate on that one. "Yes." Luther had never ignored his own instincts. They were sharper than most, which is why he made a damn good cop.

His instincts insisted that Gaby was up to something. If only he knew what.

"Well, so do I," she told him. "You want the truth, Luther? Fine. I knew something was wrong." She emphasized, "*Something*. Not that it involved Bliss, and not what it might be."

Luther could usually spot a liar, but with Gaby . . . he just didn't know. She appeared truthful, sincere.

Believable.

A small part of his subconscious insisted that the mentally insane often used sound logic as well.

No. He wouldn't think that. Gaby was, despite her upbringing and lack of formal education, more intelligent and lucid than almost anyone he knew. It was her astute perception of her surroundings that colored everything.

"My stomach cramped and my muscles burned and everything that's a part of me screamed that I had to hurry." Gaby didn't blink. "So I did."

What she described matched the way she'd looked. And that scared him. For her. "Does that happen to you often?"

"Often enough that I hate it." She started walking again, but the burst of energy was gone, leaving her to plod along tiredly. "But not often enough for me to make a real difference in anything."

What the hell did that mean? Why would Gaby, an orphan,

an eccentric loner, want to make a difference to the society she so openly scorned?

Seeing the droop to her normally proud shoulders, Luther decided not to ask her, not right now. He'd pushed enough for one night. Although he knew she'd deny it, she looked exhausted enough to keel over.

"We both need sleep." Luther slipped an arm around her supple waist. "Come on. Stewing over this won't help Bliss. The hospital staff will keep her safe tonight, and tomorrow, we'll come back to see her to Mort's together. She'll be fine."

"I hope you're right."

Gaby said nothing on the way out of the hospital. That worried Luther. He was used to her mouthy ways, her caustic wit, and her never-ending harassment.

She was likely plotting, maybe not against him, specifically, but for certain she wasn't including him, as per their agreement.

"Listen up, Gaby." When she turned tired eyes toward him, Luther almost softened. Only the need to know she'd be unharmed kept him from retrenching. "I'm going to drop you off at your apartment, and I damn well expect you to stay there."

She looked away. "I don't have any plans to leave."

"Then how about making plans to stay?"

She shrugged. "I watch over the women, Luther. Some of them work throughout the night. If something happens—"

"You'd know it?"

"Maybe. But not necessarily."

Luther still wasn't sure about her supposed exceptional intuition, but he wouldn't discount it. Throughout his career as a cop, he'd seen a lot of inexplicable things, and too many times his instincts had saved his ass. If Gaby had those same instincts, only amplified to an extreme level, then that would explain a lot.

And maybe he was just grasping at straws, wanting to trust her, to believe in her, in any way possible.

While heading across the parking lot, she moved closer. Her hand bumped Luther's, so he laced his fingers with hers.

The lot was quiet, dark. A fat silvery moon was poised low in the sky, surrounded by a million illumined stars.

It could have been a romantic night. From Luther's perspective, any time alone with Gaby lent itself to sexual thoughts tempered by emotional need.

She brought out the extremes in him. He couldn't understand it, and he couldn't fight it.

They'd almost reached his car at the farthest end of the lot when she said, "Most of the johns can be cruel, you know. They hurt the women just because they can. They're mean, nasty, and sometimes they cross the line. But they're not necessarily evil, just wretched human beings."

So her intuition didn't allow for mundane, ordinary, everyday evil? Realizing his own thoughts, Luther shook his head. He'd believe in her—to a point. But he wasn't ready to buy in hook, line, and sinker.

He decided she needed a little clarification on her observations. "Men who pay for sex are not the best of men, Gaby. Don't judge everyone by them."

"I wouldn't." At his car, she circled around to the passenger's side, then stopped and turned to face him. "But I can't judge all men by you, either."

Luther told himself to get in the car, to take her to her room so she could get the rest she needed. But his feet wouldn't budge. There was a magnetic pull to Gaby, and he always felt helpless against it.

They stood in shadows, the chill evening air still around them.

She tipped her head and looked . . . *around* him. "You're aroused," she said.

Like a moth light-struck in her glow, Luther braced his hands on the car around her, caging her in. "You think so, do you?"

Totally relaxed and almost sleepy, Gaby rested against the car. Her expression never changed as she nodded. "I see your aura, so I know you are."

"Ah. Yeah, I'd almost forgotten." Many times now, Gaby had commented on auras—always, for him, in a complimentary way.

"Your raw energy is really dancing, Luther. It's shimmering around you, all excited and jittery and warm."

Damn. She seduced him, destroyed his better intentions, without even trying. "It's been established, honey, that I always want you."

Not one for shyness, Gaby stared into his eyes. "It's pretty frustrating for me. I don't want to have sex with you. Hell, I'm still not entirely sure I understand the lure of sex. If you want the truth, what I've seen is interesting, but also a little disgusting."

"What you've seen is the dregs of society copulating." Luther couldn't keep his gaze off her small breasts. "That's nothing like a man and woman making love."

"Oh please. Don't even mention love. I don't know what it is, don't even believe in it, and it sure as hell has nothing to do with a man sticking his dick into a woman until he grunts and moans."

Luther pulled back. Damn it, her coarse ways weren't new to him. But her porn-star descriptions still had the power to shock him clean down to his toes.

She rolled her eyes. "Sorry. I can see I said too much. My point is that I want something, but I'm not sure what, and it's all pretty damned confusing and annoying and I don't like losing sleep over it."

An idea came to Luther.

A horrible, wonderful, masochistic idea. His heart thumped; his dick got hard. He licked his lips, leaned in a little closer, and said, "How about I prove a point to you, Gaby? We won't have intercourse, since you say you aren't ready. But . . ."

Her brows knit together. "But what? What are you thinking?"

To regain his calm, Luther closed his eyes for just a moment. It didn't help. His plans became visual, and he saw Gaby, what he wanted to do to her, what he eventually planned to do to her.

And the end result: Her blue eyes glazed with amazement, her body warm and fluid and . . . wet.

Shit. He had it bad, no denying that.

When Luther opened his eyes it was to take a quick look around the empty parking lot while he considered their isolated position. Even if someone did show up at this ungodly hour, his car would block any view of them, of what he'd be doing to her.

He inhaled, girding himself.

"Oh for crying out loud!" Gaby exploded. "Are you planning a murder or worse? What the hell are you up to, cop?"

In response, Luther put his fingertips on the inside of her right knee.

Her eyes widened.

"I can ease your frustration, Gaby. I can make you feel things you didn't know existed." As he spoke, he trailed his fingertips higher—under the edge of her skirt, and up to the elastic leg band of her panties.

The cotton was soft, but unadorned—like Gaby. But then, what else would he expect her to wear? Lace? Silk? Not likely.

She held herself perfectly still, watching his face the way a trapped mouse would watch a cat.

"You already feel it, don't you, honey?"

She swallowed, lifted her chin. "Maybe."

Yeah, she felt it. His chest expanded with satisfaction—and his body hurt with lust. "Put your arms around my neck."

With a surprising eagerness, Gaby did as he instructed. Luther kept his right hand between her legs, and with his left, tipped her face up more to accommodate a devouring kiss. She stood only three inches shorter than him, and he knew her to be a very capable woman.

But now, right this moment, she felt fragile and very delicate. Her compliance filled him with steam. With their mouths melded together, her tongue came out to mate with his, urging him on, easing the way for his lesson.

Against her lips, Luther said, "Men who care about women don't just rut with them. They take the time to enjoy them. I'm going to enjoy you a little, Gaby."

"Yeah, okay." She closed the small space between their lips with an insistent kiss.

So eager.

And so easy to sway when aroused.

It was a novel thing to have Gaby in an agreeable mood. He liked it. But then, he liked her even when she was contrary and antagonistic. At times, Luther felt that if he didn't have her, he'd go mad with the wanting.

When his hand cupped her small breast, she started and pulled her mouth away.

Their gazes met. Watching her, Luther skimmed his thumb over her tightly beaded nipple.

Her breath caught. "What are you doing?"

"Enjoying you."

Her lips parted and her eyelids went heavy. "Why . . . why does that feel so good?"

Oh God, it was the sweetest torture. "Because you're enjoying me, too."

Leaning into his hand, she said again, "Okay."

Against his wrist, Luther felt the static beat of her heart. Her flesh was soft, her nipple supple. She had sensitive breasts. He liked that. A lot.

After playing with both breasts, tweaking, tugging on her nipples, Luther cupped his other hand over her crotch.

She shot to her tiptoes in surprise.

"Shhh." Taking her mouth to silence her, to share with her, Luther began stroking. His touch was light and easy, teasing, over the now damp cotton of her panties.

Gaby panted, her breath coming fast and harsh. Her strong fingers sank into his shoulder muscles, almost to the point of pain, definitely with demand. She rocked her hips once, then stilled herself.

"No," Luther whispered, "don't stop. Move as you want to move, Gaby. It'll make it even nicer for you."

"I don't know about this."

"I do."

Her hands clutched at him. "I feel like a wire being tightened."

Luther bit her bottom lip, her chin, her throat as he made his way down to her chest. By her nipple, he said, "I want you pulled so tight, you snap." And then he drew her nipple into his mouth.

She cried out, curled herself around him, moaned.

No reserve for Gaby. In this, she couldn't be more honest.

"Lift your shirt for me, Gaby." As he said it, Luther worked his hand up and over into the waistband of her panties. He felt her soft pubic curls, her hot flesh.

She didn't move and he raised his face to look at her.

From the time he'd known Gabrielle Cody, he'd noticed some affliction that altered her appearance through strong emotion.

Now her blue eyes were diamond bright, somehow more catlike in shape, very exotic. Her cheekbones looked sharper, her mouth more lush.

She looked like Gaby, but different, and she was sexy as hell.

Holding her gaze captive, Luther parted her slick lips by gliding two fingers back and forth, back and forth.

Her expression constricted even more.

Slick moisture bathed his fingers.

Luther gently opened her, and with inexorable pressure, worked both fingers into her. She was small, but he couldn't imagine Gaby ever taking half measures.

She'd want to be filled.

And he wanted to fill her.

Her virgin flesh stretched, and he felt the strain of her entire body.

A sharp breath parted her lips. A mix of pain and pleasure made her eyes flare.

"You are so damn tight," he murmured, turned on by the knowledge of being the first to do this to her.

The first to do *everything* with her, wanting to be the only man to ever—*no*.

He wouldn't allow himself to think that way. Not now, not with so many unanswered questions. Not while she remained such an enigma.

As Luther pressed his fingers deeper into her, her eyelids drooped—and she lifted her shirt.

Needing no more invitation than that, he lowered his head and drew one taut nipple into his mouth. Her fingers sank into his hair, holding him to her. Heat, scented by her heightened desire, filled the air.

Luther switched to the other nipple, nipping with his teeth, tugging till she moaned and then lathing with his tongue to soothe her.

Just as she relaxed, he closed his mouth around her again and sucked hard.

A tearing groan escaped her. Her body stiffened, and knowing she was close, he brought his thumb up to her distended clitoris. Pressing, fretting her most sensitive flesh with a delicious friction, Luther pushed her—and far too quickly, she came.

Thank God they were alone in the big lot, given her savage scream. Her short nails drew blood on his shoulders. Her strong muscles clenched, quivered, then went lax.

Damn. He'd known it from the moment he saw her, how explosive she'd be, how unique and special and mind-blowing.

He couldn't wait to be inside her, to share that pleasure with her. But for now, he'd have to.

Gaby was so limp, in another second she'd be sleeping.

With her most immediate problem resolved, he needed to get back on track.

Now the real fireworks would begin.

❦

Resting the side of her face on his shoulder, letting him support her weight, Gaby yawned. Man, oh man. Talk about taking the stress away. She felt so lethargic, more than anything, she wanted her bed.

Luther's hand moved up and down her back, comforting, intimate.

They'd just shared something monumental. She knew it, but she didn't have the energy to react to it.

Yet.

In a minute, she'd figure out what she needed to do to reciprocate. She wanted Luther to feel what she'd just felt.

Oh sure, she knew he'd done that plenty of times. The man had surely practiced to be so good at it. But she wanted him to feel it with her.

She yawned again, nuzzled closer to his big, hard chest, and wondered how he'd feel in her hands, if it'd be the same for him.

"You still awake?" Luther asked her.

"Mmm. I just need a minute." Or five or ten.

He kissed her temple. "I can pick you up tomorrow. We'll have breakfast, talk, and then visit Bliss again. She should be dismissed early."

Was he nuts? Held upright by the constriction of his strong arms around her, Gaby lifted her head to stare at him.

Oh, he was ripe with sensation, his aura so bright and molten it was a wonder they weren't both singed.

When he only smoothed her hair, she asked, "What about you?"

"What about me?" He kissed her mouth, smiled like a conqueror. He even touched the end of her nose. "I got what I wanted."

He *had* to be kidding. "So what was it you wanted?" The repletion of muscles and sinew kept her loose and limp. Gaby struggled to stiffen her knees.

This confrontation demanded a little strength on her part, not Jell-O limbs.

"I wanted you to see that it's not always about men sticking their dicks in women. For men who pay to get their rocks off, sure, that might be it. But between us—"

"There's an us?" Stupid question. He'd just rocked her entire world in a very big way.

And it had only taken him a few minutes.

In a parking lot.

Out in the open.

He squeezed her bottom and said, "Whether you want to admit it or not, yeah, there is. Eventually, I'll be on top of you, Gaby. I'll be inside you—and I don't mean my fingers either."

Because she suspected it'd put a stop to his cocky assurances of what sounded vaguely like domination to her, Gaby cupped her hand over his crotch.

Sure enough, he went mute, still, even pained. His gaze froze as he stared at her, held in suspense, unsure what she'd do, and probably hoping she'd do it.

Gaby *almost* smiled over the feeling of power.

A different type of power from what she was used to.

A more satisfying type of power.

"This," she told him, squeezing a little, measuring the length of his cock by slowly stroking base to tip and back again, "is noticeably bigger than two fingers. I'm not sure it'd work."

Muscles tensed and voice rough, Luther said, "I know I hurt you—"

"Ha. Let me tell you something, Luther. That wasn't pain. Not even close. In fact . . ." While keeping him captive in her hand, Gaby let loose a wide-jawed yawn. "It was relaxing."

He closed his eyes against a private struggle. "Trust me, honey, when it happens, you're going to love it."

"More than I enjoyed that?" She wouldn't use the "L" word in any context, so he could forget it.

His big hand covered hers, but not to move her hand away. He pressed her closer. "How much did you enjoy it?"

"You want honesty, right?"

Disquiet nudged aside the sexual voracity on his face. "Always."

She inhaled, then exhaled long and slow. "I'm familiar with pain, ya know? It's a part of my daily life, coming and going in varying degrees, emotionally and physically."

"Gaby." He touched his forehead to hers.

A lump formed in Gaby's throat, and she had one hell of a time swallowing. "What you just gave to me . . . well, it's startling because I didn't know anything could feel like that. For a split second of time, I don't think I was aware of anything other than what I felt."

"That bothers you?"

"It makes me vulnerable."

"Not when you're with me. Never with me." He pulled her hand away and enclosed her in his arms. "When you're with me, you're always safe."

Gaby didn't tell him how absurdly naïve he had to be to believe such a thing. Truth was, Luther was safer with her, not the other way around.

But she supposed a big macho cop who'd just given a woman that kind of pleasure really didn't want to hear reality.

He kissed her ear. "I can tell you don't believe me, and that's okay, because I can't convince you right now. We need time enough and place proper to get naked and be at our leisure. Then you'll truly see what I mean." He smoothed her hair. "But until then, don't judge all men by the fools using prostitutes, and don't go frustrated, now that you know I can help."

Gaby eyed him up and down. Just what the hell was he

offering? "So when I need you, there you are?" She snapped her fingers. "Ready and willing?"

"Don't push it, woman." His smile took the insult out of his warning. Tugging her away from the car, he opened the car door and gestured for her to get in. "Time for us to go."

In a stupor of newfound information and physical repletion, Gaby dropped inside.

When Luther got behind the wheel, he said again, "I'll pick you up for breakfast tomorrow morning. Is eight good for you?"

Time frames didn't mean the same to her as they did to ordinary people. Unlike most of society, she didn't feel the need to keep regular hours. Hell, she wasn't even sure what regular hours might be.

Sure, she knew that people wanted to be awake with the sun, and to sleep with the moon. But for her, life wasn't that simple. Immorality erupted with an eternity of determination. For evil, the clock didn't tick, the sun didn't set.

For evil, there was no respite.

For one who fought evil, the same rules applied.

Gaby had adjusted by waking when she woke, acting when necessary, and sleeping when her conscience, and God, allowed.

"Gaby?" Luther pressed. "Is eight o'clock good for you?"

Shaking off the morbid substantiality of her existence, Gaby made a face. "I'm not a big eater, as you can tell by my prominent bones."

"I like your bones." He winked at her. "But you could stand to gain a little weight."

"Yeah, well, since leaving Mort's, breakfast has been way down there on my list of things to do."

"We can change that—starting tomorrow."

"We'll see." She looked back at the tall brick structure, well lit but still dreary. With the taint of Gaby's discordant memories, the hospital looked more like a gnarled headstone than a place of sanctuary. "I hate hospitals."

"I know, but she'll be safe here. They'll take care of her."

Gaby shook her head. "I don't know, Luther. It doesn't seem right to let her out of my sight. I have a very bad feeling about all this."

When Luther stared at her for an extended time, Gaby turned to him and said, "What?"

"You really think something will happen to her here?"

She shrugged. "I think something *can* happen to her here. That's enough for me."

After another second of contemplation, he nodded. "All right then." To Gaby's surprise, Luther pulled out his cell and put in a call, requesting a uniformed cop to stand watch.

He'd taken her concerns seriously?

Another first for her, and just as satisfying as what he'd done to her with his fingers.

"Someone will be here within five minutes." Luther dug out a card and held it toward her. "I hope that puts you more at ease."

She eyed the card, but didn't take it. "It helps."

Exasperated, Luther lifted her hand, pressed the card to her palm, and folded her fingers around it. "Promise me that if the bad feeling sticks with you, you'll call me."

Studying the card, Gaby read Luther's name, his phone numbers. "If someone's already watching over her, then why would I call and bother you?"

He didn't laugh at her. "It's what friends do, Gaby. They lean on each other in times of worry."

Friends.

Yeah, she was collecting them like cooties these days.

She could deal with it now, but somehow she figured that she and Luther were more than friends. What, she couldn't say. But even before her sexual instruction, she'd accepted that being with him was not the same as being with Morty or Bliss.

Headlights cut through the dark night, and a car pulled into the parking lot. Luther went on alert, watching the car but also studying the rest of the lot. Gaby did the same, unwilling to let a distraction with one car cause distraction over a bigger concern.

The car parked, the driver got out, and with a single click that sounded a beep and flashed his lights, locked the BMW. He'd parked in the doctor's section, and hurried inside.

Dismissing him as a threat, Luther's keen gaze studied the rest of the surrounding area.

Gaby didn't tell him that no enmity lurked. If it did, she'd know it. "I hate to break this to you, cop, but I don't have a phone."

Settling back in his seat, Luther made a face of long-suffering acceptance. "Course you don't. Why would I think you did?"

"I don't know. You're strange that way." Another car pulled in, this one a police cruiser. "Who would I call, anyway?"

Luther waited until he saw a uniformed officer get out and enter the building. "Want to go in and make sure he's set up?"

"No need." Tiredness pulled at Gaby, and she wanted to drop. While the evil rested, she needed to rest, too—because it wasn't over.

Not by a long shot.

Again, Luther believed in her. He started the car and pulled out of the hospital parking lot onto the deserted streets. On the drive back to her room, he said very little.

For her part, Gaby dozed in her seat, rethinking what Luther had done to her, and how easy it had been for him. When he pulled up in front of the building, she unfastened her seat belt, anxious to be alone.

Luther reached over and caught her arm. "You should know, Gaby, the women have been warned of a problem."

She accepted that—and how futile such a warning would be. "It won't stop them from doing what they do. It's how they survive."

"It could be how they die."

"I know." Just because she wanted to, because she needed to, Gaby leaned across the seat and kissed him. "They don't have any choice, though."

"I know." He touched her cheek with a heartbreaking intimacy. "I'm determined to do my best to figure this out, and fast. Until then, please be careful."

If he didn't stop fretting over her, she was going to start liking it. And then where would she be? "I keep telling you, cop, you don't have to worry about me."

He pulled her in for one more taste, and Gaby's toes curled inside her boots. "I'm trying."

"Breakfast," she reminded him, just to change the subject. "I'll see you then."

Gaby left the car and strode up to the building. Dawn would break all too soon, and still a few women stood outside, washed out, tired, and working toward their quota.

By way of a greeting, they made a few lewd comments about Luther. Amused, Gaby looked back, and Luther still waited, wanting to see her inside.

Bizarre.

Unnecessary.

But damn if it didn't rekindle that odd tingling deep in her belly.

Anticipating breakfast with him in the morning, she went up the stairs—and then it struck her what an idiotic fool she'd become.

For whatever anomaly of circumstances might exist, being with Luther had always desensitized her faculties, depriving her awareness of a necessary superiority. For a single moment of time, Gaby gave in to cowardly panic, wondering if, in fact, Bliss was safe, or if Luther's presence had blunted her ability to know the truth.

Opening locks with haste, she went into her apartment and to the window to look out.

Luther was gone—and still she felt no discernment of foul play. Her relief, on top of so much expended emotion, left her exhausted.

Following her basic evening ritual, Gaby cleaned her teeth and stripped off her clothes. Left in her plain, colorless panties, she again thought of Luther, of what he'd done, what she'd enjoyed.

Insane.

Wonderful.

After double-checking her locks, she fell into her bed.

Oppressive evening air engulfed her body. No breeze stirred through the open window; only cries and crashes and other emblematic sounds of the neighboring slums filtered through.

Flat on her back, her arms folded over her middle, Gaby stared at the stained and crumbling ceiling—and pondered Luther: his hands, his mouth, his warmth and caring.

She was about to doze off when the verisimilitude of the ravaged corpse, discolored, swelled with river water, skulked past her exhaustion to disrupt her thoughts. The images integrated with those of Bliss's pale face, her tangible trepidation.

For one of the few times in her life, Gaby craved something other than a normal life.

She craved Luther.

But duty demanded she defend Bliss, and that meant she'd have to cool things with Luther in order to keep her God-given advantage.

Being near him meant she risked a loss of her remarkable acumen toward evil, evil that meant to harm Bliss.

There'd be no restful breakfast for them.

For now, until she destroyed the wickedness, she couldn't let Luther drown her in that prodigious pleasure.

Her duty was a burden, but she wouldn't forsake it.

Somehow, all wants and needs aside, she had to accomplish the impossible—again.

Chapter 9

In a world-class mood of surliness, Gaby raged at the locked door to Mort's apartment building.

Okay, so she knew Mort had started locking the doors under her edict to provide an inviolable sanctuary. But damn it, she didn't mean to lock *her* out. She wanted to talk to him, to clear the way before she brought Bliss to him.

Her fist battered the door until it opened with a jerk.

"What?" demanded a slim, blond, and very beautiful woman barely wrapped in a morning robe.

Shock took Gaby back and she almost fell off the front steps: Ann Kennedy, the cop who worked with Luther, a woman better suited to him.

A woman who instilled jealousy when jealousy didn't make a damned bit of sense.

Even with her hair all frothy, her makeup faded, and her clothes missing, Gaby recognized her. So where the hell was Mort? Had something happened to him?

"Gaby," Ann said. "I wasn't . . . that is, I didn't expect you." She started messing with her hair, gave up on that and tightened her robe around her.

"What are you doing here?" Filled with suspicion, Gaby peered around her. "Where's Mort?"

"He's in the shower." Ann held the door wider by way of invitation. "Would you like to come in?"

In the shower, huh? And with Ann barely clothed.

In delayed reaction, the pieces clicked together.

They'd spent the night together. *Holy shit.* That constituted *more* than mere dating. Gaby stepped inside and said, albeit with a lot of skepticism, "You and Mort are that serious, huh?"

"Yes." Ann laughed. "I'm afraid so."

Mort's apartment caused as much consternation as Ann's presence. It was the same, but a whole lot tidier, and brighter with fresh shades on the windows and a few plants on the tables. He even had colorful throw pillows on the sofa. "Wow. He's cleaned it up."

"And replaced some things."

"Your influence?" Gaby wasn't at all sure how she felt about that. Ann must carry a lot of sway over him, and maybe that was fine and dandy. Gaby only knew that she didn't want to see Mort hurt.

Propping herself on the arm of a chair, Ann shook her head. "More your influence, I'd say."

"Mine?" How dumb. She didn't give a shit about home decorating. Never had and never would.

Probably.

Ann smiled. "You've had an incredible impact on him, or so he tells me. He claims that before you, he barely existed. Now he's more aware of everything and everyone and, Gaby, he's a lot happier."

Huh. Gaby didn't know what to say to that. She didn't want the responsibility for Mort's happiness, but how could she deny what she didn't understand?

Being tongue-tied was a first for her, and she didn't like it.

"Come on." Ann headed for the kitchen. "Let's sit down and get comfortable. We can talk. Would you like some coffee? Mort and I have only been up a few minutes, so it's fresh."

"Yeah, sure." Making note of the sway in Ann's hips, and a faint, delicate fragrance left in her wake, Gaby trailed her. In a state of dishabille on the proverbial morning after, Ann exuded fundamental, salacious femininity.

And yet, Gaby noticed, she was nothing like the prostitutes who used their sexuality to draw business. Somehow, Ann was far more provocative.

For Mort. That really bent her mind. She'd need some time to get used to the idea of Mort as a sexual being, especially when the thought sort of gagged her.

"Cream and sugar?" Ann asked.

"Sure, whatever." Gaby pulled out a chair. "So you and Mort are screwing?"

Ann nearly dropped the sugar bowl. In obvious offense, she pivoted to face Gaby in high dudgeon. "That's none of your business."

"So?" Gaby shrugged. "That's never stopped me before." Seeing hot color slash Ann's face, she sprawled back. "Never mind. I'll ask Mort."

Snapping a spoon down onto the counter, Ann said, "That's no better. You'd still be intruding."

"Mort won't mind. At least, he never has before." But then, Mort didn't have Ann before, so he'd been more than anxious to talk to Gaby for any reason. Well, for most reasons. She recalled asking him specifics on sex, and getting nowhere.

Gaby shook her head. "There have been times when he's stammered on his words, turned redder than you are now, and refused to explain."

Searching her face, Ann relented and finished the coffee preparations. As she handed Gaby a cup, she visibly formed her thoughts into words. "Mort told me you had an eccentric background."

"Master of understatement, that's our Mort." Gaby sipped the coffee. "If you're going to hang around, you might as well know that I'm a first-class freak."

Taken aback, Ann seated herself and then touched Gaby's arm. "I don't see anything freakish about you. In fact, I think you're a lovely young lady."

Flashing a look of disbelief, Gaby snorted. "Yeah, right." She stuck her leg out toward Ann. "Wanna pull the other one?"

Ann chastised her with a look. "You are *not* freakish, Gaby. Outspoken, certainly. But that's almost . . . refreshing."

"Uh-huh." Since Ann nearly choked spewing that falsehood, Gaby didn't take her words to heart.

"Mort tells me you're very capable. I think that's a wonderful quality for a young, single woman to have. Not many people, male or female, are fully independent."

Unable to help herself, Gaby asked, "So what does Luther say about me?"

Ann subdued a knowing smile, and leaned toward her. "For the most part, Luther keeps his own counsel. But when you have been mentioned, it's with frustration and often urgency."

"Huh." To give herself a moment to digest those words, Gaby again drank her coffee.

"It appears that he cares for you, Gaby."

"You're a cop," Gaby told her. "You should know that appearances can be deceiving."

"Not with Luther." At her leisure, Ann settled back in her seat, crossed her legs, and turned thoughtful. Steam rose from her cup and a lock of pale blond hair fell over her shoulder. "I've never known a man to be more rock solid, in his work, and in his convictions, than Luther."

Great. Just fucking great. All that meant is that he'd never be able to reconcile his lofty principles with Gaby's recondite purpose.

From behind her, Gaby heard Mort ask, "Are you worshipping another man, Ann?"

Gaby twisted around and found Mort striding in. His smile teased, and he went right past her to press a warm kiss to Ann's mouth.

It was . . . nauseating. For most of the time that she'd known Mort, he'd been weaselly, pathetic, and annoying. Now he seemed . . . more manly.

Gaby could barely choke it down. "Eavesdropping?" she asked him.

"Just a little." Both hands on Ann's shoulders, Mort winked at her.

Winked.

Yeah, she was definitely going to hurl. "Why the hell are you so chipper?"

At her question, Mort laughed aloud. Ann ducked her face to hide her humor.

And it struck Gaby. "Oh yeah. The whole sex thing. You got laid last night, right?" Shaking her head, a little irritated at their combined good humor, she added, "Nookie has transformed you, Mort. I swear, even your hair looks thicker."

Strangling, Mort scowled at her and smoothed a hand over his sparse brown hair. But his pale blue eyes twinkled and he stood taller, straighter. His paunch seemed less noticeable—maybe because he wore clothes with improved style, or maybe because he was now more active, more fit.

And maybe because Ann cared for him.

"Gaby has a, um, sexual question for you, Mort, so I'll take my turn showering and let you two talk."

Startled, Mort grabbed Ann's arm to detain her. "You don't have to rush off."

"Oh, but I do." She patted Mort. "I'm afraid this is out of my comfort zone."

"I doubt it," Gaby told her. "I was just curious about what Mort does to you. Luther did some stuff to me, but I'm not sure if it's normal or not."

They both stared at her.

"Well, that got your attention, didn't it?" Under her breath, she muttered, "Pervs."

Mort shook himself. "Maybe it'd be better if you asked someone else your questions."

"Like who? The hookers? Luther insists they have a different slant on things, but since Ann's not a hooker—"

"No, she's not."

Ann stiffened. "Definitely not."

"Right. So I figured she'd have a different take on the whole sexual gratification thing. I mean, Luther keeps telling me it's entirely different for women who aren't in the flesh trade."

"Oh God," Mort said. He cleared his throat. "I'm sure Luther is . . . normal in his appetites."

"And you picked that up by osmosis? You don't even know yet what he did to me."

"I'm out of here," Ann said with emphasis.

Before she could leave, Luther's voice, harsh with indignation, filled the room. "No need, Ann. I'll explain things to Gaby—again—when we're alone."

Sighing, Gaby tilted her head back and looked at Luther upside down. "You have the uncanny ability to sneak up on me."

His smile was mean. "Maybe it's just that you're not as slick as you think."

"No. That's definitely not it." She looked back at Mort with an expression that said Luther was way off base with that one. "You don't keep the door locked?"

"Usually." Sex might have revitalized Mort, but his unease in the face of Luther's obvious disgruntlement still left him stammering. "Luther. Nice of you to visit. Can I get you some coffee?"

"Thanks, no."

Because she didn't look at Luther, Gaby had to judge his heavy silence by the looks on Ann's and Mort's faces. Not good.

"You're being a bully, Luther. Lighten up before Mort pisses himself."

The insinuation that Mort lacked courage sent Ann over the edge. "That's enough!" She propped her hands on her hips. "They," she said, meaning the men, "might tolerate your abhorrent bad manners toward Mort, but I will not."

Gaby eyed her militant stance. The robe detracted somewhat from its effectiveness. "Odd. What Luther did to me was real relaxing. Almost put me to sleep." She cocked one brow up. "Mort must not be doing it right for you to be so high-strung."

Startling Mort, Ann rounded the table. For a moment there, Gaby thought the woman would attack her.

Instead, Ann stopped beside her and glared. "Listen up, little girl."

Gaby straightened in her seat. "Little girl?"

"Your obnoxious behavior doesn't fool anyone, least of all me."

She dared? Rising to her feet, Gaby growled again, *"Little girl?"*

"You can be as eccentric as you like, but if you behave like a child, then that's exactly how you'll be treated."

Gaby narrowed her eyes. "You must be hiding a pair of brass balls somewhere under that fluffy robe."

"Not impressed, Gaby," Ann shot back. "In my line of work, I've seen it all, and lady, you're not the worst, not by a long shot."

Cocking out a hip and folding her arms, Gaby grunted in disdain. "Well, that just goes to show that *someone's* not paying attention."

Exasperated, Ann threw up her hands. "I get it that you lack social skills, lady. But that is *not* an excuse for your cruelty."

Cruelty? That gave Gaby pause. "When have I been cruel?"

Though Ann was much shorter, she held herself like a woman who knew how to do combat. Police training? Luther could tell her that it'd do her no good against Gaby.

Not that Gaby had any intention of hurting her. Ann was what people called "petite." She'd feel like a fool battling with a petite little fluff like Ann.

And besides, neither Luther nor Morty would like it.

"Mort claims you're a friend, yet you take every opportunity to belittle him. You say unforgivable things, and you—"

"It's okay, Ann," Morty said.

"No, it is not!"

No, it wasn't, Gaby agreed. But in the middle of processing all of Ann's accusations, absorbing them and sorting them out, tragedy struck Gaby.

The force of it bowed her back and left her blind.

In the periphery, she heard Ann say, "Oh no, what is it? What's wrong with her?"

Luther grumbled, "Not again," while Mort said, "Get out of her way."

Seeing flames licking the sky, hearing an agonized scream, Gaby groped for the chair back and braced herself so she wouldn't collapse under the force of the image. Inside her head, the prediction blackened, the screams escalated.

It was too much. It was happening *now*.

Pushing away the hands that reached for her, Gaby stumbled from the room. If the others followed, well, she couldn't stop them—just as she couldn't stem the tide of physical torment flooding the nerve sensors of her body.

The staggering pain stole her oxygen, contorted her features, and left her teeth clenched in anguish.

"Gaby!"

Aware of Luther trying to grasp her as she fled, Gaby sucked in harsh, too shallow breaths. But this was too critical, too excruciating, to be contained by mortal means. The efficacious pain rendered her oblivious to all but her purpose.

Once outside, her senses honed and Gaby broke into a full-out run. She didn't have far to go. At the end of the block, consuming an old clapboard building, a red-hot conflagration dug fingers of heat into the sky with crimson terror.

Gaby heard the screams again, but they were silent screams trapped in her head, for her torment only.

That burning building held someone captive.

Gaby charged forward—and Luther tackled her from the side. They hit the pavement hard, him atop her; his considerable weight held her down.

Twisting her face around to see him, she met his resolve.

Pain eased, retracting its razor-sharp talons from her muscles and flesh, and at the same time, relieving her motivation to salvage an innocent life. Luther's physical contiguity blunted what should have been an inviolable defense.

Her seldom summoned humanity reared up, urging her to free herself from Luther's spell. Even with the demons gone, she knew what she had to do.

"Let me go, Luther."

He knotted a hand in her hair. "God damn you, Gaby, do you want to die? You can *not* go in there."

Closing her eyes and calming her mind against the residue of piercing cries, Gaby gathered her strength. When she opened them, Luther must have seen the purpose in her face.

He hardened himself and tightened his hold. "The building is empty."

Sadly, she shook her head. "No, Luther, it's not."

Agony darkened his gaze. His fingers left her hair to pet her jaw, frantic to convince her. "The fire fighters will be here any minute. You can hear the sirens. If you just wait—"

"They'll be too late."

"Damn you," he said, struggling with himself. "You can't know that."

"But I do." Compulsion burned her worse than any flames could. "I need to go. And you need to let me."

He shook his head. "Please don't do this."

"I have no choice." And with that simple but veracious statement, Gaby dislodged Luther's six-foot, three-inch powerful frame with remarkable adroitness. He landed on his back, stunned, and before he could recover, she'd crossed the street and broke through the crackling, blistering front of the building.

Indifferent to the smoke filling her lungs and the heat

singeing her hair, Gaby wended her way through the front room. The curtains of swirling, belching smoke left her blind, but she knew right where to find the fallen body. She felt with her hands—and encountered human flesh.

The body was small, delicate—like Ann.

Knowing each second to be precious, Gaby levered her over her shoulder and ran hell-bent for escape from the engulfing fire. Wood splintered behind her. A wall crashed in.

Up ahead, a glowing egress shone among the smoke and flames. Without faltering, she sought escape.

The second she broke from the burning building and into the fresh air, Gaby collapsed to her knees, gladly relinquishing her load to waiting firemen. They moved with an economy of take-charge action. Hoses sprayed. Men issued orders. Noise escalated.

Please, she thought, watching as firemen carried an unconscious woman to an ambulance. *Please let me have been in time.*

Just then, she heard the woman cough—and then Luther was there, pulling her to her feet, urging her toward the open door of a cruiser. Mort hovered nearby, at the same time fretting and talking with Ann.

The pandemonium kept Gaby confused for a short time. Someone pressed an oxygen mask to her face while someone else did a cursory exam.

Shoving away the helping hands, Gaby lifted the mask. "The woman. . . . ?" Simple words left her choking, coughing and ready to throw up.

Luther stepped in front of the white-clothed man. "She wasn't burned, but she inhaled a lot of smoke. She's on her way to the hospital." With infinite care, he threaded his fingers through her charred hair.

"Was I in time?"

The fingers briefly clenched. "I don't know. We'll find out soon."

The paramedic spoke. "She should go to the hospital, too."

Gaby freaked. "Fuck that. I'm fine." Shoving aside the oxygen mask and knocking the paramedic away, she started to leave. Her reaction would only cause more alarm, but her astronomical fear of medical treatment kept her unable to temper herself.

"Gaby—"

"I said no." She started walking, intent on leaving the scene before some damned do-gooder tried to strap her to a gurney.

The way she'd seen Father strapped down.

Cancer had stolen his thoughts, his personality, and left behind a stranger who required restraints.

Gaby gasped, and choked again.

Luther stepped in front of her. "Fine," he said before she could draw back a fist. "You say you're okay, then you're okay. I believe you."

Her chest hurt, and only part of it was from the smoke and excitement. "Do you?"

As black as a thundercloud, he dismissed the paramedic by saying to him, "We're actually on our way to the hospital to see a friend." His domineering attention swung back to Gaby. "If she's not breathing easy when we get there, I'll have her checked."

Holding up both hands, the paramedic said, "Not what I'd recommend, but suit yourself."

Shaken, feeling like a fool, Gaby closed her eyes and inhaled cautiously. "Thanks."

"I need you to sit. I need you to stay."

Her eyes snapped open again. "I am not your fucking pet."

His left eye twitched. "Unless you want to explain what drove you to go into that building, I need to see what happened here. But I can't do that if I don't know you're safe and waiting for me to finish."

Looking beyond him, Gaby saw Mort and Ann watching. "I'm not explaining shit."

Luther remained silent, and damn it, she felt guilty. But she couldn't explain. Not yet. Maybe not ever.

"Fine. I'll wait. But you could work a little on your verbal skills. Your idea of a request sucks." Stomping despite her enervated state, Gaby left him growling and snarling, and went to Ann and Mort.

Mort stepped toward her. "God Almighty, Gaby. Are you all right?"

"I'm fine." She pointed to a less-crowded section of sidewalk. "I'll be waiting over there for Luther. You know, if he looks for me or anything."

Ann touched Mort's arm. "Go with her. I'll see what I can do about crowd control."

Still in her robe, barefoot and hair loose, Ann took charge like an army sergeant. Wasted in mind and spirit, Gaby watched her, and admired her forceful manner and deep blue aura. "You've got a live one, Mort."

"I know. She's something, huh?"

"Her aura tells me that she's doing just what she was meant to do. That's good. Not many people ever find their true purpose." Together, Mort and Gaby went to the curb and sank down on their butts.

Chewing her bottom lip, Gaby did her best to keep any further thoughts of Father at bay.

Mort's hand slipped into hers. "That was pretty damned scary."

Looking first at his hand, then his sincere face, Gaby frowned. "What?"

"Running into a burning building? It's not what most people would ever do. In fact, I don't know anyone else who'd do it."

"I didn't have a choice."

"I know that. But have you thought about how you're going to explain it to Luther? You know he's going to ask how you knew a body was in there."

"I know." After what had happened with Bliss, he was already suspicious of her. But hell, it wasn't like she could ignore the plea of the innocent, whether Luther Cross liked it or not.

"That's not what's worrying you, is it?"

"No." She could deal with Luther. Somehow.

But images, memories, kept crowding in, suffocating her. Hurting her.

"Gaby?"

Her eyes burned, so Gaby used her free hand to rub them. "I just . . . anything to do with hospitals and ambulances and all that . . ."

"Oh." His fingers squeezed hers. "You're reminded of the guy who raised you?"

"Father didn't raise me." The state had raised her—and they'd done a shitty job of it. "I didn't even meet him until I was seventeen." And then her life, her entire world, had changed.

Someone approached with water and a wet cloth. Mort thanked them and accepted the items for Gaby.

After a big swig of water that helped a little, she wiped her face. Soot covered her clothes, her hair and skin.

Her thoughts.

She stared off at nothing in particular. "I didn't know him

long enough, but he was the closest thing to family that I had."

Quietly, Mort said, "Take another drink. It'll help take the sting out of your throat."

"Thanks."

As she guzzled the water, Mort cleared his throat. "What Ann said . . ."

"Yeah." She set the jug aside. "She's right." A trickle of water ran down her chin and dropped onto her chest. That felt good, too, cooling, so Gaby upended the jug and doused her head and shoulders. "I am a bitch, Mort. We both know it."

"You are not. It's just that Ann's defensive of me."

"She cares for you." Using the cloth again, Gaby cleaned her face the best she could—but there was only so much she could do to put off the inevitable. She owed Mort an apology. "I'm sorry."

"Gaby, don't."

"Ann hit it dead-on. I have been cruel." She snorted at herself. "Hell, I'm usually cruel."

"You're a paladin. You save people."

"Fucking hero worship." Some things never changed. "Stow it or I'll puke, okay? I'm an asshole and that's all there is to it. You deserve better."

"Okay, so you can be abrasive." In a show of camaraderie, Mort nudged her with his shoulder. He was teasing, friendly. "You *are* the best, and I'm proud to call you my friend."

Damn. How had she gotten so blessed? Gaby sat there, numb and hurt and horribly afraid—for things she might lose, things she hadn't known were hers.

Caring could be a real bitch.

Ann strode up, then sat down beside her. "Mort, give us a second, okay?"

"Sure thing, honey." He stood without another word and walked away.

"He minds well."

"Don't start, Gaby."

"Sorry." Wondering what Ann wanted, dreading it a little, Gaby waited.

Ann put her elbows on her knees and clasped her hands. Sunlight gilded her fair hair, fighting with the dulling effects of smoke. She looked like a smudged angel, like Luther's counterpart.

But she loved Mort. Gaby could see that. She doubted Ann or Mort knew it yet, but they were meant to be together.

Strange. But kind of nice.

Ann let out a long breath. "Okay, so you're the weirdest, scariest, and most capable person I've ever come across."

Well, she hadn't expected that. Closing her burning eyes, Gaby tried to meter her breaths.

"You're also the bravest."

Rasping past the numbing effects of memories and excess sentiment, Gaby said, "Bravery has shit to do with it."

"Modest, too."

Oh God. A woman could only take so much. Gaby reclined against the hot pavement and draped the damp cloth over her face.

Ann wasn't deterred.

"You didn't even know the woman in that building, did you, Gaby?"

Hell, she hadn't known for sure it was a woman until they'd reached the outdoors. "No."

"But you ran into that blaze anyway."

Gaby shrugged. It was her duty. She'd been told to go, so she went. Not that Ann would understand.

"You'd have gone in for Mort—or me."

If God told her to . . . No. She wouldn't play games with herself. Not anymore. Luther's presence had somehow counteracted God's command—and still, she had to go.

If someone, especially someone she knew, was at risk, and she could help, then it wouldn't matter what God had to say about it.

Tears burned her eyes and clogged her throat. "Fucking smoke." Using the cloth, she swiped her eyes.

"Gaby?"

"Yeah." Sitting up, she tossed the cloth to the side. "I'd have gone in for you. Happy?"

"I'd say I'm more enlightened than happy. But we're getting there."

"Dandy."

Ann laughed, but quickly sobered. "How did you know?"

Shit, shit, shit. Playing dumb, Gaby asked, "Know what?"

"That she was in there?"

Here we go again. "I heard her." Looking Ann dead in the eyes, Gaby asked, "Didn't you?"

"I didn't hear anything."

"Huh. I guess I've got exceptional hearing."

Not the least bit fooled, Ann nodded. "I guess so." She patted Gaby's knee. "It's definitely time for me to get that shower. Take care of yourself, okay?"

"I always do."

Ann no sooner left, giving Gaby some respite, than a shadow fell over her. She knew it was Luther, and she wasn't in the mood for his complaints. "Not now."

He knelt down in front of her and took her hands. "We're sharing, remember?"

His mood had changed. Again. He shifted tempers quicker

than a teenage girl on her period. Right now, he was in comfort mode, and Gaby didn't know if she could take it. Her throat felt raw, her eyes scratchy.

Camouflaging her loss of composure, she replied with acrimony. "How could I forget?"

His big hand cuddled the side of her face. "I have a bad feeling—"

"Then your feelings are dead-on, cop, because, yeah, it's related."

Luther cursed quietly under his breath. "Are you certain?"

That's it? He wouldn't question her beyond that one request for affirmation? Wonder of wonders.

Gaby nodded, and that seemed to galvanize Luther into action. He went to the officer in charge of taking names from the crowd, and issued new orders.

It wouldn't do him any good.

The person responsible had already skipped away, gone before the flames took hold, leaving Gaby with a duty that superseded his capture.

Clever mastermind? Or sick sadist bent on any form of destruction?

More would happen. A lot more.

Until the degenerate fiend got his hands on a woman to torment, he'd wreak havoc in every other way imaginable.

He needed a hooker.

Perhaps it was time for Gaby to take up a new profession.

Utilizing infinite care, Oren stowed the syringes in a small case. If they thought the mayhem would end with one measly fire—a fire that hadn't even killed the bitch he'd stowed inside the building—then they'd be in for a delightful surprise.

Not that the woman's life would matter much, one way or

the other. He'd found her nearly insensible with drugs at a crack house. Being near there had frightened him, but also given him other ideas. Addicts were easy to manipulate. So were transients. And here, in this slum area, both were plentiful.

Tonight, tomorrow, and the day after, he'd wreak havoc. He'd keep that fucking cop and beanpole bitch so preoccupied, they wouldn't have time to worry about a group of worthless whores. In fact, now that he'd seen the beanpole take money from the cop, she ranked right up there with the other sluts.

If he could get to her, he would. She'd be his first pick.

But it'd be tricky. He wouldn't underestimate her.

Against all odds, she'd charged into that fire and carried out the junkie as if misplaced heroism ran through her veins.

Interfering cunt. When he had her locked securely in his basement, he'd teach her what it meant to get in his way. He wouldn't let Aunt Dory or Uncle Myer end her tutelage too soon. She'd pay, long and dear.

By the time he finished, she'd be begging for death.

Excited by his own plans, hands shaking and smile tremulous, Oren finished his preparations in a rush. Leaving his private rooms, he headed down the stairs—and overheard his aunt and uncle talking about him. Temper prickling, he paused to listen.

"Do you know what she's going to do?"

"Don't you ever learn?" Uncle Myer snapped.

"I just forget sometimes, that's all," Aunt Dory whined. "It's . . . confusing."

Staying firm, Uncle Myer grabbed her arm. "If you slip up in front of him, he's likely to beat you to death. Do you want that?"

"You wouldn't save me?"

"I'm trying to save you *now*. Thanks to Oren, we have a

big house and plenty of money to spend, and we can feed our fetishes. Do you want to ruin it all with your stupid mouth?"

"No." Aunt Dory, never knowing when to shut up, asked, "But doesn't Oren need us, too?"

"Not anymore. Oren can be anyone he wants, and he can start over anywhere he wants."

"But . . . we know things about him."

"He knows the same things about us! Before he'd let us blab to anyone, he'd kill us in our sleep. Now shut up about it and do what you're told, what Oren tells you to do. Soon he'll have another playmate for us. Won't that make you happy?"

Glee tinged her voice when Aunt Dory said, "Yes. Yes, that'd be perfect. I can't wait. I hope Oren bags a body for us soon."

"Trust me. He's good. He knows what he's doing. It won't be long now."

Thanks to that last volley of compliments, Oren's fury faded. They respected him and what he could do. They nearly revered him. Because of that, he'd let them live.

For now.

But Uncle Myer was right. He no longer needed either of them. Living without them wouldn't be his choice right now. He liked things the way they were. But if he heard Dory blabbing about females again, he'd cut her fat throat and watch her gurgle to death.

Oren pictured it in his mind: Dory's fat face jiggling with fear, her blood running warm and wet down her flesh, her life slowly draining away until finally, her eyes went flat and empty. Yes.

He'd enjoy that.

He'd enjoy that a lot.

It was something to think about. For the future. When he got bored.

Luckily for Dory, he had other, more pertinent things to attend to right now.

Chapter 10

Stationed out front of the flophouse, mirrored sunglasses reflecting some of the late-afternoon sunshine, Gaby slumped against the outer wall. Gaze ever watchful, senses attuned to any misdeed, she heard Jimbo raise his voice and turned her head to listen.

He issued orders to the hookers, demanding that they move up the block to get more business.

Stupid prick. Lazily rousing herself, Gaby climbed to her feet, dusted off her ass, and looked toward Jimbo with a caustic intensity she wanted him to feel.

Uneasily, his gaze slithered her way. He ignored her notice and went back to berating the women, who hesitated to budge from the safety of Gaby's realm.

She'd spooked them all, being deliberately graphic in her depiction of the dead woman's body in the river, and the attempted abduction of Bliss. She wanted them to be scared enough that they'd defy Jimbo's orders in favor of their own safety.

It worked, as now all the women packed together and refused to budge.

Trying to brazen his way past Gaby's disapproval, Jimbo straightened to his full, meager height and raised a fiduciary fist at Alma.

"I wouldn't."

Jimbo redirected his anger at Gaby. "Stay the fuck out of this."

Pushing her sunglasses to the top of her head to sear him with the full impact of her hostility, Gaby strolled closer to the contretemps. "You and I need to have a talk, Jimbo."

"Fuck that. You might've spooked Carver with your witchy mumbo jumbo bullshit, but I'm not buying it."

Witchy mumbo jumbo? Seeing the fear in Jimbo's eyes, Gaby decided hey, whatever works. She stepped closer. "You do buy it, Jimbo. Even now, your pulse is sputtering and you're getting sweaty."

"It's hot out here!"

"Wise up, Jimbo. What good will dead hookers do you? As long as they're close by, I can keep them safe. But if you scatter them, I can't be everywhere—"

He slashed a hand through the air, coming within a millimeter of striking Gaby. She didn't flinch, didn't move other than to narrow her eyes, and that gave him visible pause.

He gulped, and argued, "One dead hooker doesn't put the rest in danger."

Fed up with his recusant stupidity, her gaze level with his, Gaby tsked. "You couldn't be more wrong, dumb ass. The same person who killed Lucy also tried to get to Bliss. He wants another body to play with. Then he'll want another after that. And after that, too."

"Unless *you* stop him? Right." Jimbo tried to shove her out of his space, but Gaby didn't budge an inch, and that, more than anything else, washed the color from his face. "Look, you don't even know for sure it was the same guy after Bliss."

"I know."

"How's that possible? Bliss doesn't even know who came after her." He tried for a laugh that fell flat. "I heard that one minute she says it was a guy, and the next it was a woman. You know what I think? She's fucked up and saying whatever she needs to say so she can keep resting on her lazy ass."

Deliberately bumping her chest into his, Gaby snarled through her teeth, "You want me to kill you, Jimbo, is that it?"

"God damn, bitch. Bring it down a notch, will you? I'm just saying—"

"You're saying all the wrong things."

Gaby's knife, which she'd withdrawn from her sheath without Jimbo even noticing, pressed against his balls. The second he realized the placement of the blade, his eyes bulged in terror.

Nudging the knife snug against him, Gaby said, "What I want you to say is that you comprehend the seriousness of the threat. I want you to say that you won't do anything to put any women at risk, especially these women who look to you for protection. I want you to acknowledge that I will get the bastard doing this, but until then, you'll damn well do as you're told—or suffer the consequences."

Beads of sweat rolled down Jimbo's temple. "You're fucking insane."

"Bet on it. Insane enough to castrate you without a single qualm."

His Adam's apple bobbed hard. "Jesus, Gaby. I . . . I gotta make my money."

Gaby thought about slicing him, just a little, just enough to gain compliance. Her razor-sharp blade would cut through his denim as cleanly as surgical steel sliced flesh.

She pondered the idea—and then she felt it, the transuding of depravity into her being.

He was near.

Triumph ripped through her before the calling could devour her.

She wouldn't wait for God's command. Not this time.

She'd hone her omnipotent numen and seek out the evil on her own recognizance.

Under her own tutelary power.

She'd be in charge.

"Jesus, bitch, you're cutting me!"

Oh hell. Refocusing on the idiot before her, Gaby withdrew the knife a safe distance from his crotch. "Do we understand each other, Jimbo?"

Hands cupping his jewels, he hissed, "Yeah, sure. Whatever. Just back the fuck off."

She gave him one more long look, but in light of this new challenge, Jimbo meant little enough to her. As Gaby reached back to replace her knife in the sheath, Jimbo struck out, intending to slug her straight in the face.

Fool.

Gaby dodged the blow, caught his arm, and wrenched it behind his back. His spine bowed as she added pressure to his wrist. "You would dare, Jimbo?"

Defiant even in the grip of pain, he shook his head. "You're making me look like a chump in front of everyone."

"No," Gaby said, and needing expedient measures, she twisted hard enough to make him yell out in agony. "You did that to yourself."

Releasing him with a shove, she stepped away.

The whores ran over to Jimbo, offering sympathy and assistance—and getting cursed for their efforts. Gaby walked away from them all. She didn't want to be followed, so she didn't dare run.

The invading affliction boiled to the surface, but didn't yet take over. She had time.

She'd get him. Or her.

And when she did, God Himself wouldn't interfere.

Nervousness kept Oren walking fast down the third dark, narrow alley. He had to make it quick to hedge off possible harm to himself. So far, he hadn't had much luck. Evening would prove a better time for his goal, but he lacked the courage necessary to wander the alleys, in the slums, during the dark of the night.

Like engorged veins, broken pipes climbed the outer walls enclosing the alley, trickling fluid, making the way slick. Mold grew rampant. Rats fed off refuse.

It was all so distasteful—and yet, so necessary.

Because of her.

Because of that damned cop.

Up ahead, at the bottom of concrete stairs leading farther into the bowels of hell, Oren saw what appeared to be a shrouded head.

His third, rapid target for the day.

He always saved the best for last.

To be safe, Oren slipped on gloves, then withdrew the one remaining hypodermic and prepared it for use.

The waiting body didn't move.

The nearer Oren got, the more details were illuminated. Grizzled graying hair poked out from beneath an old knit hat. Long, knobby fingers, disfigured with arthritis, clutched an all but empty bottle of booze. The reek of unwashed, aging skin and hair emanated from the huddled form.

Heavy in his pocket, the knife he'd brought along encouraged and titillated him.

He could barely wait.

The fouled drugs he'd dropped off at the crack house were amusing, giving the possibility of multiple deaths if a druggie chose to share.

The pipe bomb left near the playground, waiting for some idiot child to detonate, kept his anticipation sky-high.

But this, the promise of real bloodshed, pleased him the most.

Giddy excitement threatened to bubble over, stealing his control. Oren tamped it down. This foul creature wouldn't offer much of a challenge to his intelligence and cunning, but it'd pose confusion to the bitch and to the cop.

That counted for a lot.

Oren was only a few feet away when the bedraggled, decrepit being stirred. He looked up through watery, faded eyes, vague with indulgence and pathos.

Too stupid to sense his own inescapable death.

Lunging forward, Oren stabbed the syringe into the man's chest with brutish delight.

The victim's wrinkled mouth opened in terror; a feeble hand batted at the needle.

But already, the lethal dose of drugs scoured through his bloodstream, rendering him mute, paralyzed.

Defenseless.

Unwilling to waste time, Oren retrieved the syringe, broke

off the needle against the brick wall, and dropped it back into his pocket.

The man's head slumped to the side.

Such an easy death for him; unfortunately, he wouldn't feel a thing.

Oren withdrew the knife. For only a moment, he fingered the hilt, letting his palm become accustomed to the grip, the weight.

The man twitched, a spontaneous pinching of muscles, and that stimulated Oren, quickened his heartbeat and his glee. Laughing, he stabbed the man in the cheek.

Blood spurted out against the bricks, bathing the dull rust in glistening crimson.

Oh God, that felt good.

He stabbed again, this time sinking half the blade into the man's shoulder. Then into his chest. His thigh.

Entranced by his bloody results, at the display of gore and torn muscle, Oren slashed at the deceased man's nose, leaving cartilage exposed as the only tether keeping it on his face.

Seeing the nose dangling there, Oren tipped his head. And laughed.

The idiot drunkard looked so ridiculous.

But the enjoyment couldn't last. He didn't dare vacillate; strike and move. That was the plan. Again and again.

With one last thrust, Oren buried the knife into the man's face. It deflected off his cheekbone and slipped alongside his temple, under saggy skin and putrid flesh.

Macabre.

Oren loved it.

Oh how he would enjoy the look on the cop's face when he found the man. But some pleasures would be denied him. Oren accepted that.

Stripping off his gloves, he pocketed them, and with a cursory inspection to certify no blood splatters marred his tidy clothes, he went on through the alley and out the other side. Within half an hour, he'd be back at his house, secluded, safe, watching the news for any word of the destruction he'd wrought.

If it all wasn't such a bother, he'd be having the time of his life.

❦

Gaby was closing in on her prey when an onslaught of sensation contracted her muscles and stiffened her bones. No, *no!*

Pain of this magnitude either meant she was too late, or there were multiple threats.

Caught in an illimitable quandary, the pain intensified to egregious proportions. She stumbled, fell against a wall.

What to do?

Closing her eyes, she tried to bank the physical misery and clear her mind for instruction. Gasping in deep, fast breaths, she separated the callings, weighed them, and made a choice. For one calling, she was already too late to gain anything. For another, there was still time.

From what she prevised, only one summons would offer erudition.

God help her if she chose the wrong one.

Hating herself, Gaby gave over to the deepest encroachment of consecrated instruction. Driven forward, following a compulsion, she traversed to a dark alley. The pain blistered and popped—then settled into a fizzling ache.

Too late. She knew it, and still she hastened in, her knife in hand, her senses on alert. She was so immersed in the need to find a live body that she nearly tripped over a dead one.

She pulled back and focused on the grisly scene.

Blood drenched a human's clothes, splattered the surrounding bricks, the hard ground beneath. The body, still in a semi-upright position, was so abused, Gaby couldn't determine if it was male or female.

But it was a stranger.

And this was all for show.

Careful not to disrupt anything, knowing that somewhere here, a clue waited, she scoured the area and, eventually, descried the needle.

Bingo. The tie she needed to convince Luther that the attacks were related.

By the looks of things, the poor drunk hadn't put up much of a struggle, meaning he'd probably died before the mutilation.

Tipping her head back to see beyond the old towering buildings, Gaby peered up to the cloudless sky. "Very merciful. Thank you."

Urgency pressed in on her, reminding her that this corpse wasn't the only source of her suffering. Keeping the heterogeneous pains segregated, she decided she had to quickly notify Luther of the incident before following the other dictate.

Backing out of the alley, she went to the nearest pay phone, dug out Luther's card and some change, and put in the call.

Sounding harried and frustrated, he answered on the first ring. "Detective Cross."

"It's me."

His tone changed. "Gaby?"

"Yeah, it's me." Ever since she'd stood him up for breakfast a few days ago, and then rescued the woman from the fire, she'd avoided him. She had to avoid him in order to sense these perversions. Around him, her perception was blown to hell. "Surprise, surprise, huh?"

After a tick of silence, he asked, "Is everything okay?"

Straight to the chase, huh? Maybe he was still pissed at her. And maybe he'd finally given up on her.

She wouldn't blame him either way. "Actually . . . no. I hate to fuck up your day, but—"

"I'm dealing with three dead addicts. Believe me, my day is already fucked."

Three dead addicts? Gaby thought of that needle lying by the dead body in the alley. "What happened?"

There was a rustle as Luther probably moved away from the crowd. "Someone conveniently lost a stash of what looks like cocaine in a crack house, only it was laced with something deadly. Three women made use of it, and after the first died in convulsions, the third hightailed it to the hospital. She got there in time to shriek out the story, flail in panic, and expire. The docs tell me it was an ugly, painful death. They're still diagnosing the contaminant used."

It struck Gaby that Luther was in a strange sharing mood for a man who was through with a woman. But what the hell? She'd take any edge she could get. "What about the other person? You said there were three, right?"

"Found her dead at the crack house. Whatever they shot into their veins, it killed them quick and nasty."

Damn. Gaby wanted to ponder the connections, but she couldn't ignore the demand growing to excruciating proportions.

Hand shaking, she kept the phone to her ear. "I can trump that." She stared toward the alley, making sure no one entered from the street side. She couldn't guard both entrances at the same time, though. "Someone played slice and dice on a transient dozing in a drunken stupor in an alley."

"And you know this how?"

She heard the burgeoning anger in Luther's tone, but there

wasn't time enough, or caring enough, to apologize. "I'm looking at him. Or her. Not sure which it is, the body is so . . . dismantled. Judging by the clothes, though, I'd guess a guy."

"Give me an address."

Gaby rattled off directions, then said, "I found a needle by the body. I left it there, but I don't want you to miss it."

"No faith in my detective skills, huh?"

"Don't go wounded on me. This is too important for ego."

"Right." His tone changed. "Do not go near it again, Gaby, do you understand me? I'm coming right now, so stay on the street and stay out of trouble."

"You should hurry, because I can't stay. I need to . . . do something." She wasn't sure what yet, but if she didn't move soon, the torment would overtake her.

"Gaby!"

She hung up on Luther. Bossy jerk. What did he think— that she looked for trouble?

Hell, it stalked her, often at the most inconvenient times.

Even as she started on her way, following her instincts, each step quicker than the one before, Gaby began putting the puzzle pieces together.

Poisoned addicts.

Mutilated transient.

Trouble always came in threes, and this was trouble. Now in a full-out run, going on autopilot to expedite matters, Gaby ran several blocks away. Because she was focused inward, she didn't at first recognize the area where Mort lived, not until she came alongside the playground at the abandoned elementary school across from Mort's apartments.

Her steps became sluggish, her brain ticking like a bomb. Like a million tiny razors cutting into her flesh, the pain took her.

Oh no.

Kids of various ages and colors filled the broken concrete play area. Rusty chains on swings clashed with squeals of laughter. High-pitched voices rose like musical bells, happy and carefree despite the public squalor and misery of their lives.

Gaby saw them all.

And she saw the pipe bomb.

Her heart shot into her throat. Her vision narrowed. God no. Not a group of children.

In one agile leap, she went over the chain-link fence and loped to the center of the playground. Two youths, probably ten to thirteen years of age, noticed the bomb and ran toward it.

"*No.*"

They looked up, startled by her intrusion. Long strides took Gaby to them, and she stood directly over the bomb, using her body as a physical block. The taller of the two boys pushed tangled, reddish hair out of his eyes and glared at her. "We saw it first."

"Tough tittie, kid. I'm laying claim."

The little bugger bunched up at her. "You can't do that!"

"Watch me." Gaby spotted a cell phone in his pocket and said, "Give me that."

His soft white chin, marred with a bruise and freckled with dirt, went into the air. "It's mine."

"I'll give it back after I make a call." When he started to retreat, Gaby hauled him close and relieved him of the phone. She shoved him away and said, "Now get out of here. I'll let you know when I'm done."

"Hey!" He jumped, trying to reach it where she held it over her head. "Give it to me!"

Damn. She hated to scare a kid, she really did. But she wanted them safe, and that meant that they had to move away.

All of them.

Unleashing the darkest of her paladin essence, Gaby leaned close, stared hard. "Get out of here. *Now.*"

The kid backpedaled so fast, he fell on his butt. His buddy took off, unwilling to wait for him, screeching loud enough to wake the dead.

None of the little miscreants went far though. They huddled together, watching her, wary and curious, and Gaby knew how she must look.

For once, she was glad. Anything to keep them out of range of the explosion, should the bomb detonate.

She dialed Luther again.

He answered with a roared, *"Where the hell are you?"*

Wincing, Gaby jerked the phone away from her ear. "Jesus." Under her current deadly situation, her temper frayed. "Asshole. That *hurt.*" Then curiously, she asked, "How'd you know it was me?"

"A fucking hunch."

"Wow, you really are good," she mocked, trying to lighten her fractured mood.

"Damn it, Gaby, I told you to stay put."

"Yeah, but I couldn't. Have you seen the body in the alley yet?"

"I'm almost there. Where are you?"

"Well, that's the thing." She gulped, looked down at that damned bomb resting between her feet, and she felt sick.

"Gaby," Luther said, and it sounded like a warning. "Talk to me. Are you in danger?"

"It's worse than that, Luther." Again she gulped. "A lot of kids are."

"Kids?" Icy control replaced his anger. "Where are you?"

"Well, you see . . . I'm sort of straddling a pipe bomb that our guy put in the playground across from Mort's place."

A long, pained pause preceded Luther's moderate, composed voice. "Step away from it, Gaby. Get as far from there as you can—"

"No can do, cop. Don't you get it? It was left here on purpose so the kids would find it. And they did. I had to run the little buggers off, but you know kids today—they didn't go far enough."

"Shit."

"There're twenty or more of them playing here. If this thing blows, I don't know how badly they'll be hurt. So . . . I can't budge."

"Got it." Luther breathed fast, then went into detective mode and took charge. "I'm on my way, honey. There should be some uniforms in the area that can be there in under three minutes. They'll help to evacuate. Until then, don't move. Don't touch it. Don't—"

"Yeah right. I'm not an idiot, Luther. I'm not going to play tag with it." She eyed the audience of fascinated kids, making certain they kept their distance. "Just hurry up, okay?"

She hung up and surveyed the children. Most of them were barefoot, many were shirtless. They were thin, dirty, their hair hadn't been combed and their teeth hadn't been brushed. But thanks to naïveté, they appeared mostly happy.

Gaby couldn't remember ever being like that. Her youth had been spent in inexplicable pain, shuffled from one unwelcoming house to another, never understood, never accepted.

Never loved.

Thoughts of Father Mullond, the only person to ever accept her, filtered in. He'd made a difference to her life, and then, he was taken away. Gaby quickly blocked the memory. She needed all her faculties about her now, without the contamination of sadness.

"Hey, kid?" When the boy she'd terrorized met her gaze, Gaby pitched his phone to him.

He caught it handily. Emboldened by the return of his prized phone, he edged a foot closer to her. "S'that really a bomb?"

So they'd overheard? Damn. She didn't really want them panicked—but then again, she didn't want them too curious either.

"Yeah, looks like." Gaby locked her knees, put her shoulders back. "What's your name?"

"Halen. Why?"

"How old are you, Halen?"

Suspicion had him curling his lip. He glanced around, saw all the others watching, and struck a brave stance. "I'm twelve."

"No kidding?" He was so scrawny, she would have guessed eight or nine. "You look older."

His chin rose a little more.

"You look like a smart guy to me, Halen. A leader. How about you try to get everyone farther away, out of danger? The cops will be here any minute, and I know they'd appreciate the help."

"Why would I wanna help the cops?"

Pugnacious little runt. "Well, let's see." Gaby nodded at his hand. "If you don't, they might ask you where you got the phone."

Halen's eyes widened.

"That is," Gaby said, "if you're still alive. This bomb could go off any second, you know."

"Really?"

Gaby shrugged. "Truth is, I don't know shit about bombs. It could be a dud, or it could be remotely controlled." Her stomach curdled with the thought. "If it is, that means some mean bastard could be waiting to detonate it."

Halen considered that. "What about you? If it blows up, won't it kill you?"

Glancing down at the eight-inch metal pipe with wires, a battery pack, and an LED light attached with an excess of Scotch tape, Gaby feigned insouciance. "I doubt I'd be doing much dancing, not without legs." She looked back at Halen. "Who knows? One of my limbs could end up splattered all over you. Wouldn't that suck, to get knocked out by a bloody, burned, detached leg or arm?"

That grisly image served to commove the kid into action. He rallied two buddies to help him give orders. With a lot of mean-mugging, shoving, and insistence, Halen took charge.

"He with the cell phone rules," Gaby whispered to herself. Amazed, she observed from her custodial perch over the bomb as children were corralled out of the playground, led a safer distance away.

The next few minutes brought a maelstrom of activity. Uniformed officers arrived, and in record time, cleared the streets. Right behind them, Luther pulled up.

Unwilling to risk a single child, Gaby still stood over the bomb. Sweat trickled down her spine, her skin itched, and her nerve endings twitched. But she refused to take chances. What if someone *was* watching with a remote? Would the damn thing blow just as she stepped away?

A cop yelled, "Lady, get away from it now."

She wanted to. But . . . she shook her head. "Not a good idea."

Luther put his hands behind his head, paced once, and then started toward her.

Gaby threw up her hands to halt him. "No!"

He paused. "Then come to me."

Oh God, she wanted to. "But what if . . ."

"I know what you're thinking, Gaby. But you're fast. I've seen it."

She fought with herself. If others saw her quickness, would they wonder? Would she be giving herself away?

"You either come to me, Gaby, right now, or I'm coming to you."

Shit.

At her hesitation, he took a step, saying, "Move away, and move away *now*."

Knowing he meant it, she screamed, *"All right."*

One deep breath, and she bolted. She didn't head for Luther; she didn't want him implicated in her life with so many other officials watching. Feet flying, she soared up and over the fence with an Olympic hurdler's grace.

And almost collided with Ann.

Jolted to a halt, Gaby tripped, and stared at her.

Ann crossed her arms under her breasts. "Must you always be amazing, Gaby?"

Her mood seemed very uncertain. "I dunno. What do you mean?"

Ann laughed. "Here comes Luther, and he doesn't look happy. Please understand that his anger stems from concern for you, okay?"

"You're warning me . . . why?"

Ann gave her an unexpected hug. "I like the man, and I don't want you to demolish him. Now that I've seen you in action a few times, I know demolition is entirely possible."

Gaby wasn't given a chance to reply to that bit of idiocy before Luther swung her around and into his chest. His mouth opened, but nothing came out. Then he crushed her close in a fierce hug. Gaby grunted at the force of his embrace.

She felt . . . safe.

Secure.

God, what an illusion.

His fingers tunneled through her hair, curved around her skull, pressed her closer. "You're turning me old before my time, woman."

Knowing exactly what he meant, Gaby tried to shrug. "You would have done the same thing."

"No, I wouldn't, because I have resources. I don't have to rely only on myself, as you always seem intent to do."

In that, she had no choice. "I called."

"*After* you straddled the damn thing."

That was a difficult point, because despite what he said, Gaby knew without a doubt that Luther would have acted the same to keep a child from harm.

She pushed free of his tight hold and looked toward the playground. Sunlight glinted off the metal pipe. "Is it real, do you think?"

His hands rubbed up and down her back. "Looks real enough to me. But I'm not an expert. The bomb squad is bringing in a robot to disrupt the device, so I guess we'll soon find out."

"No shit?" Going on tiptoe, Gaby searched behind him. "A robot?"

Luther smashed her head back to his shoulder. "The police chief is closing off the streets so no more traffic can get through until we know it's safe." His arms tightened in bruising force, then released her. "And you, Gabrielle Cody, are coming with me."

"I don't know. I might be needed here."

"Why?" He cupped her chin. "Do you sense our guy is still around?"

Her eyes widened at his sincerity. Did he really believe in her?

In the long run, did it even matter? No. It couldn't—for one simple reason. "There's this big old sucky problem I need to tell you about, Luther."

His hands went to her shoulders. "I'm listening."

In one way or another, he always touched her. Right now, to anyone observing them, his casual caresses could be misconstrued for a kind of avuncular comfort.

Gaby knew they were far more intimate than that. The memory of what he'd done to her, how he'd made her feel in the parking lot, would supersede any effort at emotional distance. "You have a weird effect on me."

His eyes warmed, his mouth tipped up at the corners. "What kind of effect?"

"Not what you're thinking, so cool your jets." Gaby rubbed her head. "You know my super-keen insight? Well, you royally fuck it up."

Startled, he dropped his hands. "How so?"

"I wish I knew. It's just that when I'm around you, I don't feel things the same way."

"I'm not following you."

"You cloud my judgment, my instincts, everything. So even though I don't think our guy is around right now, with you so close, I can't be sure. Could just be that you're dicking with my perception again."

A muscle ticked in his jaw. "Want me to move to the other curb?"

"That won't help. I'll know you're there."

His arms crossed. "So how far away from you do I need to be?"

"Far enough to be like . . ." She winced, but had to say it. ". . . nowhere near me at all."

With Luther's stare boring into her, the commotion surrounding them faded to nothingness. He drew her with that look, which was both recusant and wounded. He devoured her, and her aggrandizing motives.

"Luther . . ."

His look of scorn burned her. "Anything, any way, to keep me at a distance, Gaby, is that it?"

She drew back. "Whoa. You think I'm making this up?"

"Your bullshit is so hard to follow, I have no idea."

Well. That made things a whole lot easier. "Fine. Then don't bother trying. Whoever asked you to anyway? Not me." She turned, but as usual, she'd gotten no more than a foot away before he swung her back around.

Gaby shot to her toes to shove her face toward his. "I'm getting real sick and tired of your manhandling."

He kissed her.

Right there, in front of everyone.

She jerked her mouth free. "What are you—!"

Hauling her right back to him, he kissed her hard enough to bend her back, melt her resistance and her good intentions. His arms clamped around her, keeping her arms pinned to her sides. With her back bowed and her feet off the ground, she had no leverage.

But what the hell?

She loved it. She needed it.

After suffering the agonizing possibilities of a bomb, Luther's heated attention obliterated her agitation. She reciprocated with fervor, biting his mouth, arching her hips into his.

In the next instant, her feet touched the ground and he released her.

Leaving her cold, he said, "Let's go," and with his fingers wrapped around her wrist, began dragging her across the street.

Befuddled, Gaby sucked in air and tried to shake the butterflies from her brain. In her present state, opposition was futile. Hoping he'd take her somewhere private, she asked, "Where to?"

"I have some men guarding the alley where you found the body. I want to go back there and check it out. Then I need to call in to see if anyone's found out anything about the addicts."

He wanted her along on police business? Well, hell.

"Then," he said, stressing the word, "you and I are going to calmly have a meal, talk, and go over the rules. One—more—time."

"I repeat," Gaby said, "I *called*. What more do you want from me?"

At his car, he stopped. Hands on his hips, brows fused, Luther gave her his profile. After a heavy pause, he looked at her again. "What I want is still up in the air at this point. You're uncooperative, cantankerous, angry and . . ." His voice lowered, full of uncertainty. "Crazy as it is, insane as it makes me, I'm starting to think that everything with you still won't be enough."

Chapter 11

From across the linen-covered tabletop, Luther regarded Gaby. No matter the provocation, he had to keep his cool—because he knew she wanted him to lose it.

In the muted restaurant light, the artificial purple highlights competed with the more natural bluish hues of her inky dark hair. It grew fast, already looking shaggy again, unkempt . . . sexy as hell.

He loved the feel of her silky hair, such a stark contrast to her caustic manner and cutting wit.

Other patrons wore jackets, and he felt the chill of the air-conditioning. In her sleeveless shirt and short skirt, she should have goose bumps.

But she didn't.

"Are you cold?"

Distracted, she shook her head. "No."

Of course not. Gaby often seemed immune to the trivial

discomforts that afflicted most people. She did without sleep, food, friendship, security . . . It drove him insane.

Constantly shifting, her light blue eyes kept a vigilant watch over the rest of the customers. Long dark lashes softened the intensity of her surveillance. Even pinched together, her lips looked soft, pliant, and very kissable.

He was obsessed, without knowing why.

She fed him an explanation, and even when the more rational part of his mind told him to hold back, he bought it hook, line, and sinker. More so than any other person he'd known, Gaby radiated sincerity, credibility—when her actions and words were so preposterous.

"Mort and Ann seem pretty serious."

Without looking at him, she said, "Tell me about it."

He thought of Morty Vance, and how Ann had given in to her fondness for the unlikely hero. They were a mismatched pair with Ann vibrant, professional, masterful, and beautiful, and Morty backward, insecure, and . . . dumpy.

But Ann was happier than he'd ever seen her.

"You're not surprised?"

"Not really, not after seeing them together. It's destiny."

So much surety in that simple statement. Gaby seldom had doubts on anything.

Was it Morty's connection to Gaby that led Ann to a fallacious appeal?

Whatever ethereal power Gaby possessed, she had ensnared him. Morty, after aligning himself with her, seemed to have the same power.

Watching Gaby climax once wasn't enough. Not by a long shot. He wanted to be inside her the next time she came. He wanted to ride her hard, to conquer her, and destroy all her barriers.

And he wanted to protect her, to take that abstruse sadness from her eyes.

If he didn't have her soon, he'd go nuts. But before committing that possible physical faux pas, he needed to understand her better.

He needed to know what made her tick.

It wasn't the want of money, companionship, security, or comfort. Gaby made her own way, on her own terms. She needed no one and nothing and that made her unique, not only from every other woman he'd known, but every other human being he knew.

She accepted sexual interaction with him—under duress. But even there, her acceptance was deviant, being more about curiosity than corporeal pleasure.

So . . . why did she ever give in to him?

What made her take such staggering chances with her life, just to help others?

Sagacious, mature, emotionally battered beyond the years of a twenty-one-year-old woman, she intrigued him in boundless ways.

Remembering Gaby's unfaltering and careless dash into a blazing building, her stoic stance over a live bomb, left Luther's heart palpitating and his skin clammy with dread.

"You're not still shook up over your ordeal, are you?"

She snorted. "No. Why would I be?"

Her unparalleled will would be the death of him. Either from her tragic youth, or from some other influence, Gaby lacked a self-protection mechanism. She'd protect others, but not herself.

Holding her fork in her fist like a weapon, she again scanned the restaurant. She was tense, nervous, and barely eating the burger and fries he'd gotten her.

Luther took one quick visual trip over her lithe and lean body. "Want to tell me what's wrong now?"

Her gaze darted to his. "Nothing. Why?"

He nodded to the fork held in her tight grasp. "You're not eating."

Expression pinched, she slapped down the utensil, picked up the burger, bit off a chunk, and chewed. "Happy?" she asked around a mouthful.

"Not really, no." Again, her slender throat, her smooth, unmarred skin drew his fascinated attention. For a woman who took every opportunity to leap into the most menacing of battles, she had no discernible scars. "I won't be happy until I get you figured out."

That statement choked her.

Bits of burger, bun, and condiment shot Luther's way. He picked up his napkin and, without comment, dabbed the mess from his shirt.

Eyes bugging, Gaby grabbed up her cola, took a big swig, and washed down the rest of the food. Still a little strangled, she glared at him. "Damn it, look what you did."

"What?"

She glanced around, and Luther could have sworn her face filled with heat.

Self-conscious? Unbelievable. Whenever he got near Gaby, he found new depths to her personality. "Everyone chokes, honey. It's not a big deal."

She didn't agree. Pushing aside her food, she announced, "I'm done. Let's get out of here."

Enthralled, Luther studied her. "I never thought to see you embarrassed."

Anger deepened her blush. "Kiss my ass."

Humor sparkled above his irritation. "Eventually, I'd love to." He watched her, saw her incredulity. "I'd like to kiss you everywhere." He put his elbows on the table, and repeated softly, "Everywhere."

Her mouth fell open.

"What? You don't like that idea?"

"I've never seen the hookers do anything like that."

For such a hard-ass, her innocence never failed to amaze him. "Prostitution is all about haste. The less time it takes, the more the hooker makes per hour. But when a man and woman make love, they take their time, and anything is possible. Anything that gives them pleasure."

Her level gaze never wavered. "Sounds perverted to me."

"I'll eventually show you." Luther sat back. "That is, if you stop fabricating reasons to keep your distance from me."

Gaby reached again for her fork, no doubt to gig him, but Luther caught her hand. "No physical violence in a public forum. It's ill-mannered."

That only infuriated her more. She jerked her hand away and sunk down into her seat, almost sitting on her spine, indulging a good sulk.

After a moment, she muttered, "It was ill-mannered of you to bring me here in the first place."

"Why?" The restaurant was a favorite of Luther's. Casual but upscale, with good, home-cooked food. He'd take it over a fast-food joint any day.

When Gaby didn't answer, he shrugged. "If you don't like it, you should have said something. Where would you prefer to eat?"

Her mouth constricted.

"The silent treatment?" An interesting twist for Gaby. "I see you're like other women after all."

She came out of her seat and up over the table in a fluid rush. Palms flattened on the tabletop, fury palpable, she hissed low, "I am *nothing* like other women and you damn well know it."

He carefully caught her wrists. "Then what's the problem?"

"I feel on display here, you jerk. I'm an aberration who doesn't fit in. Are you a glutton for punishment? Is that why you always drag me to these places?"

Wow. So much sizzling energy and emotion.

It turned him on. *She* turned him on—even when giving him hell.

Yes, he was definitely a glutton for punishment. "Please sit down, Gaby. People are starting to stare."

Her eyes flared comically. In a whisper, she said, "You dick."

Her insults, on occasion, bordered on amusing. "You're the one causing a scene, not me."

On a heartfelt groan, she melted back into her seat. Face in her hands, she said, "I'm going to strangle you for this."

"How about you just relax and enjoy the food instead. You never eat enough."

Her fingers opened so she could peek at him. "You saying I'm too skinny?"

"Whatever you are, I like it."

She rolled her eyes.

"It's true. I know you're . . . unschooled in some things, but you're smart all the same. You have to have figured it out by now that I have a very serious thing for you."

"A *thing*?"

Cavalier, Luther smiled at her. "Yeah. I've never had it before, so I can't really pinpoint what it is. But I want you. I like being with you. And even though I can't always understand you, I very much admire you."

Gaby could trade insults with ease, but a compliment always made her defensive.

"Poor Luther," she remarked with a good dose of sympathetic scorn. "I keep telling you—that makes you as much a freak as I am."

"Maybe." Luther reached over and trailed his fingertips up and down her arm. "For a soft woman, you sure do pack a lot of bravery."

She snorted—but didn't pull away.

"Because I care, you scared me half to death today. But at the same time, I was so proud of you."

She flinched as if insulted. "Proud?"

"Shocking, huh?" Had no one ever been proud of her? Probably not. Gaby hadn't ingratiated herself to many people. According to her tales of Father Mullond, the priest had cared for her, but he'd been a strict guide, not a doting friend given to praise. "You don't even realize how heroic you are, do you, Gaby?"

"Oh gawd. I've already spewed food on you. Do you want to make me puke, too?"

"What you did was amazing. Very brave." Luther began tickling her forearm again. "Maybe a little foolhardy, too, but you kept kids alive, Gaby. Did you see how those little faces looked at you?"

Uneasiness rounded her usually proud shoulders. "They're just dumb, desperate kids who don't know any better."

"They watched you with starstruck awe. You swept in and did what their own parents seldom do—you put their well-being first."

"Go ahead, break out the violins, why don't you?"

Each caustic word hid a hurt so deep, Luther felt her pain. "If I had a violin nearby, I'd give it a try."

She grunted. "Fine, but then don't blame me if you end up with vomit on you."

Slipping his fingers around her wrist, and then down to

twine with her own fingers, Luther held her hand. "You were scared, weren't you?"

"Well, duh. If that bomb had exploded, it would have blown off my moneymaker. That'd scare anyone."

Luther sputtered over that descriptive prediction. "Your moneymaker?"

She shrugged. "That's what Bliss calls it. The other hookers call it a hoo-haw, or a—"

"I know what they call it." Trying to stifle a laugh, Luther carried her hand to his mouth and kissed her knuckles. "I'm glad you're in one piece, moneymaker and all."

"Well, yeah, me, too."

"If you're not going to eat, then we need to clear the air."

"We could do that better outside."

Luther shook his head. "Here is fine." She could more easily avoid him outside. "Explain to me how I interfere with your perception of things."

To his surprise, she plunked her head down on the table and locked her hands behind her neck. So much visible struggle unnerved him. Whatever Gaby's issues, she believed them, which meant he had to give them credence, too.

After a moment, she propped her chin on her crossed arms. "Before I bother—do you believe me that I know when stuff is about to happen?"

"I've seen it, so yes." Soon as he got a chance, he'd do some research on extrasensory perception. As a cop, believing in such far-fetched things went against the grain. He liked proof that he could touch, motives he could dissect.

But in an effort to understand Gaby . . . he'd bite the bullet and try a little faith.

Wary, she squirmed in her seat, but it wasn't in Gaby's nature to be demure—in anything. "You'll have to accept that when I feel the evil, it hurts me."

He'd seen the pain contorting her, and the fact that she'd finally explain, encouraged him. "Hurts you how?"

"I can't describe it really. It's an awful twisting agony that pervades me. Everywhere."

"The way your features . . . alter . . ."

"Yeah, that's a new one for me. Until you told me, I didn't know I looked different. Can't say I'm happy about that either. I thought it was only the—" Her gaze clapped on his, and she swallowed the rest of her words.

"What?"

"Never mind."

Luther rubbed the bridge of his nose in frustration. "You thought it was only . . . someone else who changed?" She frowned at him, but didn't acknowledge his guess one way or the other. "You may as well fess up, because I'm not letting it go."

"Nosy bastard."

"I'm a detective," he told her, losing some of his calm. "I'm supposed to be nosy."

She struggled with herself, and it fascinated Luther to watch her, to see her weighing the consequences of trusting him.

She looked at him again, and he saw the expectation in her eyes. She wanted him to mock her, because that would free her.

"I figured it was only the evil that looked different."

Around Gaby, he had to choose his words with care. Playing along seemed his safest bet to keep her talking. "For me, evil people don't look any different. That's the problem. If they did, solving murders would be a piece of cake."

"You're not me."

Her scorn nudged him that much closer to anger. "No, I'm not."

She watched for signs of ridicule, but Luther held himself phlegmatic.

Her gaze sharpened. "For me, the truly immoral people look different."

A possibility struck Luther, and with the thought that he might finally catch on to her, he asked, "Their auras?"

Her fingers toyed with the fork. "That's part of it."

"What else?"

She withdrew. He saw it, felt it.

"Look, the important part of all this is that when you're around, I don't feel the pain as sharply as I should. Your presence somehow . . . weakens it."

Honesty seemed his only recourse. "I'm glad." Anything that made her more . . . normal, suited him just fine.

"You don't get it, do you?" Petulant in her need for him to understand, she leaned closer again. "The pain is what helps me to focus. It's what guides me."

"Into burning buildings and playgrounds ready to explode."

"Yes. Without it, I can't . . ."

"Can't what? Play hero?"

Her fist struck the table. "Damn you, I am not playing!"

Mired in conflicting reactions, Luther said nothing.

Gaby didn't like that. Her lip curled. "What are you thinking now, or do I even need to ask?"

"You won't run away from me?"

Her back stiffened, and she braced herself. For more hurt? It's what she always expected.

"I don't run from anyone."

True enough. She didn't even run from a bomb. "I figure you're either certifiably nuts . . ." Needing the touch of her warmth, the assurance she was real, Luther reached for her hand. ". . . or you're a truly gifted phenomenon."

She pried her hand free with disgust. "More like a cursed delegate, but hey, whatever. Are we done here?"

"No." Musing over her choice of words brought Luther to a new consideration. "How long have you had this . . . affliction?"

"Since birth, far as I know."

Which could explain a lot of her background. "That's why it was so difficult for you to fit into the foster homes?"

"Part of the reason, yeah. But I'm a natural loner, anyway. Cute little family circles have never much appealed to me."

He didn't believe that for a minute.

In the oddest ways, Gaby created a family unit everywhere she went. First with Mort, and now with a pack of lonely, desperate hookers.

Trying to be subtle, Luther moved her plate closer to her. She took the hint and started eating again.

While she dug into her food, he mused aloud. "At Mort's, with me standing right behind you, you sensed the fire, and that someone was trapped."

"Yeah." She thought about that. "I probably would have known sooner without you there."

Humoring her wouldn't hurt anything. For now. "But you still knew. So my presence doesn't completely obliterate whatever . . . aptitude you have."

"No, not completely." She shook her head. "But I can't take that chance. I need to know that Bliss is safe."

"And you can't trust me on that?"

"What do you have to do with it?"

The insult hit home, but taking Gaby's unique lack of social skills into account, he tamped down on his annoyance. "I have officers keeping watch over her, and Ann is there more often than not. She knows what she's doing."

"Maybe." After finishing off her burger, Gaby started on her fries. "But when it comes down to it, I trust me more than the two of you put together."

Damn it. A man could only take so many insulting barbs before losing his temper. "All right, Einstein. Since you've got this all figured out, what do we do next? How do we catch the psychopath?"

"I have a plan."

Luther's blood ran cold. "What plan?"

"Can't tell you, cop, sorry." She waved a French fry at him. "Even with all this soul-baring, I figure it'd be a bad idea to include you. For sure you'd have a conniption, and the truth is, I'm not going to change my mind about it, so . . ." She held up both hands. "Why hassle over it?"

Putting both elbows on the table, Luther closed the space between them. Voice low, he issued a warning. "You will tell me your plans, Gabrielle Cody, right now, or so help me I'll—"

"What? Arrest me?" Unconcerned, she chomped down another fry.

"Damn right. If that's what it takes to know you're safe, then that's what I'll do."

Now that Luther had lost his cool, her appetite had returned with a vengeance.

"Fine. Go ahead. It'll fuck me over real good, but if you're such a control freak that you don't mind doing that to me, then I guess I'll know where I really stand with you—once and for all."

Damn her, she'd turned the tables on him. "How will it fuck you over?"

"Oh, come on, Luther. You know I'm wallowing in anonymity. The very last thing I need is to be in the system."

One of his worst suspicions, laid on the table. "Are you wanted by the law?"

"Not yet, no." Luther started to relax, when she added, "No one knows who I am, so how could anyone pin anything on me?"

God Almighty, she made him insane. "Are you saying that you—"

"I'm saying if you get me fingerprinted, I'll skip out of here the second I can. New name, new identity, the whole shebang. It's the truth I'd miss you something awful, but . . ." Gaby shrugged. "I guess that's the price I'd have to pay."

She'd miss him? Somehow he had his doubts. "Would you?"

"Disappear? In a heartbeat."

He shook his head. "No, I meant would you really miss me?"

"Ah, what is it, cop? You need a little stroke to the old ego?" Plate now clean, Gaby shoved it away and mirrored his position with her elbows on the table. "Okay, if you want the truth—"

"Always."

"Fine. I think about you every five minutes." Her gaze went to his mouth; her voice lowered. "Sometimes I dream about you, too. And after what you did with your fingers . . ." Her eyes closed on a sigh. "Yeah, I'd miss you."

Before Luther could relish that admission, she added, "But that wouldn't stop me from disappearing if you forced me to."

Because he knew Gaby, he believed her. To buy himself time to think, Luther asked her, "Dessert?"

"No thanks." The offer made her shudder. "I ate the meal for you, but I don't want to stay here any longer than necessary."

She'd eaten for him? Giving up, Luther signaled the

waiter for the check. Eventually, he'd accustom Gaby to some of life's little pleasures. For now, he could accommodate her idiosyncrasies.

As he tossed several bills onto the table, Gaby raised a brow in question.

"When I dine out," Luther told her, "I always leave a nice tip. I believe in good karma. You know, what goes around comes around. An angel's smile, and all that."

"No such thing, Luther. Bad stuff happens to good people all the time. It's the way of things. But if it gives you a false sense of security, go ahead, suit yourself."

People did indeed look at her when she stood, but Luther thought it was more Gaby's striking attitude than how she dressed or acted. Her confidence, her capability was a live thing, and it touched everyone within her realm.

It was one of the things he'd first noticed about her.

After casting a black look on one particularly nosy woman, Gaby strode beside him with her chin in the air and her manner more abrasive than usual. But then, that was Gaby, always on the defense, always combative.

Curious about her take on heavenly intervention, Luther said, "You don't believe in angels?" Her faith in God was more intrinsic and personal than anyone he knew. At times, she spoke of Him as if they were cohorts.

Under the bright sunlight, Gaby slipped on sunglasses. "Course I do. Angels are always among us."

"They are?"

Her long-legged walk nearly left him behind. "Sure. Just as evil lurks, so does good. But I prefer to rely on my own ability." She stopped and looked at him over her shoulder. "It'd be nice if you'd have a little faith in my ability, too."

"I see your capability." He beat her to the car so he could open her door for her. "What you don't understand is that when you care for someone, every awful possibility that could steal them away from you always comes to mind. It makes people worry, even when they know someone is skilled."

Proving she'd gotten used to his gentlemanly tendencies, she sat in the car without comment.

Luther closed the door and walked around to his own side to get in. Gaby stayed silent.

It was the oddest thing, Luther thought, trying to seduce a woman who preferred insults to flattery, who kept an illegal and lethal blade strapped to the small of her back, who spoke as candidly as a porn star but shied away from any signs of affection.

"So." He started the car and steered out to the street. "How about you tell me what you have planned, and I'll do my utmost not to interfere."

"No."

The phlegmatic, cool refusal dismantled Luther's quiescent mood. His muscles contracted and his teeth came together.

One of these days, he swore to himself, she'd stop treating him like an afterthought.

"It's possible, you spiteful little irritant, that I could be of assistance to you."

"Little? I'm almost as tall as you."

She didn't dispute the irritation or spiteful attributes. "I outweigh you by at least a hundred pounds. And the few inches I have over you are all muscle, compared to your skin and bones."

"So you're bigger. That doesn't make you better—at anything." Remaining apathetic, she shook her head. "And no, it's not even remotely possible that you'd assist me. Trust me."

Reminding himself of her incommensurable life and

attitude, Luther sought an even, convincing tone. "I do. Trust you, that is. And before you start rolling your eyes or threatening to throw up, try to understand that worry and mistrust are two different things, ruled by two different emotions. Okay?"

"That still doesn't mean you'd like my plan."

Which must mean her plan was dangerous and foolhardy.

For the next mile, they rode in silence. Luther had almost lost the fight for equanimity when Gaby finally spoke.

"If you really trust me, then give me three days."

Where it concerned Gaby, so much could happen in seventy-two hours. "Why?" Suspicions rose like sharp needles. "What happens in three days?"

"It's just that I have details to work out." She reached back and adjusted the knife at her back, reminding Luther that nothing with Gaby would ever be mundane. "After that, after I've given it a lot of thought, I'll decide if I should share with you or not."

Fuck. It wasn't easy, but Luther managed a nod. "Fair enough." A compromise was the most he'd get from Gaby, at least for now. "Just tell me, will you be in any danger in the next three days?"

Putting her head back against the seat, she stared out the window. "Danger lurks everywhere, cop, you should know that by now. Sometimes it comes calling whether I want it to or not. Practice that hyped faith in my ability, and maybe you'll do less worrying, okay?"

Giving up, but only for the moment, Luther nodded. "I'll try."

As Gaby relaxed, it occurred to Luther that her idea of danger and his were worlds apart.

Not being an idiot, he'd keep an eye on her, and when he couldn't, he'd enlist the aid of others.

Tonight, he'd make a visit to Mort.

He wanted to check up on Bliss anyway, and while there, he'd recruit Mort and Ann for his cause.

Whether Gaby liked it or not—and for a certainty, she wouldn't—she'd have backup.

That's what friends were for, even when you denied having friends.

Chapter 12

While contriving her next move, Gaby wrote with a near electric ebullience. The pages disembogued, the drawings came to life, and within a few days, she'd all but finished the latest graphic novel.

All she needed now was an ending, but she couldn't write the ending until things . . . ended.

Knowing what she would do to ensnare and extirpate the menace, she'd already depicted herself as a haphazard hooker who, as the graphic novel progressed, dealt harsh commination with grisly precision.

Satisfied with her latest efforts, she sat back on her stool and stretched her cramped muscles. When she relaxed again, her eyes caught on her last sketch.

Lush, colorful details were nonetheless menacing. Looking more closely at the scene of conflict between a looming, hyperbolized version of herself, and a bloodcurdling depiction of her nemesis, she saw Luther's faint outline in the background.

His usually compassionate eyes watched her with nocent intent.

What the hell? Gaby picked up the page. She didn't even recall putting him there. Even in her imagination, he intruded.

Laying that page aside, she stood and picked up each visual for the novel. Like a dark, heralded sidekick, she found Luther's form repeatedly interwoven into the story and graphics.

Damn it. Somehow, regardless of how she tried to block him, he appeared on almost every page, sometimes advising, sometimes protecting, sometimes . . . enticing.

And a few times, his presence served to portend her demise.

Slapping the pages aside, needful of fresh air, Gaby stood and crossed to a window. Night had fallen with atramentous gravity, enshrouding the moon and stars, smothering the weak illumination of streetlamps and blinking neon bar signs.

Pressing a fist to her chest, Gaby tried to deny the growing ache there, but the severity of it refused to be modified. Luther had no place in her novels.

He had no place in her head or heart either.

And yet, she couldn't rid herself of him. Luther might believe her show of feigned indifference, but Gaby never lied to herself.

He meant far too much to her.

In her dreams, Luther emblematized a desperate craving for normalcy. For caring.

And love.

He was everything she wanted to be, but wasn't.

Well, except that Luther was all male, and given his

preposterous attraction to her, she was thankful for the femaleness she'd often scorned.

Leaving the window, Gaby went into the bathroom and did her best to scrub the ink stains from her fingers. She trimmed her nails, cleaned her teeth, combed her hair, inspected her rumpled clothing and, with a shrug, found her ankle boots. She stepped into them and left her room.

On her way out, to the hookers who greeted her, Gaby said, "I'll be working tonight, too, just so you know."

Betty paused in comical confusion. "Workin' on what, sugar?"

Gesturing down her own body with her hand, Gaby said, "You know. What you do."

Betty's eyes widened. "The hell ya say."

Posy twittered a laugh, saw Gaby remained unsmiling, and coughed. "But, Gaby, you ain't never . . . well, you know. You ain't never done that."

Gaby examined a nail. "Yeah, so? How hard can it be?"

Opal stepped in front of the other women. "What are you up to, girl?"

"Don't worry about it. We all know I'm not competition. But I have my reasons, so just tell me where I should stand."

"I won't. Jimbo would skin me."

Rolling her eyes, Gaby surveyed them all. "None of you has reason to fear him. If he gives you any problems, just let me know."

"There'll be problems, all right, if you traipse out there all set on sellin' yourself." Opal shook her head. "We'll all catch hell, and that's the truth."

"Fine. I'll clear it with Jimbo first. Happy?"

They all stared at her.

Giving up, Gaby asked, "Where is he right now?"

"Down the corner, takin' care of some business."

The way Opal said that left Gaby leery. Jimbo did a lot of business: drugs, stolen goods, arms. But something in Opal's tone didn't sound right.

Gaby put her hands on her hips. "What kind of business?"

Opal clammed up. Posy looked to Betty, and tried to slip away.

"Not another step." Gaby closed in on them, and as one, they crowded back against the peeling wallpaper. She looked at them each in turn. "No one leaves until I know what's going on."

Betty let out a long, aggrieved sigh. "It ain't nothin' for you to get involved in, Gaby."

"How about you let me make that decision, okay?"

"But it's the truth, you sometimes overreact," Posy confided.

"I won't this time."

Opal snorted. "Yeah, right. And I'm headin' to sainthood."

The three of them guffawed.

Gaby tapped the toe of her boot. Damn it, if she was going to carry through with this farce, and she was, despite her personal dread, then she wanted to get on with it. "If we stand here all night, none of you can work. Then how happy will Jimbo be?"

That possibility stifled their humor. Another minute passed before finding results.

"Oh, for Chrissake," Posy blurted. "A john roughed up one of the girls. He paid extra for it, though, Gaby." She wrung her hands. "You know some of 'em enjoy doing that sort of thing."

"It gets 'em off," Opal added.

Oh God. Gaby felt ill. While she'd been writing, a

woman had been hurt. Damn her selfish need for expression. Of course, that type of abuse wasn't the sort of thing that ignited her senses. She should have been on the street, where she'd have seen the trouble.

Ice filled her veins. "How bad was she hurt?"

The women shared a pained look. Posy said quietly, "He knocked one of her teeth out, left some welts on her back, and . . ."

Opal cleared her throat. "He burned her a couple times with his cigarette."

Tension snapped Gaby's back straight. For only a moment, her vision blurred. Honing her anger inward, she focused on retaliation. "Who was it?"

"Marie."

Her heart squeezed. Poor old Marie. She was more mature than the others, heavier, homelier. Because of that, Jimbo often ridiculed her. She never made as much as the younger women, and often took the riskier propositions—with Jimbo's blessing.

This time, he'd be sorry for his lack of defense.

Gaby nodded to the women. "Thanks for telling me. Don't worry. I'll handle it."

Opal grabbed her arm, but whatever she felt had her snatching back her hand with alacrity. She blinked twice before getting the words out. "Gaby, please. We don't need no more trouble."

"He's payin' Jimbo extra for the problems he caused," Posy offered.

Sick bastard. Fuck that.

Gaby felt no deep calling, so he wasn't the one who'd killed Lucy and tried to take Bliss.

But for now, he'd do.

"Yeah, he'll pay," Gaby agreed. "Now all of you, get to work before Jimbo suspects you of ratting to me."

And just like that, they scattered, leaving Gaby alone on the steps.

She couldn't butcher the man, although she wanted to, although she could. Not out of pleasure, but out of justice. Some people didn't deserve to take up space on Earth.

Anyone who would abuse a woman, even a woman for sale, fit the category of unworthy.

Sex was one thing. Physical maltreatment was something else entirely.

Under burning intendment, Gaby went down the flight of stairs, out the front door, and to the walkway. Even the blackness of the night couldn't conceal Jimbo's loathsome dealings. Gaby saw him a block up, with another man, and a cowering woman.

Marie.

She didn't realize she'd moved until she found herself a mere yard from the men.

"How can she work like that?" Jimbo demanded. "It'll be two days before those burns heal."

"I ain't paying you more'n that," the man raged. "Fifty bucks extra is compensation enough for the likes of her."

Under implied threat, Jimbo scowled at him. "Well I say it isn't."

Gaby strode into the middle of the fray. "For once, Jimbo, we're in agreement."

All eyes turned to her. Marie's poor face sported multiple bruises. Her lips were bloodied. On her neck, a small round burn, haloed by inflamed red flesh, still oozed. Dried blood encrusted her swollen nose. Her hair hung in matted tangles. Torn clothes barely kept her covered.

Gaby inhaled a slow, steadying breath—and it didn't help. Not one iota.

Anxious to dissuade her of involvement, Jimbo snarled. "Butt out, Gaby."

He was as insignificant as a gnat—so Gaby ignored him. "Where else are you burned, Marie?"

Quivering all over, Marie said, "I'm . . . I'm okay, Gaby."

"Show me."

Marie sent a nervous glance toward the two towering men.

Gaby hardened her resolve. "Show me *now*."

Cringing, Marie lifted her torn blouse to display a worse, deeper burn on her ribs, right below her left breast. Bruises and welts surrounded that wound.

Fierce rage fulgurated.

Rock-steady, primed to contravene the sight of mistreatment, Gaby turned to the man. "You hurt her pretty damn bad."

Beefy in the way of a street brute, he stood at least five inches taller than Gaby. Thick brown hair hung over his ears, and bright green eyes twinkled with mirth. "She's a whore, so what do you care?"

Tipping her head to the side, Gaby smiled.

Jimbo sucked in air. "Oh shit." He rushed closer. "God damn it, Gaby," he hissed low, "I'm warning you—"

Without looking at him, Gaby struck out with her elbow, and hit Jimbo square in the nose.

He exploded, cursing, stomping, threatening her with evil retribution that they both knew carried no weight, not against her.

Gaby spared him a glance. "You let this happen, Jimbo. For all you know, he could be the same perverted asshole who murdered Lucy."

The man snorted. "What are you talking about? I ain't murdered no one."

Holding his bleeding nose, Jimbo frowned at Gaby. "Well, he's not, now is he?"

"No, he's not. But you didn't know that, and you did squat to stop him. Far as I'm concerned, that makes you as guilty as him."

Trying to sound reasonable, Jimbo explained, "I wasn't there, bitch, so how could I have stopped him? And if you'd stop nosing in, you'd see that I'm trying to settle it with him right now."

"Oh no." Gaby shook her head. "You're trying to compensate off Marie's pain. That's not the same thing."

Desperate, Jimbo grabbed her arm and spoke low. "Money is the only thing most people understand. If it costs him, he'll be less inclined to ever do it again."

Realization struck Gaby. Huh. Maybe Jimbo wasn't as inhuman as she'd always thought. "Okay, so you get an A for effort."

"Hallelujah."

"But this time," she continued, "the cost of money isn't near enough."

Shaking with his anger, Jimbo tried to take her attention off the man. "It's none of your damn business, Gaby."

Slowly, Gaby looked down at his hand on her arm, then into his eyes. "I'd suggest you back off, Jimbo, and let me do my thing. I'm done playing with you right now, and if you don't let me vent where I most want to, I'm going to vent on you next."

Just that quick, he released her. Exasperated, he threw up his arms, turned his back on her, and marched a few—safer—feet away.

The man in front of Gaby roared with hilarity. "I'll be damned. He's afraid of you, ain't he?"

Just below the surface, Gaby's savage temper bared its teeth. "He's not as stupid as he looks."

The man continued to chuckle. "Little sis, you sure talk a long line of shit, I'll give you that. But I wonder if you can—"

Gaby struck out hard and fast, using the heel of her palm to punch him in the throat. With his larynx traumatized, he gargled and choked, reeling back in utter shock. While he remained off balance, she landed a solid, dead-on kick of her boot heel against his head.

The blow felled him and, dazed, he dropped to the side. But he was a hardy one, and after a second of choking, he shook his head to clear it. In slow motion, he lifted his bruising face to glare up at her. "Just who the hell are you?"

"Tonight," Gaby told him as she advanced, "I'm vengeance. And that, you sadistic pervert, makes me your worst fucking nightmare."

Issuing a roar, the man lumbered back to his feet and charged her.

Braced for the attack, Gaby went with the impact of his brawny body, rolled to her back, and kicked him away in one adroit move. It never even dawned on her to draw her knife. She needed physical release, and this was as close as she'd get.

Gutting him would end things too soon. She'd rather beat the shit out of him.

And so she did.

While he tried to get back to his feet, bracing up on one arm, Gaby kicked out his elbow. It snapped, and a splintered section of bone sliced through the skin. Blood poured out. The man screamed in agony.

In glacial hostility, Gaby stepped over him. "Get up, you pussy."

Sweat bathed his face as he lolled to the side in agony. "You broke my fucking arm, you crazy cunt."

Again making use of the heels on her boots, she stomped his solar plexus. "Sticks and stones, buddy. Now *stand up*."

It took him a minute, but he got awkwardly to his feet. Holding his arm, he snarled at her. "If my arm wasn't broke—"

"What?" Gaby taunted. She folded her arms behind her back. "Now we're on even ground." And so saying, she kicked his thigh, almost buckling his leg. Before he could recover his balance, she kicked his knee, and he went back down again.

Screaming at the pain it caused his broken arm, he curled into himself.

Heaving, Gaby kept her pose, arms behind her. "I'm not done."

Horrified, he looked at Gaby. "What the hell do you want? I can't fight. I can't do anything."

"Wanna bet?" She stomped his ankle, wrenching another raw scream from him. He had powerful lungs, and soon a large group of local denizens converged to watch the entertainment. Gaby paid them no mind. "Get up, or I'll break your jaw."

Tucking his uninjured arm over his face, he cringed tight. "I can't, I tell you."

Her fury made that unsatisfactory. "Stand up or so help me, I'll destroy you where you are."

He tried, she'd give him that. But while he was still on his knees, shaking badly, white as a ghost, Gaby accepted that he'd be no challenge now.

Disgusted, she put her boot to his face and shoved him

back down. He sank backward, and she delivered one last debilitating blow to his nuts.

Maybe that, more than anything, would encourage him to think twice before hurting another woman.

"Jesus." Jimbo dared to muscle his way in front of her. "Stop already. You're going to kill him."

Redirecting her wrath, Gaby fired on Jimbo. "And you fucking care? After what he did to Marie?"

Jimbo backpedaled.

Shaking all over, Gaby looked at the fallen man, at the blood splayed around him, his battered face and cowered position—and it didn't help. Not even a little.

Softer now, her voice strained, she asked of no one in particular, "Do you really think *I* should fucking care?"

Marie touched her shoulder, and flinched when Gaby whirled to face her.

Through swollen lips, Marie tried a tremulous smile. "Thank you, Gaby. I'm okay now. I promise. You did more'n enough."

Unseeing, heaving in her anger, Gaby put her head back and howled like a wild animal until her lungs hurt and her throat felt raw.

Why? Why did it not help?

But she knew. This pathetic excuse for a human being was only a poor substitute for her real target. God hadn't even bothered to direct her to his misdeeds. What he had done, others did every day to women.

But that changed nothing.

Just like the guy who'd tortured Lucy, he deserved nothing less than death, but . . . Gaby turned away from him and went to Jimbo.

Again he backed up, then caught himself and withdrew a knife.

Gaby kicked it out of his hand without even thinking about it. "Ever pull a knife on me again, and you'll regret it, Jimbo, do you understand?"

Red-faced and rigid, he refused to reply.

Gaby bumped her chest into his, so close that she breathed in his foul air, and smelled his acidic fear. "From now on, there will be no corrupt deviants who take pleasure in causing pain. You got that?"

His eyes narrowed. "Does that include you?"

Struck, Gaby locked her jaw.

Sensing that he'd hit a nerve, Jimbo pushed into her, backing her up a few steps. "Cuz bitch, it sure looked to me like you enjoyed yourself."

"Shut up."

Jimbo laughed. "I gotta tell ya, Gaby, I think that's the only time I've ever seen you smile."

The truth of that pierced Gaby, hurting her and leaving her sickened. She never had much reason for smiling—but taking on a sadist . . . yeah, that gave her pleasure.

She looked Jimbo dead in the eyes. "Maybe you should take that as a warning, huh?"

"Yeah, sure." He shoved his way around her and went to the man on the ground. "Now who the hell is going to take care of this?"

"I can have a cop here in two minutes." Just to piss off Jimbo, she fashioned another smile out of her starched lips. "Will that make you happy?"

"Fuck no." He turned to Marie, looked her over with a frown. "Go fetch a few of the ladies. Get them up here real quick." As she started to go, he stopped her with a hold on her arm. Ill at ease, he frowned some more before saying, "After you send them here, go on to your room and soak in the tub or something."

Surprised, Marie nodded. "Okay, Jimbo."

Awkward, Jimbo still hesitated. He dropped her arm and ran a hand through his hair. "Look, if you think you need a doctor or something . . ."

"I don't."

That reply didn't really satisfy him, but he accepted it. "All right. Get going then." Glaring at Gaby as if the bout of conscience was her fault, he pulled out his cell phone and put in a call.

Moving closer, Gaby listened in.

"This is Jimbo. Get your sorry ass over here double-time. I have a job for you."

After he'd stowed the phone again, Gaby crossed her arms. "I take it that wasn't an ambulance?"

He moved with palpable agitation. "That'd be worse than the cops. I have a guy coming over to get him out of here."

Dire possibilities occurred to Gaby. She had no real concerns for the man, but hell, if she'd wanted him dead, she'd have killed him herself.

"Where will your friend take him, Jimbo?"

"What do you care?"

Annoying jerk. "If you're planning to dispose of him, after I did a number on him but refrained from killing him, then I have a right to know."

"God damn, you're a bloodthirsty bitch. No, I'm not going to *dispose* of him. What the hell kind of crazy talk is that? I'm in the flesh trade, not the murder biz." Twitchy with impatience, he waved a hand toward the fallen man. "I want him out of here, off my block, before anyone links him to me. That's all."

Selfish prick. She should have known.

The man groused a complaint, proving he was still very

much alive. Jimbo looked down at him. "Hang on, you ass-hole. Don't you dare die on me."

"I need a doctor."

"Yeah, well, tell me where you live and my man will take you there. What you do after that is your own damn business, but I suggest you figure out a story that keeps me and my girls out of it."

The threat hung in the air until the man finally nodded.

"As long as we understand each other. Now where should we dump your miserable ass?"

The man gave his address, and Jimbo nodded. "Got it. In less than ten minutes, you'll be out of here." Under his breath, but loud enough for Gaby to still hear, Jimbo added, "And then you're not my problem anymore."

Drawn to him again, Gaby strode over to the wracked body. Seeing the wounds she'd so easily inflicted left her cold and indifferent.

Kneeling down at his side, she put her knee *almost* on his throat.

"I could still kill you," she told him in an eerily serene voice. "And as you now know, I don't need my knife to do it, either. Your size and strength didn't help you one bit. Bullies always meet their match—eventually."

"Yeah, I get it." Face pale with pain, he favored his arm. "Like I told Jimbo, I just want to get my arm fixed, that's all. I don't want no more trouble."

Gaby wasn't satisfied. "If it wasn't for Marie, the woman you burnt . . ." Her lungs constricted with anger all over again, and she had to take a cleansing breath before she could continue. "If it wasn't for her, I might have killed you tonight, and you and I both know the world would have been a better place for it."

Pathetic and afraid now that he couldn't harm anyone, he tried to turn away from Gaby.

Knotting her fingers in his thick, cool hair, Gaby brought his face back around. "You'd be smart to learn from this reprieve, because if I ever again hear of you harming anyone for jollies, man, woman, or child, I'll hunt you down, and I'll make you suffer a long time before killing you. I won't leave a single bone unbroken, and just before you die, I'll chop off your balls and carve out your black heart."

Horror flashed in his eyes.

"Believe it." Gaby released him and stood.

"God Almighty, woman," Jimbo whispered. "Let it go now. He sees the error of his ways."

"He better."

With Jimbo mumbling and huffing beside her, Gaby turned and started to walk away. When she saw Posy and Opal rushing toward them, she paused and, thinking of them, turned back to Jimbo.

At her aggressive approach, his brows arched into his hairline. *"What now?"*

She leaned in close so only Jimbo would hear her. "Blame any of the other women for my actions tonight, and you and I will have more than words. Am I clear on that, Jimbo?"

"Yeah. Real clear. Now get the fuck out of here, will you? I have to clean up the mess you made before we're all fucked because of it."

"You promise you're just taking him home?"

"Yeah, cross my fucking heart. Now *go*."

Gaby studied Jimbo, decided he meant what he said, and headed off. Maybe she wouldn't play at being a hooker tonight. She wasn't in the mood. It'd wait. Right now, she felt no evil.

Except for the evil brewing inside her soul.

It was an awful thing to know she possessed the capacity to maim, to murder—to behave exactly as the wholly evil did.

God had made her a paradox.

He'd made her a paladin.

And in the process, she'd become an abomination of all humanity.

Sometimes, she didn't even trust herself.

Chapter 13

From a safe distance away, Oren cowered in the obscuration of heavy night shadows, watching, waiting, drawn again and again to the tall figure.

Woman?

With the way she fought? He was starting to doubt it.

Flesh and blood? Definitely.

But she possessed abilities he'd never before witnessed. How could she look so plain, and yet be so spectacular?

Unlike the other stupid sluts he'd taken captive, this one would prove to be worthy of his time and refined effort.

She would fight to the bitter end. Never would she give up and surrender to death as an easy escape from the pain, as the other, weak adversaries had.

Not that one.

Adulation kept Oren glued to the spot until she disappeared into the adumbral night. Without her magnificent presence to

hold him ensorcelled, Oren's attention wandered to the grue-
somely battered body of the man she'd just dismantled.

Ah. They had that in common: *a love of corporal punishment*.

While disciplining the big man, she had glowed with vi-
vacious energy. Her face, usually so ordinary, had taken on
an ethereal beauty.

Oren's heart rate accelerated with sweet anticipation.
Would she glow like that when he had her strapped down,
naked and helpless? Would she still exude energy even as he
issued a tantalizing test of pain-filled judgments against her
lack of morals?

All along the sidewalk, people milled, seeing the beating as a twisted form of entertainment in their pathetic
lives.

Did he dare make use of this golden opportunity? He'd
done so much thus far without being stopped, without suspicion. Oren closed his eyes and drank in the sweet taste of
bold arrogance.

Tonight he would extend his reach for the thrill of seeing
what he could get away with.

Not about to lose this golden opportunity, Oren slipped
away to get his car. Taking only enough time to change his
disguise and, still maintaining a discreet but diagnostic distance, he drove up the block and waited in the idling car.
Only a few minutes passed before another vehicle arrived to
retrieve the injured man.

It took two of the hookers to help get the idiot into the
car. They were more concerned with haste than gentleness,
and given their curses, the man had considerable weight.

It could be a problem, but somehow, Oren knew he'd
manage.

With the man stowed in the backseat, the vehicle drove away.

Oren followed. They drove for fifteen minutes or more before slowing. The car pulled in to a quiet but lower-middle-class neighborhood. Headlights turned off, Oren pulled up and waited. The driver got out, went around to the back, opened the door, and without ceremony or care, dumped the big man to the curb.

The car sped away.

Oren waited, but when the big man sat up and still no porch lights came on and no one came to investigate, he decided it was safe enough.

Slowly, cautiously, he pulled up and, when nothing seemed amiss, he got out and approached the big bruiser.

In a childlike voice, he asked, "Mister, are you all right?"

A raw, wretched groan made Oren's hair stand on end. After scrubbing a hand over his face, the man said, "Help me up, kid."

Thanks to his broken arm, he sounded nearly in shock, heightening Oren's bravery.

"Oh my gosh," Oren enthused. "You're hurt, aren't you? You need to get to a hospital."

"Yeah, a hospital." The man tried to stand, but he went back to his butt in misery.

God, Oren despised gutless cowards lacking internal fortitude. Hiding his repulsion, he reached for the man's beefy upper arm. "I'll help you."

After urging the brute to his feet, Oren opened the rear door to his car. "You'll have to get yourself into the backseat. Can you do that? Then I can drive you to the hospital where the doctors can make you comfortable and take care of your pain."

The man struggled, sweated, and cursed. His broken arm,

now blue and grotesquely swollen, was of no use at all. Seeming confused but cooperative, he strained and finally managed to load his crushed and cracked form into the backseat as instructed.

"That's it." Oren reached into his pocket. "Now just lean back and close your eyes. I'll try not to hurt you." He withdrew a syringe, panted with his ebullience, and stuck the man in the thigh.

The guy was so far gone, he barely flinched at the prick of the needle.

Within seconds, he went entirely limp—which was a blessing, because at least now he wasn't whining and whimpering. Oren rushed around to the front of the car and got behind the wheel.

Contemplating the sadistic delights in store made driving a challenge. Anticipation sizzled and sparked.

Going straight to the house, Oren jiggled in his seat. He could barely wait until Aunt Dory and Uncle Myer saw the surprise. They'd both been annoyingly antsy without anyone to play with. From the looks of things, this man wouldn't last long, but then, he didn't need to.

Oren parked in a rush, locked the garage door, and went to the intercom system. In a singsong voice, he said, "Uncle Myer, Aunt Dory, I need you to come to the basement. Right now."

Five minutes passed, testing Oren's forbearance, before his aunt and uncle arrived. Disheveled and sleepy-eyed, still in their bedclothes, they stepped off the elevator.

"Come, come," Oren told them, his voice tinged with febrile intent. "We have to hurry before he awakens and causes a ruckus."

"He?" Uncle Myer rushed to Oren's side. "Who is he? What have you done?"

"Why, I've brought you a present to feed your ardent fetishes." Oren opened the back door of the car with a flourish to display the large, unconscious man lolling in the seat. "Ta-da!"

Wary, Uncle Myer eased closer. His eyes widened. "A man? Is he dead?"

Idiot. "Not yet, no."

"But who is he?"

Chafed by the questions, Oren stepped back from the car. "That, Uncle Myer, doesn't concern you."

Aunt Dory peered over Myer's shoulder. Her eyes sparkled and a wild pulse thrummed in her throat. "Oh my. He's awfully bloody already." Her ripe nipples showed beneath her nightgown, turgid, elongated. "Did you do all that to him, Oren?"

At least she appreciated the gift. "No, of course not. I found him like this, and decided he'd make an excellent playmate."

Uncle Myer rubbed his chin. "He doesn't have any family looking for him, does he?"

Growing more splenetic with each sign of his uncle's hesitation, Oren crossed his arms and glared at each of his relatives in turn. "He'll be bloodier when the two of you finish with him."

Aunt Dory twittered, and her homely face lit with burgeoning excitement. "Really?"

Smiling at her fervor, Oren held out his arms in grandiose presentation. "Absolutely. Do what you will with him. Anything you desire."

Breathing hard now, Aunt Dory pressed a hand over her breast. "Anything?"

"By all means. He's a gift. Indulge yourself in whatever means pleases you."

Uncle Myer wasn't convinced. "But, if he dies . . ."

"He most certainly will, and that's fine. I want him to." The man groaned, stirring a little, and Oren stroked his thigh. "Shush now, my friend. You're going to delight my relatives, and when they're done with you, why then, you'll serve a higher purpose. Your miserable life won't be a waste."

Laughing now, Dory said to Myer, "Hurry. Let's get him on the rack before he comes to."

"I prefer women," Myer complained, even as he reached into the backseat and hauled the man out by his uninjured arm. He collapsed onto the basement floor.

"And you'll have a woman," Oren promised. "A sublime woman. A woman like no other." Saying it aloud excited him. "A woman who will last."

"You're so good to us, Oren." Aunt Dory danced to the side of the man to help elevate him.

As Dory and Myer dragged the man toward a specially designed restraint, Oren watched. Once locked into place, there'd be no escape for him. "I'll procure the woman for you next—but not until the time is right."

Myer grunted as he arranged the man onto the platform. "Any idea when that'll be?"

"Soon. Very, very soon." Talking about it excited Oren unbearably, so he forced the image of the tall, dark-haired girl out of his mind. "But for now, would you rather I leave Aunt Dory to her pleasures and give you chores to do?"

"No, course not."

Sullen idiot. "Then hurry it up and get him fastened down. I think he's in shock. If you keep dallying, he'll die before you can even get started."

That warning spurred Myer to haste. As he and Dory worked with industrious delectation, Oren went up to his rooms to change from his frumpy, dirty clothes. He detested the garb he had to wear to fit into the slum neighborhoods. He much preferred finer things, but he was adaptable enough to do whatever was necessary.

Leaving the intercom open so he could hear the frenzied activity in the basement, he stripped out of his costume and changed into his regular clothes.

At one point, he laughed aloud at Aunt Dory's rapture. She was such a rutting pig that her groans of pleasure could be heard over the man's hoarse screams of agony.

And Uncle Myer, for all his protestations about preferring a female, wallowed in the ministrations of pain with the vigor of a man half his age.

The high-pitched wails were like music to Oren, feeding his soul. He'd missed this so much. Thanks to the tall woman, it had been too long since he'd luxuriated in his preferences.

When the coordinated blend of tormented outcries and squeals of carnal pleasure began to fade, Oren knew the man had expired. As he'd suspected, the brute hadn't lasted long.

Because of his personal bent toward inflicting pain, Oren often read up on various medical afflictions. He knew that shock could cause a sudden drop in blood pressure, a faint pulse, and if left untreated, death.

Of course, shock had only hastened death. The overindulgent tendencies catered by his relatives had done the most to terminate the man's life. They had never learned to savor opportunities, but in this instance, Oren didn't mind. Their lack of mastery over their obsessions had, for once, served his purpose.

Resolute in his whims, tingling with impassioned expectancy, Oren made a casual descent to the bowels of the grand house. As he reached the cool basement, the scent of death, excrement, and sweat assaulted his nose.

Lifting a hand to shield his nostrils, he ventured forward into the tableau of pain. The mangled body of the man, now stained with blood and his own body fluids, as well as secretions from his relatives, showed signs of grotesque abuse.

Like children denied the last bite of succulent candy, Aunt Dory and Uncle Myer stood there, silent and sullen.

Her desires not yet fully sated, Aunt Dory still quivered with need.

Uncle Myer, for all his protestations, looked well glutted.

Buffoons.

They lacked all finesse, and neglected all sense of advantageous detail.

Walking past them and the bloodied remains, Oren approached a mahogany cabinet. On the outside, apparatuses of various use hung in arrangement according to size and application. Accoutrements of torture filled the many drawers. The amount of paraphernalia his relatives had procured through the years belied their ability to control themselves.

After searching for the best device to suit his purposes, Oren retrieved a long surgical blade from a golden hook. From a velvet-lined drawer, he withdrew elbow-length rubber gloves. Inside double doors at the base of the cabinet, he took out a long plastic apron.

His mouth trembled. His hands shook. Deforming a corpse added no felicities to his perversion, he assured himself.

But he'd do this.

The end result would bring immeasurable pleasure to him.

It would be the best joke of the century.

❧

Ann sat on the edge of his desk, flirting without meaning, annoying for the fun of it.

"Luther, Luther, Luther."

"What?" he asked, trying to concentrate on his papers despite her physical disruption.

"After all the women who've thrown themselves at you." She tsked. "Mmm, mmm, mmm."

Laying his pen aside, Luther looked up at her. "Really, Ann? Harassment from the woman who's sleeping with Morty Vance?"

Umbrage put her shoulders back. "His name is Mort, not Morty."

"Whatever."

After a moment, she treated Luther to a Cheshire cat smile. "He's adorable, isn't he?"

Not in the least. "If you say so."

She stood, stepped behind his chair, and rubbed his stiff shoulder muscles. "So what about you?"

"What about me?" God that felt good. Lately, he stayed so knotted up, he felt like a walking lump of tension.

Leaning around to see his face, she specified, "Are you sleeping with little Miss Sunshine?"

He wished. "You're awfully nosy all of a sudden."

"There's a method to my madness."

"Yeah, and that'd be?"

She went back to rubbing, which kept her out of his view. "Have you seen Gaby lately?"

"No. She wanted a few days to herself." Gut instinct started churning. But then, he always felt uneasy when thinking of Gaby. "Now why do you ask?"

"Huh." Stepping to the side of the desk again, Ann lifted a wrist and looked at her watch. "Our shift is up. Are you ready to go?"

Dodging his question? "I don't think so. Not until you tell me what's going on."

She wrapped both her arms around one of his and tried to lead him toward the door. "I'll tell you, but only after we're outside and in your car."

Planting his big feet, Luther refused to budge. "My car, huh? Should I take that to mean you'll be riding somewhere with me?"

"Yup. To Mort's." She cleared her throat. "Because that's where Gaby's at."

Oh hell. The way she said that . . . Luther shut down his computer and grabbed up his suit coat. "Let's go."

Trotting in her high heels to keep up, Ann said, "Just that easy?"

Where Gaby was concerned, Luther had learned a second's hesitation could be too long. "Yeah, just that easy."

"She has you twisted up pretty good, Luther. I'm not altogether sure that's a good thing." Once they were in the hallway, she pulled back on his arm. "Slow down, please. My shoes aren't meant for sprints."

Luther moderated his pace, but his determination burned. They stepped outside to a setting sun and humid skies. "Okay. So what's going on?"

"Well, two things, really. And I want you to hear me out, okay?"

"Fine." He opened the passenger door for her, practically tucked her into the car, and hurried around to the driver's door.

Ann laughed. "I didn't mean to alarm you. Gaby's visiting with Bliss. From what Mort said, she'll be there a little while yet."

"Unless she decides to leave."

"Well, yeah. She does make mighty abrupt decisions, and her mood switches faster than light."

"Trust me, I'm well aware of Gaby's personality quirks."

Grim, Luther started the car and pulled out of the parking lot. "So what specifically about Gaby being at Mort's made you think we needed to get over there?"

"You won't like this."

"That much I already know."

Ann half turned in her seat to face him. "Given what Mort overheard of the conversation between the girls, Gaby wants to know the particulars of being a prostitute."

"So? She's always curious about . . ." Luther trailed off. Ann didn't need to know about Gaby's preoccupation about, and inexperience with, sex. "Never mind."

She waved that away. "I don't think you're getting me, Luther." Ann touched his arm. "Gaby wants to know what she should do, and how she should act, to convince others that she's a hooker."

Disbelief slammed into Luther. His hands tightened on the steering wheel. Damn her. So that was her harebrained plan?

At least Mort and Ann had done as he'd asked, and notified him posthaste of her foolhardy plan.

Resigned to Gaby's perfidies, Luther said, "She hopes to set herself up as a hooker in order to catch the cretin who'd killed Lucy."

"I think so. That was Mort's impression. He couldn't think of any way to dissuade her, so he called me, so I could tell you . . ."

Striving for a calm that was well out of his reach, Luther said, "I appreciate it. Thanks."

Ann sat back. "Well, bravo. And here I thought you'd be up in arms about it."

"There's no need to get upset because she's not doing it."

"She's not?"

"Hell no."

Seconds ticked by as Ann studied him. She settled back in her seat and folded her hands over her lap. "Well, I'm curious as to how you plan to stop her. From what I've seen, Gaby is an unstoppable dynamo who does just as she damn well pleases."

"I'll stop her." Luther flexed his hands on the wheel. One way or another, he'd force her to see his reasoning. "That's all you need to know."

"Luther . . ." Ann's hesitation diverted his attention.

"What?"

"You know I love you. As a friend and partner, I mean. I can't help but worry about you."

He'd said as much to Gaby; friends worried, and nothing could change that. "What's on your mind?"

"I don't want to anger you. But you're so eaten up with this girl, I'm not sure you're seeing things as clearly as you should—as clearly as you *normally* would."

Luther glanced at Ann. Eaten up? Yeah, he was. Gaby had him twisted up in a dozen different ways. He stared at the road ahead of him. "Let's hear it."

And still Ann fretted before finally saying, "How did Gaby know that there was someone in that fire? No one else knew, right?"

"She claims to have this incredible intuition." Feeling idiotic, but unable to stop his defense of Gaby, Luther attempted to explain. "You know, like a cop's instincts that tell him something isn't right. You've done it. So have I."

"Not like that, Luther. Gaby knew someone was inside. She didn't just suspect it."

He didn't have an answer for that, so he said nothing.

"And after just stumbling on that dead vagrant, how did she then go several blocks away, only to discover a pipe bomb in an old playground?"

Oh God. He should have asked himself those same questions. But when he was with Gaby, his need for her blunted his suspicions. She made him believe in her.

Probably because he so badly *wanted* to believe in her.

"I don't know." Luther shook his head, growing more tense by the moment. "It could all be bizarre circumstance."

"I suppose that's possible." Ann's hand tightened on his arm. "But, Luther, you're a cop. You have to accept the other possibility—that Gaby knows these things, because . . ."

He didn't want to hear it. He didn't. "Ann—"

"She knows, because she's the one responsible for them."

Fuck. *Fuck, fuck, fuck.* Luther tightened his hold on the steering wheel. Acid burned his throat and his guts churned. But he needed to hear it all. "You've gotten to know her some, Ann. In your personal opinion, do you think she's capable of that?"

"Capable?" She answered without equivocation. "Absolutely. I've never seen anyone more capable. But do I think she did it? No."

His lungs filled. "No?"

"I was there when she stormed past that fire to save someone she didn't know. I was there when she stood over that damned bomb. You heard from the bomb squad. If it had detonated, there would have been no more than little bits and pieces of Gaby left."

So he wasn't the only one under Gaby's spell? Nice to know, but under the circumstances, not a whole lot of comfort.

"Gaby is hurting. I see that, too, Luther. And people in pain can do astounding things. Mort trusts her with his life."

"They have a screwy friendship." A smile took him by surprise. "Want to hear something funny? When I first met

Gaby and got to know Mort, I thought they had something romantic going on."

Ann smiled, encouraging him with her silence.

"I was jealous." Feeling raw, Luther laughed at himself. "That's pretty fucked up, huh?"

"You know what I think?"

He wasn't sure he wanted to. "What?"

"I think Gaby is incapable of causing such carnage, but she knows a whole lot more than she's telling you. And regardless of our personal feelings on it, we're obligated to explore every possibility."

Luther pulled up to the curb in front of Mort's apartment building. "Meaning you want me to count her a suspect?"

"I don't relish Mort's reaction to such a thing. He'll feel betrayed, and that's sure to cause a rift between us." She opened her seat belt. "But do we really have any choice?"

"No." They were about to get out when a call came in.

Ann answered, saying, "Detective Kennedy." After a moment of listening, she closed her eyes and rubbed her forehead. "I see." She listened again, then said, "Oh God. Yeah, we'll be right there."

Seeing the strain on her face alerted Luther to the seriousness of the call. As soon as she disconnected, he asked, "Trouble?"

"That's an understatement." She looked at him with sympathy. "We have to make this visit short."

"He got another woman?"

"No, this time it was a man. We're being called in because he was tortured pretty badly, in a similar way to our first victim."

Ice cut along Luther's spine. "Where'd they find the body?"

"About two blocks from where Gaby lives." Ann reached

for his arm. "It's worse than the female victim, though. They say this guy had his testicles and heart removed. They were left on either side of his head, so no one would miss the . . . significance."

"Christ." Luther looked up at the building holding Gaby. Somehow, he just knew she was involved.

"There's more, Luther."

Ah. Just as he figured. "There always is."

"An anonymous source claims that Gaby fought with this guy the night before last. He said he witnessed her beating him to within an inch of his life."

Numb, Luther looked at Ann, and asked the only thing he could think of. "Why?"

"Something about the guy abusing one of the hookers. I guess Gaby took exception to it."

"She would."

"The thing is . . . the witness says he overheard her threaten the guy with further punishment."

Dread formed a cold lump in his guts. "Let me guess. She told him she'd cut off his balls?"

Ann nodded. "And carve out his heart."

Luther scrubbed his face and laughed. "Leave it to Gaby to let her arrogance bury her neck deep in shit."

Leaving it up to Luther, Ann asked, "What do you want to do?"

Patting Ann's hand, he silently thanked her for the support. "Gaby's not stupid, you know. She wouldn't openly threaten a man, and then kill him and display him for all the world to see."

Ann considered that. "They said the corpse is pretty mangled."

"Yeah, and that, Gaby could do."

At Ann's surprise, Luther shrugged. "If the man hurt one

of the prostitutes bad enough, I have no doubt Gaby would have beat him nearly to death. She's ferocious in her protection of anyone she thinks is smaller or weaker than herself."

"I've noticed that."

Luther's thoughts churned. "In all honesty, I believe she could even kill the guy." He looked Ann in the eyes. "But if Gaby murdered someone, no one would ever know about it. The body would never be found."

Refraining from judgment, Ann sat quiet.

"I guess we should go."

"A few uniforms are holding the site for us." She softened. "If you want to stay here to talk to Gaby, I can head over there without you—"

"Forget that." Luther opened his door. "This is going to be quick."

Ann hurried out of her side of the car. "And if Gaby is resistant?"

He strode toward the front door. "She won't be. Not this time." Luther swore it to himself, and hated what he knew he'd have to do. But damn her, she had his back against the wall.

What happened next would be on her. She'd brought this on herself.

But knowing that for truth didn't alleviate Luther's consuming guilt one little bit.

Chapter 14

Edginess had been creeping in on her for days. Not the feverish diminution of strength and thought that usually accompanied a true calling, but a more frenetic sensation that left her discomforted, antsy.

Something had happened—but what?

Everyone she cared about was safe; she trusted in that. If any of them, any innocent person, was in great peril, she'd know.

Bliss droned on in great reluctance, schooling Gaby on patent costs for various deals of prostitution. Blowjobs, handjobs, visuals, and extra participation . . . it all sounded repulsive and far-fetched. But to catch her guy—

A disturbing premonition of dread invaded Gaby's thoughts. Bellicose urgency brought her to her feet, but unlike her other episodes, this impending doom affected her differently.

This had to do with Luther, not evil incarnate.

"Oh fuck."

Bliss grabbed her hand. "Gaby, wait."

"Can't. I need to get out of here. Now." Gaby jogged to the front of the house and caught Mort just as he started to unlock the door to Ann and Luther. "Don't."

He turned to her in surprise. "It's okay. It's Ann—"

"I know who it is." Pulling him away from the door, Gaby studied his face, praying for the support she desperately needed right now. "Mort, you know me, you *trust* me."

His earnest gaze never faltered. "One hundred and fifty percent."

"Well, Ann and Luther don't."

Sympathy darkened his features. "Gaby . . ."

"They don't know me, and they sure as hell don't trust me."

Luther's fist rattled the door. "Mort! Open up."

After glancing at the door with nervousness, Mort put his shoulders back. "What do you need me to do?"

Thank God for friends. Gaby headed for the steps. "Stall them while I sneak out through the basement."

"I changed that window, Gaby." Mort turned her around. "Go out through the kitchen door and into my shop. In the backroom there's a window you'll fit through. It'll put you in the alley."

How had she gotten so lucky? "You're my hero, Mort." Changing routes, Gaby rushed through the house.

Bliss stayed hot on her heels. "Gaby, wait. I have to tell you something."

"Not now."

In an uncharacteristic display of backbone, Bliss smacked Gaby's shoulder. "Yes. *Now*."

Caught in a quandary, Gaby nodded. "Fine. Follow me and talk along the way."

They both heard the front door open, and Luther's voice questioning Mort. She didn't have much time.

Holding a finger to her lips, Gaby held open the door leading into the graphic novel shop connected to Mort's living quarters. Bliss went through, and Gaby closed it again with a quiet snick of the latch. "Come on."

Unlike the dusty, disheveled shop of old, Mort's establishment was now well-organized, colorful, but at this time of early evening, empty of customers. The front shades were lowered, leaving the interior in deep shadow.

Gaby made her way to the back of the shop, through a door to a private office complete with desk, phone, fax, and other business devices. "Huh. Mort's really stepped up in the world."

Pulling over a chair to enable her to reach the locked window, Gaby started to climb.

"Luther's in trouble."

Sharp fingers of dread yanked Gaby back. She spun to face Bliss. "What are you talking about?"

Bliss rubbed her temples. "I'm sorry I ain't more clear, Gaby. But everythin' is jumbling around in my brain."

"Just tell me what you see."

Nodding, Bliss looked up, bit her lip. "I see Luther in that awful room."

Gaby's heart stuttered, and she reached for the chair-back for support. "The room where Lucy was tortured?"

Tears tracked Bliss's cheeks. "And Gaby? I see you there, too."

Contrary to Bliss's reaction, that relieved Gaby so much that her knees almost gave out. "I'm with him? You're sure?"

"That's what I keep seeing, yeah."

Glancing heavenward, Gaby whispered, "Thank you, God." If she was there, she could keep Luther from harm. What happened to her didn't matter so much. "I have to go."

Openly crying now, Bliss clung to her shirt. "But why do you have to go? I'm scared."

Gaby disengaged her fingers. "A man was killed. I don't know why I didn't know that sooner. Maybe because I really hated him and didn't care if he died."

"Who?"

"It doesn't matter anymore. The problem is that Luther will think I'm involved, which means he'll be honorbound to take me in for questioning—or more."

Bliss shook her head hard. "No. Luther cares about you. He's a good man."

"I know he is, and that's why he'd arrest me." The need to see her safe, even if behind bars, would motivate Luther as much as suspicion on her involvement. "But, Bliss, I can't protect him if I'm under arrest."

Angry footsteps sounded in the hallway, spurring Bliss to panic. "Okay, okay, get on your way then. Hurry."

"Go back into the next room so Luther doesn't immediately know how I left." After a quick hug, Gaby waited for Bliss to exit the office.

The girl rushed out, inadvertently leaving the door ajar, and Gaby didn't waste time closing it. She stepped up onto the chair, unlocked and opened the window, and hoisted herself out. She was just dropping down into the dark alley when she heard Luther's booming voice calling her name.

Poor Luther.

He said he trusted her, but he didn't.

He said he believed in her ability, but how could any sane man believe what she did?

She'd convinced herself of many far-fetched dreams, and now the demiurgeous intrusions of her life brought reality crashing in.

Knowing Luther would feel betrayed, Gaby couldn't make

herself go. She adjusted the window so it appeared shut. Resting against the brick walls of the alley, she fought with her conscience, hopeful of Luther saying anything to belie the urgency for her escape.

In the next second, she heard Luther barge into the room with Bliss. "Where is she?"

In a teeny, frightened voice, Bliss said, "She's gone."

Two heartbeats later, he exploded. *"God damn it."*

Ann's much calmer voice chastised his language. "Luther. Bliss is upset."

"Where is she going, Bliss?"

"I don't know. Really I don't."

To Ann, Luther said, "I guess this is all the proof I needed, huh?"

"Proof of what?" Mort demanded.

Trying to soothe him, Ann said, "We just got a call about a murder victim, a man mutilated much like Lucy, except his heart and testicles were removed."

Oh shit. Gaby knew it was the same man, the one she'd threatened with just that retribution. Someone had heard, and was setting her up.

Mort now matched Luther's outrage. "You think Gaby was involved?"

"She split, didn't she?" Luther shot right back.

Bliss started crying again. "She went because of *you,* Luther."

"What the fuck does that mean?" Rage vibrated in his every word.

Hiccupping, Bliss said, "She knows you're in trouble and I guess she knew about the dead guy—"

"Of course she did."

"—and she said she can't keep you safe if you arrest her."

"Perfect. Just fucking perfect." Luther laughed without

an ounce of humor. "God save me from Gaby's half-witted delusions of grandeur."

An anvil of hurt crushed Gaby's chest. She gasped with the pain of it, the humiliation. Slumping against the wall, she almost crumbled.

But she couldn't be weak.

No matter what Luther thought of her, he was in trouble. She believed Bliss, believed the authenticity of her portent.

Trying to contain the hurt, Gaby pressed a fist to her heart and staggered away from the alley.

Half-witted, he'd called her. Delusional.

That's what Luther really thought of her, and it mattered, when she'd never before cared what anyone thought.

Or so she'd convinced herself.

Now, she had to admit to her own vulnerability. She'd trusted Luther. Against a lifetime of learned response, she'd opened her soul to him.

God, she *was* stupid. And delusional. He had that right. Only a half-witted fool would believe the two of them had any sort of future.

At a corner pay phone, in plain sight should Luther leave the apartment, she called him.

He answered on the first ring. "Damn you, Gaby, where are you?"

Unemotional, barren of feeling, she said, "Nowhere that you'll ever find me."

"You have to go back to your apartment sometime."

"For what? I don't have a life, Luther. You know that." She didn't explain to him that she could get in and out of her place—and would—with the expertise of a wraith. Luther would never see her. No one would. From now on, she'd be invisible.

"Gaby, you have friends . . ."

"Who think I'm delusional with visions of grandeur. Yeah, I know."

He went silent, then she heard his footsteps as he rushed through the apartment with the realization that she'd overheard him. "Where are you? We can talk. Let me explain—"

"I'm gone, Luther. Stop chasing shadows and listen to me." She drew a pained breath. "It doesn't matter what you think of me. Not anymore."

"You have no idea what I really think."

"Yeah well, like I said. It doesn't matter now. So listen up. I'm only going to say this once. You have to be careful."

"I can take care of myself."

"You sound like me." A small, poignant smile teased her before Gaby realized it and wiped the expression away. "If you hear from anyone who wants to meet you, possibly an anonymous source, you can't go alone. No matter what he says. Do you understand?"

"If you know something I should know—"

"I know a lot of things you should know, but we're no longer cohorts. I'll be in touch." She hung up and faded back into the alley. For tonight at least, Luther had Ann with him. He'd be safe.

Probably.

But as Gaby went through the alley and over a broken wall to cut back to the street, doubts gnawed on her peace of mind. She hadn't made a conscious decision to follow Luther until she found herself near her car with the need for haste prodding her.

It proved a simple thing to drive back to Mort's, wait near the curb, and follow Luther when he left. Gaby kept a distance so he wouldn't notice her, but she never let him out of her sights. He stopped at a grocery store, went inside for about ten minutes, and exited with a bag of items. Next he stopped to put gas in his car.

Impatient, Gaby hung back, watching, noticing the limpness of his clothes, his posture. Frustration and tiredness etched every line of his big, muscular body.

Before an ominous moon, evening breezes scuttled shadows and disrupted Luther's dark blond hair. With one hand he held the gas nozzle to his car, and with the other he tugged at his tie.

She'd wanted to know him—in every way.

She'd wanted to touch him—everywhere.

And he'd ridiculed her to her friends.

Little by little, grating outrage shoved aside the anesthetizing hurt.

How dare he accuse her of insanity?

Gaby snorted to herself. She wished her only issue was a little lunacy. Her life as a crazy person would be much, much easier than that of a paladin.

Luther got back in his car and pulled out to the road.

At a discreet distance, Gaby followed.

No, she wouldn't let anyone hurt him. But she made no promises about what she'd do.

Before long, impecunious surroundings gave way to bourgeois dwellings; tidy homes with immaculate lawns lined the streets, enhanced by compact cars in the driveways and landscaping of flowers and shrubs.

Gaby slowed to a crawl when Luther's turn signal came on. He pulled into a driveway and his car lights went off. Seconds later, she heard the closing of his garage door. A streetlamp illuminated him as he hauled out his grocery bag and strode to the front door of a small Cape-style home.

Keys in hand, he unlocked a wooden door, went inside, and the porch light went on. The door closed.

Gaby sat back and studied his house. Showing his bachelor status, Luther had a well-kept lawn, but lacked flowers of any kind. A tall oak tree grew in the front. A stone walkway led to the porch. At the right side of the house, a tall brick chimney climbed to the top of the roof.

Colonial blue wood siding and cottage windows with black shutters added agrestic charm.

It was a beautiful home. A *real* home.

Longing and regret lacerated the last fragile thread of Gaby's temper. As silent as the breeze, she opened her car door and slunk out.

She'd peer in the windows, that's all. Nothing more. Not right now.

Avoiding the streetlamp's glow, she dashed across the street and onto the cushiony lawn. Thanks to the settling of dew, she could *smell* the friggin' grass.

Starved for any taste of normalcy, she paused to stroke the rough bark of the towering tree and let her lungs drink in the fresh air. Somewhere nearby, a cricket chirped.

Her eyes closed, her heart ached—

"Spying on me?"

Gaby struck without thought. The heel of her palm came up with killing force. Quick reflexes saved Luther from a broken nose, or worse. Instead, her palm clipped his chin, snapping his head back.

Appalled, she stifled the next automatic move. "Luther!" Well damn. She was pissed, yeah, but she didn't want to damage him.

He didn't fall. He worked his jaw—and the next thing Gaby knew, he had tripped her and that dew-wet grass kissed all along her back. Luther's crushing weight compressed her lungs.

Incensed, he breathed fire against her face, while at the same time, one of his legs shoved with brute force between both of hers.

She wasn't moving much, either by way of objection or defense, but still he caught her wrists in an iron grip and wrested both of her hands high above her head.

His mouth *almost* touching hers, he said, "Answer me, damn it."

For most people, her current position would be alarming. For Gaby, it didn't matter. Not even a little. "You startled me."

His whole big body vibrated with rage, and then he kissed her, hard enough that it wasn't fun.

When he lifted his head, Gaby fried him with a glare. "I wouldn't suggest you try that again."

"Or you'll do what? Stalk me?"

She head-butted him, and the solid thwack even made her see stars.

For a single instant, Luther loosened his grip and slumped over her, giving her the opportunity to twist out from under him.

She shot to her feet.

He rolled to his back, a hand to his forehead.

Now standing over his supine form, Gaby said, "I could destroy you, you arrogant bastard, and *that* is not delusions of grandeur. If you don't believe me, then come on, big boy. Let's go. Right here, right now."

He lay there, a forearm covering his eyes. Even his breathing seemed to still.

Oh hell. "Luther?" Had she knocked him out?

Gaby nudged him with her foot. "Say something, damn it."

He dropped his arm. "What do you want me to say? That I'm sorry? Fine." His gaze bored into hers; his voice softened with rueful sincerity. "I'm sorry."

No! She would not be drawn in so easily. "Get up, damn it."

"To fight with you? No thanks." At his leisure, he propped himself on an elbow. A swelling knot showed on his forehead.

"Why not? Chicken?"

His lips twitched. "You know, if you don't lower your voice, my neighbors will call the police." He looked struck with that possibility. "Or they might call me—since I *am* the police."

Her heartache swelled to impossible proportion. "You think this is funny?"

"I think I'm bewitched. There's a difference." He patted the ground beside him. "Come here, Gaby."

"No."

"Why? You were enjoying the grass." His expression remained impassive. "And the tree."

Oh God. "How do you know that?"

"I could see it on your face." His gaze ranged over her, head to toes and back again. "It's not just danger, or evil, or . . . bad things that transform you. You're like a chameleon, forever changing on me, always unpredictable."

After many vicissitudes of disappointment, she'd had no choice but to change in order to survive. "That's nonsense."

"You're a beautiful woman, Gaby. Not in the typical sense of shallow society standards. You're more striking than that."

"I must've hit your head too hard."

"Even when you alter—"

"Morph?"

"Semantics. But even then, your looks are compelling. And sexy." He patted the grass again. "Now don't be cowardly. Accept the compliments as truth."

"How can I when you're delusional?"

"Possibly. But I'm trying hard to see things clearly. With you, that's always a challenge." He held up a hand. "Come down here so we can talk more comfortably."

Instead, she took a step back. She didn't trust him in this awkward, sensual mood. "What do we have to talk about anymore?" Far as she was concerned, it had all been said.

"Life," he offered. "And possibilities—for the past and the present and the future—"

She almost kicked him. "There *is no* future."

"For us, you mean? I think you're wrong."

That stymied her, so she addressed his most recent insult. "I am not a coward."

"Not usually, no. But I scare you."

He did. So much. Resistance fading, Gaby said, "The ground is wet."

"And mosquitoes are likely feasting on me in hordes." He sat up, brushed off his arms and the back of his head. "Okay. How about we just sit in the grass, then? You can lean against the tree. What do you think?"

Gaby couldn't get herself to move. Filled with skepticism, she asked, "What are you sorry about?"

"A lot of things. Let's start with I'm sorry for being a cop, and therefore being bound to certain types of conduct and practices."

"Meaning the edicts that would have you arrest anyone suspicious."

"Yes."

"You think I'm suspicious."

"Tell me what really happened, and then I'll decide."

Putting her chin in the air, she said, "Fine." She dropped down to sit yoga-style and leaned her back against the tree. "I hear the insects."

"They're hungry little bastards." One finger moved up her arm. "And you're tasty."

Gaby snatched her arm away. "Some deranged asshole hurt Marie."

"But he wasn't the guy we want?"

"No. Just a cretin with an abusive streak."

Luther didn't question her authority on that. "How badly did he hurt her?"

Feelings, visions, demitted her cloak of bravado. "It was awful, Luther," she whispered. "He knocked out one of her teeth, beat on her, and . . ." Her throat hurt, and it seemed impossible to swallow. Gaby touched the choker Luther had given her, the choker she never removed, as if that could relieve the restriction. "He burned her with his cigarette. Twice."

Comforting, lending strength, Luther's hand rested on her thigh. "And you being a champion of all the little people, delivered your unique form of retribution?"

Her muscles tightened all over again. "Mock me all you want. I don't care."

"Actually, that was my asinine way of accepting you for who you are. You are a champion, Gaby. A defender. You know and care about Marie, but you'd have done the same for anyone you considered an underdog. I know that."

"Well, whatever you want to call it, I pulverized him."

"Describe pulverize, please."

"His arm was broken beneath his elbow."

"You're sure?"

"The bone was sticking out."

Luther made a face. "Definitely broken."

"When I finished with him, he was pretty bloodied and battered. I only stopped because he couldn't fight anymore. But before I left him, I told him that if he ever again hurt anyone to get his jollies, I'd cut out his heart and remove his balls."

Luther winced. "But you didn't kill him."

"No, I didn't." She picked at a sweet blade of grass, brought it to her mouth. "There were a lot of people there. Jimbo, the hookers, shop owners, renters. Any spectacle is entertaining."

"What happened to the guy?"

"Jimbo had a friend take him home where we both assumed he'd have someone take him to the hospital."

"And you think it's possible that our guy got to him instead, and killed him to set you up?"

Dropping back against the rough tree trunk, Gaby shook her head. "I think he killed him because he gets his rocks off that way. Setting me up is just a bonus."

While contemplating that, Luther began stroking the bare skin of her leg, over her knee, higher on her thigh. "You're especially sensitive about anyone hurting women, aren't you?"

"Or kids."

Using his hold on her knee for leverage, Luther sat up, moved closer. Whenever he touched her, the size of his hands struck her. He was a large man all over—a large, capable man who helped society without walking the fine line between corruption and morality.

He cupped her face, making her feel small, fragile.

"Tell me, Gaby. Is that because, at some point in your life, someone hurt you?"

Chapter 15

Luther saw the memories slipping through her thoughts, and he saw her reticence to share with him. He'd hurt her with his careless words, and now he'd have to make things right.

If he could.

"Gaby?" Catching the edge of her chin, he brought her face around. "Will you forgive me for losing my temper and saying things I didn't mean?"

In the most relevant show of vulnerability he'd ever witnessed from Gaby, she avoided his gaze.

The moonlight limned her features. Somewhere nearby, an owl hooted. It was a romantic night—but with Gaby, that'd mean very little.

She glanced back at him. "Are you sure you didn't mean them?"

"Positive. It's just that I'm human, and sometimes prone to the same failings as any other man. I get pissed, and idiotic garbage spews from my mouth. It's just venting, honey, not my real feelings."

Gaby frowned. "So what are your real feelings? And be honest. I can take it."

He cupped her chin again. "I think you're one of the most intelligent women I've ever met."

"Yeah right." She made a sound of disdain. "Did you forget my lack of education?"

"With you, it doesn't matter. You're smart, sharp, perceptive, and savvy. And for all your lack of formal schooling, you have something better. You have street smarts."

"So then why were you so pissed?"

Luther searched for the right words to help her understand. Gaby was smart, but she lacked the social skills that would enable her to understand the give and take, the ups and downs, of a relationship.

"I get insulted when you want to protect me, just as any six-foot, three-inch tall man would be. I lashed out—but I didn't mean it."

"So you know I could kick your ass?"

Luther stalled. Damn it, she always had to push him, but for once, it didn't infuriate him so much as exasperate him. Trying for judicious neutrality, he said, "I know you're exceptionally well trained in fighting. And that's another question—who trained you?"

She shook her head in pity. "Poor Luther. You persist in trying to find logical explanations for every facet of my being."

"Logic is good."

"Sure. But it doesn't apply to me, because no one trained me. I just know what to do and when to do it. Don't ask me how I know, though."

If she lacked formal training, then had a lifestyle of abuse fashioned her reflexes? He hated to think so, but . . . "And my other question?"

When she started playing with the grass again, Luther forced her to meet his gaze. He felt a fine tension in her that hadn't been there moments before.

As gentle as he could be, he said, "You spent a lot of time in the foster care system. Not everyone is in it to help kids in need. And you had special concerns . . ."

"Guess you just answered you own question, huh?"

Hearing her say it devastated Luther. The thought of anyone hurting a child, but especially someone as sensitive as Gaby, made him want to rail against the world and all the injustices.

Uneasy, she chafed her arms and frowned. Somehow Luther knew it wasn't the subject matter that affected her—but something extraneous, something unforeseen and exigent.

Reacting to her shift of demeanor, Luther went on alert. "What's wrong?"

In a voice unrecognizable, she whispered, "I feel sick."

Praying for a mundane cause, Luther asked, "Have you eaten?"

"No . . . but that's not it." She went to her feet in one swift, lithe movement, and turned a circle, seeking everywhere. "Something's wrong."

With the fine hairs on his nape at attention, Luther stood. "Tell me what you're feeling Gaby."

"Shhh. Let me think." She stepped away from him, into the longest fingers of a streetlamp, and he saw her features, watched them sharpening, her muscles coiling.

She fascinated him, and she scared him. "Gaby . . ."

She took two steps toward the street—and a bedraggled boy appeared. He limped, crying, coming toward them.

Gaby poised for attack.

"What the hell?" Incomprehension smothered Luther's unease. "Gaby, what are you doing?"

"It's him."

The kid's clothes were torn, his arms wrapped around himself. Luther could hear him sniffling. "Listen to me, Gaby," he said, trying to reach her while she grew more remote.

Before his eyes, she swelled with purpose, with depredatory intent. The air around them crackled with impending disaster.

"He's a kid, Gaby."

"No, she's not."

"She?" Luther looked into Gaby's eyes—and saw a great void of emotion. It was as if she didn't see him, didn't see the kid, but saw something, someone, altogether different.

Spooked, he tried to take Gaby's arm, and she shook him off so easily, his alarm escalated. He didn't want to hurt her.

But he didn't want her to hurt the kid either. "Gaby, stop."

Instead, the kid stopped. And contrary to his abused appearance, he . . . smiled.

Caught up in a bizarre dream, *Gaby's dream*, Luther faltered—and something stuck him in the neck. Not the bite of an insect, he knew, but not a knife blade either.

He twisted around only to see an elderly gentleman stepping back out of reach. Everything blurred.

Oh fuck.

Gaby had known, had seen it all, but he hadn't trusted her. *Fool.*

His knees gave out and he fell into a black abyss.

The last thing he heard was Gaby whispering his name.

Blind with the sight, Gaby kicked out at the man who'd just assaulted Luther, and sent him to his back. Certain she'd broken

a rib or two, she turned back to the boy, and an old lady jabbed her in the back with a needle. The odd sensation of a foreign substance filtered into her bloodstream, burning like fire, ravaging her senses.

Gaby snapped her elbow back into the woman's face. Blood splayed, bone crunched, and the woman dropped in a heap with a broken nose, maybe more.

Moments slithered away. Gaby turned a circle, watching the man, the woman, and the kid in turn. The drug attacked her omniscient sagacity, slowing her movements, her thoughts.

And the kid said, "Settle down, whore, or we'll cut his throat and leave him where he is to bleed to death."

Unwilling to risk that outcome, Gaby gave up.

"Put your hands behind your back."

Even disoriented with drugs, her nature rebelled. "I can't."

The woman, spewing blood and vitriol alike, jammed another needle into her, then again and again, more for spite than anything else since she'd emptied the hypodermic on the first stab.

Her vision gave way to shadows, but her hearing remained acute.

"Stop it, you moron. I want her alive."

"But, Oren—"

"Shut up and get the car."

Fear for Luther left Gaby malleable; the drug distorted everything. Cruel hands half-dragged her to a car and shoved her into a backseat. Luther's heavy frame landed against her.

And then, as the car drove away, a great black void swallowed her whole.

❦

Oren danced in his seat. "You see how I got both of them so easily? It takes superior cunning and great planning—something you both lack—to gain such great rewards. Maybe now, as my co-horts, you'll recognize my superiority."

Aunt Dory sniffled and snuffled in a nauseating display. "But she broke my nose," she complained in a nasal whine.

Seeing her bleed everywhere, Oren felt like slapping her. "Stupid bitch. I told you to watch her, to stay out of her reach. It's your own fault for being fat and stupid."

Uncle Myer cleared his throat. "Dory is slow, but it was more that the woman is so fast. Faster than anyone I've ever seen."

"Not fast enough for me." He twisted to look at her in the backseat. The big cop was out cold, boneless, defenseless. His head slumped against the passenger door.

But the woman . . . She remained more upright than otherwise, and her eyes hadn't closed. They were the clearest blue, unseeing, unmoving. But looking right at Oren.

A shiver of concern scraped down his nape. Feeling al-most . . . obeisant, he stared back. "She has the eeriest eyes I've ever seen." Using caution, Oren waved a hand in front of her face. "She doesn't blink, but I can almost swear she still has cognitive ability. It's as if she's looking right at me, even comprehending what I say."

Aunt Dory wailed in new terror. "She's a demon, Oren. That's why she's so fast. Please, let's just cut her throat and dump her here. Right now."

Animus cut through the layers of Oren's generous nature. He stared at Dory with contempt. "Because of your pusilla-nimity, you want me to leave that much evidence behind? Must you always prove your stupidity?"

Aunt Dory snuffled. "Pusi what?"

Ignorant fool. "Oh, just . . . shut up." Oren gave his atten-tion back to the woman. He was invincible, he knew that now. If she was a demon, well then, she'd be the perfect adversary for him. He needed someone worthy of his ability. Maybe she'd be the one.

Look at all he'd done so far, all with nary a glance of suspicion cast his way. Why, he could cut Dory and Myer's throats and no one would ever know.

More to himself than his relatives, Oren said, "My indomitable intelligence and keen understanding surpass the feeble effort of law enforcement. I can do just as I please—even to a demon whore."

Uncle Myer glanced in the rearview mirror and almost caused a wreck. While trying to get the car steady again, he shouted, "Oh dear God, she's smiling! She's smiling!"

Dory screamed loud enough to pierce Oren's eardrums.

Startled, Oren again looked over the seat at the woman, and saw her expression hadn't changed one iota. Incensed beyond measure, he clouted Uncle Myer, chastising him for inciting a panic.

"She's drugged, you buffoon. How can she smile?"

"I swear she did!" Myer insisted. "Jesus, God Almighty, Oren, I have a real bad feeling about this. Real bad. I don't want anything to do with her."

He sat between two fools, unworthy of his time or effort. "You're both gutless recreants. If she frightens you so, then fine, she'll be my treat, and mine alone."

"Thank you, Oren."

"But they're a package deal. You don't get the man either. I have plans to use him in order to break her down." He laughed, imagining the scene, her helpless reaction. Oh yes, it'd be grand. Very grand. "Maybe I'll even show you how it should be done."

Aunt Dory and Uncle Myer stayed silent.

And although Oren spoke with great élan, he kept a wary eye on the woman for the remainder of the drive.

Pinpricks pierced Gaby's brain by the thousands, little by little dissipating the drug-induced fog. She kept her head hanging, her hands loose.

Thanks to her omniscient replenishment, she'd never lost consciousness, only the ability to move or react. Her mind stayed sharp and she'd had plenty of time to devise her counterattack against evil's little minion.

Throughout her years she'd known a lot of assholes, but Oren surpassed others in depravity. Luther was threatened, so this kill would be easier than most.

Rough ropes bound her wrists to wooden chair arms. Another rope cut across her throat, lodged just beneath her choker, and yet another around her waist.

But her legs were unbound, and that would prove to be Oren's downfall.

Showing no obvious signs of awareness, Gaby flexed her muscles, testing her agility, ensuring her limbs didn't still sleep.

In the background, she heard Oren talking, and she heard the clink of instruments being laid on the table.

Gaby lifted her head and did a quick assessment of the tableau of torture set before her. Knifes, clamps, saws, pliers, electrical cords, and more, all created a shining array of intent.

At the opposite end of a small, square wooden table, Luther had been bound in a similar fashion, but without the cord around his throat. Still unconscious, thank God.

He didn't need to see what would happen.

In the corner, huddled together in fear, were the two idiots who'd accosted them. The woman's grotesquely swollen nose gave testament to Gaby's accuracy. The old man held his ribs.

They, Gaby realized, were astute enough to know the error in trying to take her prisoner.

Someone had stuck her knife, tip first, into the wood in the middle of the table, next to Luther's gun. When Gaby got her hands on her knife, they'd realize the folly of that taunt.

Giggling, Oren fingered a pair of steel clippers. "I hope they awaken soon. I'm anxious to get started."

"I'm awake now, asshole."

Oren jerked around so fast, he stumbled. His mouth formed an absurd "o" of surprise—but his eyes . . . his eyes held fear and his brow revealed the cold sweat of a coward.

The woman wailed again.

"Shut up," Gaby told her. She didn't raise her voice, didn't even sound particularly insistent. But she looked at the woman, and the simmering rage in her unequivocal stare encouraged the woman to clamp her lips together.

The man pressed to the wall, wild-eyed and ready to abscond at the next provocation.

Pointing at his relatives, Oren said, "Both of you, be still." He snapped the clippers down onto the table and strode toward Gaby. "No one orders my aunt around except me."

Gaby leaned as far forward as the rope allowed. "I'm going to kill your aunt, Oren. I'm going to slice open her fat throat and watch her blood spill out. And then I'm going to get your uncle, too."

"Shut up!"

"Just as you cut off that abusive jerk's jewels, I'll remove your uncle's. The skin there is thin, easily separated. I won't even have to—"

Oren slapped her. "Shut up!"

Gaby's head barely moved. Conjuring the deepest necromancy into her appearance, she stared up at Oren, and made a promise. "You I'll kill last, and by then, you'll be pleading with me like the pathetic little boy you pretend to be."

Losing composure, Oren screamed in frustration and slapped her again, and again.

Then he bolted back, breathing hard, insane and irrational. The sting in Gaby's cheek only made her more determined. She relished the proof of life—a reason to fight, and win. At all costs.

She narrowed her eyes. "You will beg, Oren. You will cry and beg and whimper. But it won't do you a bit of good."

Visibly rattled, Oren snatched up the clippers and moved toward Luther.

Gaby's heart clenched. "Anything you do to him," she warned, "I'll do to you tenfold." She looked at the older couple frozen in horror. "And to them."

The man went white, his jaws flapping in horror. The woman fainted dead away, and fell off her stool to hit the floor, unheeded, in dreggy abundance. Her broken nose oozed blood again.

Oren faltered. Face screwing up, he turned to taunt Gaby with false bravado. "How can you do anything, you ignorant bitch? You can't even move. You're bound securely. I saw to that myself."

"I know you did."

His back snapped straight. "You don't know anything!"

Gaby fashioned her lips into a spiteful sneer. "Oh, but I do."

Oren straightened. "Impossible."

"Nothing is impossible, not for me. You think you're invincible? You think you're my match? Not even close, Oren. And I'll prove it—very soon."

The man whispered, "You were looking at us. In the car, I mean. You were, weren't you?"

Gaby didn't take her attention from Oren. He stood far too close to Luther with those lethal clippers in his hand, clippers strong enough to cut through flesh and bone.

"Because of that foul drug, I couldn't speak. But yeah, I heard every word, saw every movement." And to prove it, even though she didn't look his way, she said, "Your wife is coming to. Keep her quiet, or I will."

He jumped to the floor, shushing the woman's moans of confusion and fear.

Gaby tipped her head at Oren's veiled surprise. "Oh, Oren." She shook her head, ignoring the rope that rasped the soft flesh of her throat. "I know you think yourself superior in a sick, perverted way, but the truth is, you're so fucked up in your head, you put other psychopaths to shame."

Showing his teeth in a grimace, Oren bunched his shoulders. "I am *not* a psychopath."

"Ah, come on, Oren. You're the definition." If Oren snapped and started hurting anyone, Gaby wanted the anger directed at her—not Luther. She'd do whatever she could to ensure that end. "Personality disorder, manifested in aggression. Check. Amoral, antisocial, and depraved. Check."

She needed Oren closer to her. Very close. "Confused and alone?" Gaby snorted. "I've never seen anyone more confused. The mental ward would have a field day with a specimen like you."

Trembling with hatred, Oren stared at her. "You're wrong."

The mockery cut deep, Gaby could see that. "And you know, Oren, that's all you are, really—just one more pathetic, lamentable specimen among all the lame little mongrels of society. I see you for what you are—and to me, to the real world, you're as insignificant as a gnat."

Ready to come unglued, Oren paced away—going closer to Luther. Gaby prepared herself, willing to break her own bones to escape the bonds if it proved necessary to protect Luther.

But at the last moment, Oren paused. More composed, he turned back to her. He laid aside the clippers, and picked up Gaby's knife.

"Careful," Gaby taunted him. "That's a real weapon, for a *real* woman."

Oren's head snapped up.

"What? You're surprised I know? I already told you, I see right through your masquerade."

"No."

"You thought you fooled people?" She laughed, further riling him. "Now put down that knife. It's not meant for a fucked up mental case who can't decide on her own sexuality."

That did it. Oren gave a banshee scream of rage and charged Gaby with the knife raised high in a clenched fist.

Finally. Gaby flattened her feet, clenched her knees, and just as Oren reached her, she kicked up and caught the maniac in the jaw.

Like the frail female she was, Oren pitched to the side and landed hard on the floor with a moan. Gaby's knife clattered free, and skid a few feet away.

Oren's uncle started shouting for Oren to get up, but it wouldn't happen. Not now.

The aunt screamed and screamed.

Gaby stood the best she could, walked over to Oren, and with all the strength in her body, she stomped her wrist. The blow was hard enough to break all the delicate bones.

Oren cried out, tried to curl in on himself, and Gaby stomped the other arm, shattering an elbow.

The shrieks escalated to a cacophony of human terror from multiple sources.

It affected Gaby not a whit.

But it did cause Luther to stir. He was the type of man that, even drugged, couldn't be immune to the panicked cries of humanity.

He twitched, mumbled quietly to himself.

Well hell. Not yet, Gaby prayed. Rushing now, she pivoted and slammed the chair into the wall, nearly rattling her brain loose. The chair held so she did it again, then once more. The force of the repetitive impacts would leave her spine and limbs bruised, but that beat the alternative. At last, with one more crash to the wall, the wooden seat and arms detached, still tied to her, but no longer hindering her.

Oh yeah. Gaby looked down at the wooden chair arms strapped to her from elbow to wrist. This would work. The wood served as the perfect blunt weapon.

She looked up at the aunt and uncle—and could smell their fear.

"No!"

"Yes." With the uncle trying his best to flee, Gaby clubbed him in the head. He buckled, and fell to the dirty floor, out cold.

The aunt was too scared to move, and Gaby whacked her right across the forehead.

They were now unconscious, but that didn't suffice. Not by a long shot.

None of them could leave here. Not ever. She wouldn't trust the faulty judicial system to keep them away from gentler, more innocent society.

Luther moaned, tried to lift his head but couldn't. "Gaby . . ."

Damn. He needed her, but she couldn't go to him, not yet.

Urgency propelled Gaby to the concrete wall of the basement. In furious haste, she slammed her back against it, further splintering the broken pieces of the chair. With the rope on her throat loosened, she cracked the wooden arms against the wall until the wood broke away.

Please, Gaby prayed, *let me finish this before Luther awakens. Please don't make this one more wall between us.* Knowing what had to be done, Gabe freed up the use of her hands. She needed to be able to flex her fingers.

She had to pull a trigger.

Groaning and grunting with pain, both arms broken and useless, Oren struggled into a sitting position. Blood oozed from his lip, and his jaw swelled enough that Gaby figured she'd broken it.

He looked at Gaby's knife lying on the floor a few feet away.

"I don't think so," Gaby told him. Even knowing Oren couldn't lift it, not with his smashed arms, she picked up the knife. It felt good in her hands—but she couldn't use it. Not for this.

In a pain-filled mumble, Oren said, "You *are* a demon."

"Yeah, I am. And you're too stupid to accept that you're a young lady, not a boy. What is it, Oren? A mean mommy? An abusive daddy? What happened to fuck you up so bad?"

"I was meant to be a man, that's all. Women are only useless whores. All of them."

Gaby shook her head. "You're wrong, Oren."

"My mother was a whore," he spat. "After she died, my father had whores over all the time. Mean whores."

"They were cruel to you?"

"What do you care?"

She cared. She hated to see society feasting on itself. Unfortunately, it happened all too often. The wicked begat more wickedness, and the cycle never ended.

"I'm *omnipotent*," Oren bragged, splaying blood her way. The outburst depleted him, and he swayed, eyes drooping. "I'm powerful. Powerful enough that I decided to be a male years ago, right after I killed my father. No one knew. No one even suspected me." His laugh sounded pained. "I fooled everyone."

"You didn't fool me."

"You're still calling me Oren," he pointed out, with absurd, giddy delight. "You're calling me by my male name."

"Consider it a small concession to your insanity. I feel a little bit sorry for the criminally deranged." Picking up Luther's gun, Gaby took aim. "Unfortunately, you were too cruel to satisfy your sick yearnings with harmless fantasy, and that makes you too evil . . . to live."

Seeing that barrel pointed at his chest, Oren blinked hard and fast. "No wait."

But she couldn't. Luther might awaken at any moment. "Sorry, time's up."

"Please!" Panicked, Oren again tried to stand, but his crushed arms offered no leverage, and he fell back down. "Please, no."

Gaby drew in a breath. She took no pleasure in saying, "Told you that you'd beg."

Tears fell. Blood gurgled from his mouth. *"Please."*

With deadly accuracy, Gaby shot Oren in the heart.

The force of the gunshot drove him to his back again. His mangled arms flailed wide. He whined, gargled . . . and died.

The aunt and uncle hadn't moved. Things needed to look authentic, believable, so Gaby walked back to the table. With one quick flick of the razor-sharp blade on her knife, she freed Luther's hands from the restraints. The tight bindings had chafed his skin, leaving behind angry red welts—and destroying any regrets Gaby might have felt with her decision.

After throwing his restraints toward the center of the room to mingle with her own, Gaby curved Luther's left hand around the knife hilt. She squeezed his fingers to imprint his identity. His natural reflexes kept the knife lax in his hold.

Next she put his gun into his right hand. As testament to the core of Luther's nature as a lawman, he grasped it on his own. Even unconscious, he was one with the weapon.

Standing behind Luther, Gaby took aim, and from that distance, shot the aunt in the head, the uncle in the throat. By ensuring her and Luther's safety, an instantaneous lifting of her rage-fueled intuition left her depleted. With the threat from evil ones obliterated, she'd completed her calling.

Gaby knew that she'd done the right thing, moral or not, but that wouldn't help her in a world of legality.

Roused by the blasts of gunfire, Luther mumbled again, his voice stronger this time, and his gun hand flinched, lifted, dropped back to rest on the tabletop. To finish her chore, Gaby went to her knees beside him, put her head on his thigh, and rested.

She'd protected Luther, but at what cost?

Would he believe the setup? Or would this be the final straw in testing his gullibility?

A short time later, Luther came to with alacrity. He lurched into defensive mode, and Gaby hoped he wouldn't drop the knife and slice her throat by accident. She kept very still, ready to play her part.

Ready to do whatever necessary to insulate Luther from the ugliness of her purpose in life.

Chapter 16

Throbbing pain jerked Luther from his drugged slumber. A subconscious urgency prodded him to open his eyes, but at first, he saw only a great blur. His gun hand raised and at the ready, he willed himself to full awareness.

Little by little the fogginess cleared, showing him foreign surroundings.

What the hell?

He started to lift his other hand, felt a heavy knife falling, and found himself fumbling with two weapons, a knife and his gun.

He had no recollection of drawing either one.

"Jesus." Shaking his head to clear it didn't help much; he didn't understand any of this.

What had happened?

The last thing he recalled was sitting on the grass in front of his house with Gaby. He'd wanted to make love to her, had planned to work around to exactly that.

Now he sat in the shadowed, dank darkness of a basement, and a foul stench—the fetor of death—burned his nostrils on every breath.

A scene of utter carnage surrounded him. Blood sprayed the walls. Brain matter, gore, covered an area of the floor.

In the middle of it all . . . a dead boy? He wasn't sure of the age or sex, only that, given the lifelessness of the body, whoever it was had expired. Farther away, an older couple lay in tangled, bloody demise.

Luther looked at the gun in his hand. His head pounded as memories intruded, and he squeezed his eyes shut.

This was the room Bliss had described to him, but how had he gotten here? Manacles hung from the wall, nooses from the ceiling. Makeshift cages held restraints of all kinds; it didn't take great intuitiveness to know that innocent people had suffered great and immeasurable pain here.

Where was Gaby? What had happened to her? His chest hurt and his guts cramped. No, he wouldn't think the worst.

He wouldn't. He had to figure this out, and fast.

Hearing nothing and no one, but unsure of any other threats, Luther started to stand. A warm weight shifted against his leg. He glanced down—and found Gaby slumped beside him.

"Oh my God."

When her head lolled to the side, his heart threatened to burst. More scared than he'd ever been, he put aside the weapons and cupped her shoulders. "Gaby?"

She mumbled, but didn't awaken.

Luther shook her. "Gaby!"

Sliding off the chair to his knees, he gently laid her onto the floor and checked her over for wounds. Her arms were badly bruised, and a nasty rope burn encircled her pale throat.

His muscles coiled in fury. "Fuckers. I'll kill them all."

Drawing a ragged breath, his hands trembling, he smoothed back her hair. "Honey, talk to me, please."

Her eyes opened.

To Luther's astute gaze, they appeared clear, bright with perspicacity. She frowned. "Luther?"

He shoved aside his suspicions to help her into a sitting position. "Are you all right?"

With sluggish inelegance, she put a hand to her head and looked around.

Eyes narrowed, Luther watched her. She showed no signs of shock at the tableau of horror. No signs of shock.

Eyes direct, voice unshaken, she turned to him and said, "My God, Luther."

He swallowed hard. "I know."

Her beautiful blues didn't blink. "It's amazing."

"It is?"

"Well, yes. Look at what you did."

He drew back, uncertain, confused, no memory of doing . . . anything.

Gaby wrapped her arms around him. "You killed them all, and you saved us. The city should give you a commendation or something." Her warm breath touched his neck. "It's over, Luther. Finally, it's over."

❦

After Luther made a call, it didn't take long for authorities to arrive. They swarmed the place, filling the upscale community with flashing lights and a flood of officials. Affluent neighbors came out to their porches, disgruntled by the disturbance to their peaceful and prosperous lives.

As more uniformed men shoved past her, Gaby asked, "Who the hell are all these people?"

"Detectives, crime scene technicians, medical examiner,

photographers . . ." Luther shrugged. "It takes a lot of people to lock down a crime scene and gather the evidence the right way."

"Seems like a lot of ballyhoo to me when it's already clear what happened."

His gaze sharpened on her. "And that is?"

Gaby shrugged. "Sick freaks grabbed us, you killed them all, you're a hero—end of story."

Luther didn't buy that. He ran a hand over his head, a little pained, a lot disgusted. Hands on his hips, he turned away from her to stare at the bodies. "You were right."

"About what?"

"He's not a boy."

"Well, duh." Gaby shook her head. "He's not even a he."

"How did you know?" Luther flexed his jaw in frustration. "You were so certain about it, when no one else knew. So how did *you* know?"

Time to tread carefully. Gaby tried for a look of indifference. "He's the same kid I saw in my area way back when, that's how."

"Before Lucy was taken?"

"Yeah. You remember. You asked me why I was chasing him, and I told you then that I didn't know for sure."

"But you knew that he—strike that—*she* was suspect even then?"

Gaby didn't like where the questions were leading. "He/she looked too clean-cut and uppity to be hanging out in my neck of the woods, that's all. I just sensed that something was off."

"And as always, you were right."

"Lucky me." She, too, glanced at the body. "You know," she said softly, "she prefers to be addressed as he."

"*He* is dead, so what does it matter what he prefers?"

It didn't, not really. But still . . . She glared at him for confusing her more. "Look, Luther, it was him and his two twisted relatives there—"

"How do you know they're relatives?"

Good grief. Would he grab on to her every word trying to find plot holes?

Trying for a patience she didn't possess, Gaby inhaled. "Okay, here's how it went down. Are you paying attention?"

Luther stiffened. "Just spit it out."

"They—the warped relatives—stuck you with the drug before they got to me, so you probably don't remember as much as I do. But before that, before they drugged me, I heard a lot. The lady who likes to impersonate a boy is called Oren, and the other two are his aunt and uncle."

"You actually have memory of all that?"

"I guess you don't, huh?" Gaby patted his arm in bogus sympathy. Poor Luther, he hated the loss of details, his weak grasp on the happenings. "The uncle injected you first. You got in one good hit that knocked him down, but it was too late—the drug was already in you and doing its thing. While I was moving to help you, the loony aunt stuck me, not just once, but a bunch of times."

Luther paled. "Show me."

Why not? Gaby turned and lifted her shirt.

"Jesus, Gaby." Gentle fingertips smoothed over her skin. "She did a number on you."

"Yeah. But I clocked the bitch in the nose, which is how it got broken. I'd have done more, but then I passed out and the rest is as much a mystery to me as it is to you." She lowered her shirt again.

"You need to be checked."

"Forget that, cop. I'm fine."

Concern warmed his face. "It's important that we both go—"

"Ha." Gaby shoved away his hands. "You might have to follow orders, but I don't." To keep him from getting pissed again, Gaby changed the subject. "Do you realize that this room is exactly as Bliss described it?"

Sickened by it all, Luther nodded. "I imagine all dens of torture look similar. It's a grisly sight." His gaze locked on hers. "You don't seem bothered by it though."

Gaby forced a shudder. "Yeah, it's creepy." She slugged him in the shoulder. "Thank God you played hero and took care of them, huh? If it wasn't for you, we'd probably both be—"

Luther squashed a finger over her lips. "No." He lightened his touch, caressed her lips. "Save it, okay?"

"Um . . . what does that mean?" Gaby prayed that he wouldn't start doubting her rendition of things. She wasn't up to full disclosure. Not yet.

Probably not ever.

"You'll have to tell it again at the station. There's no reason to go over it all now."

"Oh."

He looked tender, forbearing, and pained.

How should she interpret all that?

Luther put an arm around her shoulders. "There's no reason for us to stay down here. Let's go get some fresh air."

Because he looked like he needed it, Gaby agreed. "Sure. If that's what you want."

Ann was at the other side of the room with two other detectives. Luther walked over to her. "We'll be out front if anyone needs us."

She surveyed him with a critical eye. "I'd prefer you head on to the hospital to get checked out."

"I'm feeling better by the minute."

"We need to be safe. You can't remember anything, and what if it isn't a drug? What if you have a concussion?"

"I wasn't hit in the head."

"All right, fine." She tried a different tack. "It wouldn't hurt to get a blood sample, just in case the drug is still in your system."

"I guess it can't hurt. I am still sluggish and a little on the queasy side. If you want to line up someone to drive me, I'll go."

"I'll have Sergeant Faulkner take you. If the doc gives you the okay, you can come back then. God knows we're going to be here awhile."

After that agreement, they both looked at Gaby.

She frowned. "What?"

Luther gave her a suspicious once-over. "It's odd, given how I feel, that you don't seem at all adversely affected by the drugs."

So now she recovered too quickly? Nitpicking jerk. "I guess I'm hardy, huh?"

Ann's expression pinched. "Yeah, I'm sure that's it, Gaby." She shared a look with Luther. "Go on outside. The stench in here is enough to try even the hardiest stomach. Sergeant Faulkner will be right with you."

Once they reached the steps, Gaby nudged Luther. "When Ann first got here, she spent a lot of time clinging to you."

"She's a friend, and she knew I could have died. That's all there is to it."

"She's a really touchy-feely friend, isn't she?"

Luther sat with a groan, not giving her concerns much attention. "You were offended by it?"

"No. I know she's got a thing with Morty." She joined him on the top step. The clear, star-studded sky blanketed the area. It amazed Gaby that a night so beautiful could shadow such evil. "From what Ann said, I guess they'll be here for a long time?"

Luther leaned into a post. "Maybe all night. It's important to collect evidence in the proper way. They're hoping to tie the other deaths to this scene. Even in the worst situations, it's good to give victims closure."

"With all that blood and stuff in there, that shouldn't take long."

"They'll get search warrants and go through the whole house." Luther paused. "You know, it's possible they might find more bodies inside."

"They won't," Gaby said, before she thought to censor herself. She made haste to cover her error. "Oren was too cagey for that. I have no doubt he's killed others, but they're dumped somewhere, someplace where they might not ever be found."

Just then, several men brought out the plastic-wrapped corpses to transport to the county morgue.

"It's weird, isn't it?"

Luther watched her through the darkness. "What is?"

"The house is so beautiful—and it hid the basest evil imaginable. If you ask me, they should burn this place to the ground."

He pulled her against him. "I understand one sicko running amok, wreaking havoc on innocent lives. But how the hell do these crazies find each other to conspire together?"

Closing her eyes and resting her head on Luther's hard shoulder, Gaby recited something she'd read long ago while trying to understand her own predilection. "Bloodthirstiness can stay clandestine inside the most trustworthy people, and no one would ever know it's there. Societal teachings and moral principles lock it down and keep it well hidden, but it smolders there, torpid, idle, until the right circumstances call forth the appetite—and serenity is forever shattered."

Luther's mouth touched her temple. "You are a fascinating woman, Gaby."

She was a scared woman, a woman wanting things she was never meant to have. In a mere whisper of sound not intended for Luther's ears, Gaby spoke her deepest thoughts. "If only I'd figured this out in time to save Lucy."

Luther kissed her again. "You did your part, honey. Yours, and mine."

Gaby's eyes widened.

The sergeant stepped out of the house. "Sorry to have kept you waiting. My car's right over here."

Luther stood. "Come on, Gaby. We both have to get checked, repugnant as it seems, so we may as well get it over with."

"I hate hospitals," she told him as she tugged to her feet.

"But you'll have me with you. And that, Gabrielle Cody, can make anything more bearable—if you'll only let it."

Two weeks had passed since Oren and his aunt and uncle were stopped in their deadly occupation of torture; two weeks of mundanity, the tedium melding one hour into another.

Gaby had a lot of decisions to make, but circumstances gave her time aplenty to make them.

Luther, her biggest decision of all, stayed busy with the details of the case, gathering information, and filling out reports.

Accolades for his work were pouring in. Jimbo read the papers daily—a shocking revelation for Gaby—and he kept her informed without being asked. So far the police chief and even the mayor were heralding Luther as a hero. They said his dedication, professionalism, and cool head under pressure had spared the community further, unspeakable crimes.

Cool head under pressure? Gaby snorted. Yeah, being threatened with prolonged torture would qualify as pressure, for sure.

Luckily Luther had endured a drugged sleep through it all.

And she . . . well, she'd only been pressured to dispatch the abominations without Luther being injured, and without him knowing. By all accounts, she'd succeeded.

And so went the banausic nature of her life.

During cooler nights and quiet days, Gaby completed her novel and mailed it anonymously to Mort. In less than a day he'd read it and now he enthused to any and all who'd listen that this was the best Servant graphic novel yet.

Gaby appreciated his praise, just as she appreciated the purgative effect of writing and illustrating this most recent harrowing segment of her duty.

The artistic nature of the work cleared her head, but not her conscience.

As her biggest fan, Morty now had Bliss reading the novels, when she'd never been much of a reader of any kind. There'd been many changes in Bliss's life, and Gaby thought it was time for her to leave the streets. The girl needed a job that didn't involve the flesh trade.

Jimbo wouldn't like it, but she and Jimbo resided in strained, semi-respectful peace, and he wouldn't want to disrupt that, not for one hooker.

Bored with herself, Gaby strode to her window and looked out at the night. In such a short time, the weather had changed. Heat still ruled the days, but evening temperatures were more comfortable.

Maybe tonight she'd sleep.

Maybe tonight she'd make a decision—the right decision— and remove herself from Luther's life.

Turning away from the window, she went into her meager bathroom, washed up, and brushed her teeth. Wearing a tank top and panties, she headed for bed. She had one knee on the mattress when a disturbance erupted in the hall. Before she could reach her door, a fist pounded on it.

Outraged that anyone would dare, Gaby crossed the room with a stomping, barefoot stride. "Who is it?"

"Open up, Gaby. *Right now*."

Luther? Had something happened? Jerking the door open, and then seeing him whole and unharmed, Gaby prepared to blast him with her distemper.

Then she noted Bliss fretting behind him, and wide-eyed Mort behind her. Seeing her in her underwear, Mort gave her a surprised once-over. Bliss gave her a look of apology. For what?

"What the hell's going on?"

"No more." With that cryptic roar, Luther shoved his way past her attempts at blocking him, and kicked her door with unnecessary force. It didn't quite shut. Being reinforced made it heavier than Luther had anticipated and he turned with a dark scowl to examine her door.

Gaby gaped at him. He was . . . in her room!

No one got into her room. It was her private sanctum, the one place she could let down her defenses. Here, the signs of her extreme defense toward society, along with her aptitude for writing and illustrating, were evidenced.

In a near panic, Gaby scoured her room. The tools she used for her graphic novels were stored away. But the locks on her bathroom door were obvious to the naked eye. And if Luther looked, as detectives often did, he'd find not only her knife but a gun as well.

"What the hell is this door made of? Solid steel?" He lifted a hand to appraise her many locks.

Apprehension nearly took her breath, making speech strained. "What. Do you think. You're doing?"

Giving up on the door, Luther transferred his scowl to her. "You're thinking of running out on me again. And damn it, I've had enough of that." His finger pointed, almost touching her chest. "I have my hands full wrapping up this case, fending off bloodthirsty reporters, and thanks to you, I've also got half the city wanting to pat me on the back."

Feeling smaller, more vulnerable than she ever had in her life, Gaby backed up a step. She kept her gaze glued to Luther, unsure what he might he do, or when he might realize the scope of her anomalous existence. "Thanks to me?" Being surrounded by her own damning evidence left her near to panting. "What do I have to do with anything?"

Luther propped his hands on his hips and surveyed her with a critical eye. Voice less caustic, but still inflexible, he said, "This is unnecessary, you know."

A knock sounded on her door, and he yelled, "Not now."

Through the door, Bliss said, "But Luther—"

"I'm handling it."

"It?" Gaby asked. And what was unnecessary?

"You." Luther gestured at her room. "This."

Her heart threatened to punch through her rib cage. "You should get out. Now. While you still can."

He advanced on her, and by sheer instinct, Gaby reacted, throwing a kick that he blocked, an elbow that he dodged.

She found herself tumbled onto her bed, pinned down, and . . . kissed. And, oh God, she felt starved for it, for him—even knowing she should have already left the area.

She jerked her head to the side, and Luther brought it back around.

"Settle down, Gaby." He touched his nose to hers. "I have something to tell you."

Uh-oh. She didn't like the sound of that at all. "What?"

"I'm going to keep your secret."

Alarm skittered all along her nerve endings. "What secret?"

He ignored that to trace her choker with one finger. "You're going to have to learn to trust me, you know."

How could she? He didn't realize how she'd fabricated everything just to suit her purpose. She'd protected herself, and lied to him in the bargain.

Luther's gaze met hers. "It's not always easy for me, Gaby. It goes against the grain to be drawn into falsehoods." Luther's earnest expression never wavered. "I'm not a liar, and even a lie of omission eats at me. But I understand it. Hell, if I hadn't been so busy trying to catch maniacs, I probably would have seen it sooner. But I see it now."

Oh God, oh God. She shook her head, words beyond her.

Luther held her face in a gentle hold. "I see this, your apartment. And I see your life, what you've done and why and what you'll still have to do. And most of all, I see *you*."

Fear, hope, choked her. Around the tears that tried to escape, Gaby said, "You're nuts."

He had to be. If he saw the real her, he'd want nothing to do with her. He couldn't. He was a law-abiding man, and so much of her life fell outside the law.

One corner of his mouth kicked up in a compassionate smile of acceptance. "It's okay, Gaby. You're an admirable woman, a woman I can like despite your . . . individuality."

She stared at him, saw his grin widen before he said, "And it just so happens that you make me hot as hell, too."

Another tentative knock sounded on her door.

Luther said, "Not yet, Bliss."

Mired in a jumble of foreign emotions, Gaby licked her lips. "Why is Bliss here?"

Reaching down, Luther wedged his hand to the inside of her thigh, opening her legs wider so he could settle between. Then he propped himself on his elbows and stared down at her.

"Well, you know she was dead-on about the basement, right?"

"You believe that now?"

Teasing, he bent to kiss her lips. "You don't?"

She'd always believed. So many things couldn't be explained by science or logic. "I know Bliss has a gift."

"Good. I'm glad we're on the same page for once. Because that's why I'm here."

She didn't understand any of this. "You're here to talk nonsense and molest me?"

He laughed. "Sorry to disappoint you, but no, I won't molest you. I won't have to. We'll be together whether you like it or not."

That bold statement pushed her ridiculous reserve to the back and brought out her truer nature. "If you think to force me, cop, think again."

"Silly." He pushed off the bed, grabbed her hands and hauled her up. "That bed was far too tempting, and I guess it's time for you to talk to Bliss anyway."

"I don't—"

Luther hauled open the heavy door.

Red-faced and worried, Bliss almost fell inside. It was obvious she'd been trying to listen in.

She wiggled her fingers in a half-hearted wave. "Hi, Gaby."

Standing behind her, offering silent support, Mort watched them. And now Ann had joined them, too.

Unsure of herself and the situation, Gaby just waited.

Ann said, "Do you know what you're doing, Luther?"

"For once, yes." He nodded at Bliss. "Tell her."

Looking down at her feet, rounded shoulders hunched,

Bliss sighed. "I see the two of you together, Gaby. Just as Mort and Ann are meant to be, you and Luther are—"

Gaby slammed the door. No. Bliss couldn't possibly know that.

Time stood still while she struggled to reconcile the impossible with a dream.

Luther touched her back. "Take a breath, honey."

"You!" Gaby turned on him. "Are you out of your fucking mind?"

"Probably, but it doesn't change anything."

It hurt. More than anything ever had, it hurt. Gaby shook her head.

"I know you care about me. By now you have to know that I care about you. And Gaby? Nothing else matters."

He caught her when she would have turned away. Jerking her into his chest, he reiterated, *"Nothing."*

"That's because you don't know."

He went solemn, serious. "I know I didn't kill Oren or his relatives. I know you protected me. And I know I'm glad to be alive."

Gaby's brain went blank. How could he . . . ?

He swayed her from side to side. "I know that Bliss confirmed what I'd already suspected."

"Oh God, Luther, you should stop now, while you can." If he didn't stop, she might be convinced, and then they could both be doomed.

"I can't. We're an item, Gaby, now and forever." He kissed the top of her head. "It's meant to be."

Desperation clawed at her heart. "Because Bliss said so? You don't even believe in that stuff!" He didn't believe in her.

But . . . he hadn't turned her out for lying about Oren. In fact, he'd almost sounded grateful.

"What can I say, Gaby? You've made a believer of me." Luther set her away from him. "Now, much as I realize you're pretty superhuman—"

Her mind stalled on that description. Not a freak, but . . . superhuman.

"—I'm still just a man, and I'd prefer we ease into the physical part of this relationship little by little. Perhaps tomorrow works for you? I can get out of the station early. What do you say?"

Her brain was still contemplating the odd compliment he'd given. "What are you talking about?"

"I need to make love with you, Gaby." His gaze skimmed down her body, and came back to her face. He inhaled. "But I'm throwing a lot at you all at once, so I'm trying to be noble. I want to give you time. I want you with me every step of the way."

Oh, when it came to the sexual side of their relationship, she was with him. "How much time?"

He smiled. "Tomorrow sounds good to me, after we've had a chance to talk things out, figure out how we're going to do this. But for right now . . . Being this close to you with you dressed like that and a bed right there is testing my control."

The shock of Luther's proposition wore off, and the possibility of acceptance presented itself. Gaby looked at her bed. Did she dare?

Luther took her hand. "What do you say, Gaby? Want to go out to dinner with our friends?"

Their friends.

Just like a normal couple.

Gaby turned her back on Luther, desperate for a clear thought. But from the first, he'd kept her thoughts jumbled and skewed her perspective.

And maybe . . . just maybe, that had been God's plan all

along. Was it possible she needed to learn acceptance? And in acceptance, could she have it all?

It was worth the risk. It had to be.

Keeping her back to him, but unable to keep her heart any longer, Gaby nodded. "Okay, Luther. I'd like that."

And now a special preview of the next book
in the chilling new series by L. L. Foster

SERVANT: The Kindred

Coming soon!

God, please, not now.

For long minutes, what began to feel like an eternity, Gabrielle Cody fought the inevitable. Naked on Luther's king-sized bed, she stretched taut as sweat beaded on her skin and her teeth locked.

The agony grew.

And she fought it.

As her heart buffeted too hard in her chest, she repeatedly fisted her hands, clenching and unclenching them as she grasped the smooth, clean sheets beneath her. Exiguous moonlight snaked through a part in his heavy bedroom drapes, sending a silvery dart to cross the floor and crawl, with painstaking slowness, up the wall.

Clean. Organized. Masculine. Everything about his home, a *real* home, felt nice, smelled nice.

So inappropriate to the likes of her.

That Gaby could hear Luther in the bathroom finishing up

a hot shower was the only salvation, the only measure to fight the staggering call. It dragged at her, commanding acceptance, gnarling her muscles, relentless in its claim on her.

She squeezed her eyes shut and thought of Luther, remembered his pleasure as she'd capitulated to his demands.

Demands to join him, to try for a normal life—to give them, as a couple, a chance.

He was a fool. *She* was a fool for accepting even the slightest possibility of a normal life, a real relationship.

Before excusing himself for the shower he'd smiled at her, thrilled to have her in his home, anticipation bright in his eyes. Luther thought he'd gotten his way. He thought he had Gaby where he wanted her.

Be careful what you wish for.

Another shaft of pain pierced her. It was always this way—the bid to fulfill her duty was a wrenching agony she couldn't fight. Whenever she'd tried, the pain had grown insurmountable.

As it did now.

Sweat trickled down her temple to soak into Luther's pillow. Already she soiled his fine home. If she stayed, she'd turn his entire existence black with depravity.

Her breath caught as the shower turned off. Luther would not expect to find her in his bed. No, he thought she was downstairs, waiting, where she should have been, where he'd left her. He wanted to go slow, to give her time.

But God knew, time wasn't always something she had.

Tonight, right now, her time had run out before she'd even begun.

Damn her plight. Damn her *duty*.

For so long now, Detective Luther Cross had tried to worm his way into her dysfunctional, psychotic life—and she'd resisted.

With good reason.

No matter his claims of "knowing" her, of "accepting" her and her strange eccentricities. He might think he had an inkling of what she did and why. But he didn't, not really. He couldn't.

Why had she come here?

Tears, salty and hot, trickled along her temples, mingling with the sweat. Her body strained as she tried to find just a few minutes more, just enough time to have Luther. Once. A memory she could keep forever . . .

But the relentless pull and drag on her senses, the encompassing pain that twisted and curdled inside her told her to stop being fanciful.

Should she leave without telling him? Make a clean break of it and let him wonder, let him worry?

Let him give up. On her.

On them.

Or should she try trusting him?

No, no, never that. She couldn't.

The pain lashed her, impatient for obedience, and Gaby knew she couldn't resist it any longer. As she sat up, she cried out—and the bathroom door opened.

Luther stepped out, buck naked, tall and strong and oddly beautiful for a man. That stunning golden aura swirled around him, bright with optimism, with promise of all that was good.

All that was the opposite of her.

Seeing her, he drew up short, stared for a moment. His hot gaze moved over her body, but not with lust as much as concern. "Gaby?"

"I was waiting . . ." She gasped, nearly doubled with the physical torment of the calling. "For you. I was willing, Luther. I was anxious. But . . ." She staggered to her feet, unseeing, choked with the need for haste. "But now I have to go."

He remained strangely still, watching her. "Where?"

How could he remain so composed, so . . . detached, in the face of what she was, what she had to do? "I don't know yet."

She fumbled for her shirt and dragged it on.

Words hurt. Leaving felt like death.

But she was a paladin, and being interested in a man, even a man as good as Luther, didn't change that.

Luther didn't ask any more questions, he just dried with the speed of a man on a mission. "I'm coming with you."

"Don't be fucking stupid." She stepped into jeans, almost fell, and had to stop, had to gnash her teeth and squeeze her eyes shut in an attempt to contain the overpowering draw. But she knew the only relief would be to give in. And she would— once she was away from Luther. "I work alone."

"Not tonight." Already dressed in a black T-shirt, jeans, and sneakers, he reached for her. His hand touched her face, smoothed back her damp hair, and some of the awful, distorting agony dissipated. Almost sad, definitely accepting, he whispered, "Not tonight."

He'd always affected her this way, bringing clarity in the midst of the blind calling, easing her misery, calming her heart.

With the short reprieve, Gaby slapped his hand aside and pushed her feet into casual shoes. "I'll say it once, Luther. Stay out of my way."

And then she gave herself over to her duty.

Once accepted, it lashed through her, shocking her body, rolling her eyes back, straining her spine. In the peripheral of her senses, she felt Luther there, not touching her, not deterring her, but keeping pace as she moved forward, out of his bedroom, out of his house—and into the hell that was her life.